MURDER IN THE
ABSTRACT

Hi Dorothy —
I hope you, as a mystery reader Supreme,

MURDER IN THE
ABSTRACT

•

Susan C. Shea

like this!

Susan C. Shea
6/28/10

AVALON BOOKS
NEW YORK

Published by Thomas Bouregy & Co., Inc.
160 Madison Avenue, New York, NY 10016

Library of Congress Cataloging-in-Publication Data

Shea, Susan C.
    Murder in the abstract / Susan C. Shea.
        p. cm.
    ISBN 978-0-8034-7768-1 (acid-free paper)   1. Artists—
Crimes against—Fiction.   2. Art museums—Fiction.
3. Fund-raisers (Persons)—Fiction.   4. Murder—Investigation—
Fiction.   5. San Francisco (Calif.)—Fiction.   6. Santa Fe
(N.M.)—Fiction.   I. Title.
    PS3619.H39985M87 2010
    813'.6—dc22
                                                                            2009054251

PRINTED IN THE UNITED STATES OF AMERICA
ON ACID-FREE PAPER
BY HADDON CRAFTSMEN, BLOOMSBURG, PENNSYLVANIA

For Tim, forever.

Thanks to my writing group—Terry Shames, Ruth Hansell, Diana Orgain, Martha Jarocki, and John Gourhan—who coaxed me toward a stronger story, and to Terry for the title. I am immensely grateful to mystery authors Louise Ure, Ceil Cleveland, Rhys Bowen, and Linda Peterson for reading all or part of my book; to another stellar mystery author, Cara Black, for constant encouragement; and to Doris Herrick and Helen Shepherd, the first and last readers, respectively. My agent, Kimberley Cameron, is a gem beyond compare. The talented Peter Samis of SFMOMA lent his first name and a nifty plot suggestion in addition to giving me some inside perspectives on the museum business. In Santa Fe, Police Department Investigations Section Commander Gary Johnson, Detective Sergeant Tom Wiggins, and the city's PI Officer Laura Banish were very helpful. My sons, Brian and Steve, also are writers and share the highs and lows of this life with good grace. Where I got something right, the good people of my writing village can take a bow. Where I didn't, the error is mine alone. While the worlds of art, fund-raising, and society may suggest characters and plots, every person and circumstance in this book is a fiction sprung from my imagination.

Chapter One

I was hiding in the third floor ladies' room when my cell phone began to jangle. Struggling with the oh-so-cute clasp of my Kate Spade evening bag, I cursed the weakness for fashion that had made me choose an accessory that was almost as useless as it was expensive.

"Yes?" I snapped when at last I pried open the handbag. I had been congratulating myself for getting my boss an appointment with a gold-plated venture capitalist after listening to the man tell me more than I wanted to know about his collection of Oceanic art. If it led to a donation for the Devor Museum of Arts and Antiquities, I might get a nice raise. Right now, all I wanted was a few minutes to repair my lipstick and recharge my batteries.

My business is convincing wealthy people to give away large sums of money or precious objects, and it can be hard work. It's an honorable profession, for the most part, although some folks see us more as thieves, car salesmen, or carrion crows. When I was married to money, and I certainly was for a short time, my mother-in-law made it clear that was how she saw me.

I learned a lot about money during my four years as Mrs. Richard Argetter III, consort of one of San Francisco's wealthiest young social lions. For one thing, all those clichés about money not making you happy? I now know they're mostly true. I'm awed on a regular basis, though, by wealthy people with good hearts and generous instincts who do great deeds.

"Better get down here, Dani," a voice barked into my ear. "All hell's breaking loose."

"Len?" Len Hightower's our security chief, much given to drama. "What are you talking about?"

But I could already hear a change in the tone of conversation outside the restroom door. As gregarious as an open bar and the presence of their peers rendered San Francisco's social butterflies at a party like this, the anxious quality of this particular hum set it apart.

"Get down here. Peter needs you."

"I'm on my way." Peter Lindsey is my boss. He's also the director of the Devor Museum. I may be a senior executive, too, but when he says jump, I do.

Snapping the phone shut, I quick-checked my reflection. The new green eye shadow did nice things for my hazel eyes, but the flame lipstick had to go. On my large mouth, it looked like clown makeup. I swiped it off and settled for lip gloss.

Nudging the door open with my shoulder, I reached for the pager. The display showed Peter's cell phone number. I speed-dialed while easing my way past guests, a few of whom were looking over the railings of the central staircase that runs up the spine of the handsome old Edwardian building to the glass-roofed atrium.

Something was wrong, but I couldn't see what it was when

I peered over the heads of the shifting, murmuring crowd. Was there a fire? I sniffed but didn't smell smoke.

Squeezing past the outstretched arms of the two museum guards standing at the third-floor landing after getting a nod of recognition from one of them, I hurried down the carpeted stairs. It looked as though the guards' orders were to keep people from coming down, which surely meant it wasn't a fire. But what the hell was it?

The bar had been set up in the large first-floor lobby for tonight's preview of Matthew Barney's multimedia installation, so, naturally, that's where the biggest crowd was. I paused at the second-floor landing and looked toward the two-story glass entrance doors installed a few years ago over the howls of architectural purists. Strangely, because our liquor license from the city forbids Devor Museum guests from loitering outside the entrance, there seemed to be as big a crowd on the sidewalk as inside the building.

As I peered down, an elevator opened into the lobby, disgorging a score of black-clad, dot-com types and a security guard—a temp brought in for the evening, by the look of him. They merely added to the crush. I made it down to the first floor, maneuvering past a flock of twenty-somethings in Prada and Jimmy Choos who were chattering about guys with cute butts, while craning their pretty necks and sniffing the tension in the room.

Even though I'm tall, I couldn't spot Peter over the heads of the crowd. Len is short, a matter of some sensitivity to him. I worried he'd need one of those bicycler's flags to stand out right now.

"What happened?" I asked a portly man blocking my path to the information desk, where I guessed staff might be gathering.

"Someone said a body just landed outside," he replied without taking his eyes off the glass doors.

Landed? What did he mean? Landed in a plane? Landed off a skateboard?

Suddenly, someone shouted my name. Len was standing on a chair behind the dark walnut information desk, beckoning me while simultaneously talking into his walkie-talkie. Our little Napoleon, living his dream at last.

The red lights on the roofs of the emergency vehicles in the street raked the dark, wood-paneled lobby walls. My adrenaline started to pump, and my heart responded by drumming in my ears. I pushed past people, muttering apologies and wondering how long it would be before they morphed into a panicky mob.

"Where's Peter?" I shouted up as I reached the desk.

Barely an hour earlier, Peter had been standing in the same spot. My best friend, Suzy Byrnstein, had grabbed my arm as I cruised past and shouted over the cocktail-fueled voices, "Say hello to RR."

Rowland Reynold, an art collector based in Santa Fe, is a very rich man, and Peter had been sucking up to him big-time, at my urging.

"Has Peter been telling you about the Toulouse-Lautrec the museum purchased?" I had asked, shaking hands. A software developer rolling in new money after a successful IPO had given the museum six million dollars to buy a Toulouse-Lautrec café painting at a Sotheby's auction.

"Our donor's pretty pleased," Peter had murmured.

No doubt. It would guarantee the man or his wife a seat on the Devor's board of trustees within the year.

Suzy had winked at me. Short, with spiky brown hair,

dimples, and a wardrobe that plays off her zaftig curves, she's a serious painter and wise to the ways of philanthropy.

"How's our rising star?" Reynold had drawled. His gray hair, sharp incisors, and the almost colorless irises of his hooded eyes made him look wolfish. "Ready for Basel Miami Beach, the Venice Biennale, and the MOMA show in New York?"

Ignoring the fact that the artist in question, Clint Maslow, was not mine in any sense of the word, I'd shrugged. "I'm guessing Clint's frantic right now, although I know how grateful he is to you for making this happen. Have you seen him tonight?"

"No," Reynold had replied, his voice turning icy and his cold smile to a grimace. "Maybe he's scouting for bigger fish."

Reynold had been supporting Clint for several years by purchasing most of his work and bringing him to the attention of powerful art dealers in New York and London. If Clint was neglecting his benefactor now that he had hit the big time, it was bad politics.

Now, an hour later, I didn't see Peter, Suzy, or Reynold in the lobby. The security chief clambered down from his perch. At the same time, a phalanx of uniformed San Francisco cops swarmed through the glass doors. The mayor was here tonight, which probably explained the impressive show of force. One of the cops held up a megaphone and barked an order to step back. The crowd shuffled ever so slightly away from the doors. The amplified order came again, this time with more force, and the shuffling became a backward march of sorts. I looked around for Teeni Watson, my assistant, but remembered she was working the fifth floor, home to the contemporary art and sculpture galleries.

"Peter's with the mayor," Len said, raising his voice to be heard. "They're in the security office. But he's going to your office from there, using the freight elevator."

"My office?"

"Yeah. You and I need to get up there too."

"Why? You haven't told me what's happening."

"I'll tell you on the way. C'mon." He paused to confer with a uniformed cop. I heard the policeman say the scene outside was under control and that no one was being allowed to enter or leave the building. My worry was the scene inside, since, in a way, this was my party. Many of the VIP guests now milling around the landings and peering over the iron balustrades were my responsibility.

For an instant, my eye landed on a movie star who commutes from LA. Earlier in the evening, I was playing my private game of awarding points to the best and worst dressed people in the room, and she had been the hands-down winner, a size zero decked out in a black body stocking, pink tulle skirt, and five-inch heels. For best, I mean. I'm smart enough to know that if I showed up in the size fourteen version of that outfit, someone would call security.

As we made our way through the crowd, I saw her again, posed artfully above the crowd on the staircase. *Give the girl credit,* said my inner voice. *She smells a photo op in the making.*

"Someone fell from a window upstairs. Yours." Len pulled me back into the moment as we hustled onto the elevator and he punched the fifth-floor button.

"Who?" I croaked. "How do you know it was my window?"

Len's shoulders rose. "Witnesses said it was the fifth floor. Your window is the only one facing the street that can be opened. And the guy in the security office says your alarm's on."

"You've got to be kidding."

Before Len could respond, the elevator door slid open. Up here, I could tell that artists had infiltrated the crowd. Some had purple hair, a good number sported Keds high-tops, and there wasn't a manicure in the lot. Also, when invited to museum events, artists tend to bring along friends who excel at stripping bare lovely tables of food in minutes. My feeling is, since any one of them might turn out to be the next Rothko, Warhol, or O'Keeffe, one makes the best of it and tries to figure out who in the crush around the tables paints and who merely eats for a living. My boss is more uptight, as he should be, since the skewered lamb, sliced figs, and asparagus spears come out of his budget.

I resisted the impulse to cover my ears with my hands. We had decided to put the techno band in the fifth-floor foyer, overlooking the stairwell and atrium. The noise level up here was like a dance club at 2:00 A.M., on top of which the alarm was wailing to its own beat. Worst, someone was screaming, and the sound was coming from the staff wing beyond the elevators.

The guard who had the bad luck to be assigned to this area was waiting for us at the open door to the staff wing, red-faced and slump-shouldered. He tugged his navy blue uniform pants up over a bulging middle. "It wasn't me who opened the door, Mr. Hightower. One of those temps did that when we changed shifts. But I didn't let anyone in."

"Reinforcements are on the way, Carlos," Len barked. "Be sure to send Mr. Lindsey in to Ms. O'Rourke's office as soon as he gets up here."

Carlos pulled the walkie-talkie, which was starting to crackle, off his shoulder as Len and I hustled past the door, propped open with one of the caterer's fancy waste bins. All of a sudden, I felt a warm breath on my neck and heard a murmur in my ear that still pushes my pulse into overdrive.

"Hello, cupcake. Fancy meeting you here."

Damn and double damn. Dickie Argetter III, my ex, charming millionaire about town, unfaithful husband, source of many of my insecurities, the burr under my saddle.

"What are you doing here?" I blurted as I spun around. He has that effect on me in the best of times, which this was not.

"The building's flooded with cops, someone's screaming, and you and the general here are headed to your office at a trot. I figured you might need help." So saying, he smiled his patented crooked smile, put his hand on the small of my back, and steered me in that direction, following a fast-moving Len Hightower.

I didn't have time to answer. The screaming had stopped by the time Len reached my office, but the alarm was loud in the enclosed space. Lisa Thorne, the wife of an artist on the invite list, was hunched in a chair, clutching her handbag in her lap and staring down at the floor. She didn't even look up when we came barreling in. Teeni was perched on the edge of the couch, her hands over her mouth, her brown eyes wide open, staring at the open window behind my desk. I had never seen it open before.

"Stay where you are," Len said.

Since the two women were frozen in place, it seemed like an unnecessary command, but that's Len.

"What's going on?" I asked. "Why is the window open? Teeni?"

She looked up at me and took a few noisy breaths. "I

heard something and came in. The window was open and . . . and . . ." Teeni gulped and put her hands back over her mouth.

The sound of sirens and loud voices wafted up from the street, bouncing off the newer, taller buildings that surround and are beginning to dwarf the Devor's stately Edwardian presence.

Dickie, ignoring Len's command the same way he ignores everything he doesn't agree with, covered the few steps to the window behind my desk in two seconds, stuck his head out, then moved aside to make room for Len. The security chief leaned out and looked down. He jerked his head in suddenly, banging it on the frame.

"Ouch," he said, wincing. "Don't touch the window frame, Mr. Argetter. It might have prints."

Before Dickie could reply, a voice from the door said, "Anything I can help with?" Rowland Reynold poked his head in. Len snapped, "How did you get in?" at the same instant Dickie turned and said, "It's not pretty." Reynold ignored Len, poor guy, and raised an eyebrow toward my ex. "Some guy is down there on the pavement," Dickie explained. "He looks, well, I hate to say this, but he looks dead. Dani, take it easy."

That last probably because I was sucking in air and blowing it out noisily. It was that or faint. Black spots in front of my eyes, ears humming like radio transmitters, I dropped onto the couch next to Teeni and put my head between my knees the way they'd taught us in junior high. My God, someone who had been standing here in my office just a little while ago had died a horrible death by falling five stories. Who could it be? And why had he been in my office in the first place?

When I lifted my head, two uniformed cops and Peter

Lindsey had joined what was fast becoming a crowd. And, judging by the set of his jaw and the intensity of the glare he shot my way, Peter seemed to think this whole mess was my fault. Oceanic art collection or not, it didn't look as if he would be approving a raise for me anytime soon.

Chapter Two

One of the uniformed cops leaned out the window, then ducked back in and spoke into his walkie-talkie. The alarm stopped like magic. In my ears, the sudden silence sounded like a roar. For a couple of seconds, no one spoke. Then Teeni jumped up and glared at the security chief.

"At last," she said. "Took you long enough. Didn't you get my message?"

Hightower's face reddened, and he opened his mouth to protest. Before he could say a word, the cop with the walkie-talkie jumped in.

"Okay now, Miss . . . ?"

"Teeni. Teeni Watson." In an instant, her voice dropped an octave. It sounded husky, sexy. Even at this moment, with a dead body five stories below us, Teeni was sizing him up. His expression was neutral, but it was hard to believe he wasn't noticing her too. With black curly hair, small waist, and big hips, turned-up nose, and skin the color of toffee, Teeni Watson can stop traffic when she wears her red, four-inch heels

11

and one of her dozens of short skirts. That's what she had on tonight.

"Ma'am," the cop said, seemingly unmoved. "This officer is going to take everyone's names, and we will want statements from each of you. For now, I'd like everyone"—and here his gaze swept the tiny office—"to stay put. Please don't touch anything," he added sharply as Dickie absently reached for a pencil on my desk. Dickie put his hands up, palms open, widening his eyes and aiming his trademark smile at the policeman. The cop stared hard at him, and Dickie's smile faded. He shrugged, jammed his hands into his tuxedo trouser pockets, and stepped away from the window to slouch against the wall near the door.

The cop who was doing the talking swept his glance around the room again. Len, still standing near the window, was rubbing his head where he'd banged the window frame. Lisa Thorne was staring blankly at the carpet. I could see Reynold in the hall with a few members of my staff, who were peering around the door frame with worried expressions on their faces. Either Carlos had fallen down on the job of guarding the hall door, or there was a suspicious number of staff members working in their offices tonight.

Peter, his Roman nose twitching with impatience, turned to the cop. "Officer, I am Peter Lindsey, director of the museum, and I need to know what has happened. I have six hundred anxious guests who are beginning to gossip wildly, a security staff that does not know what to do with them, and absolutely no idea what the hell is going on."

"I understand, sir," the cop said. "If you'd step outside." At which, he marched out, shooing the people in the hallway back toward the elevator area. I heard him instruct someone to get everyone out of the wing and close the door again. Peter and Len hurried in his wake.

The second cop who had come into my office pulled a notebook and a pen out of his shirt pocket and took down our names and addresses as he went around the room, subsiding into watchful silence afterward, hands clasped behind him, body rocking forward and backward ever so slightly. In the quiet room, his thick-soled shoes squeaked audibly. Lisa closed her eyes after reciting her address in a whisper. Teeni, on the couch next to me, was alternately examining her ridiculously long, rainbow-hued fingernails and eying the cop.

I caught Dickie's eye and smiled in apology for his bad luck in trying to help. Since the cop wasn't looking at me, I raised my eyebrows and my shoulders a fraction and looked at the window. Dickie shook his head. If we were speaking the same body language, he saw me ask if he knew who it was and said he didn't. A lock of blond hair fell into one eye. Old habits die hard; I was itching to go over and push the hair back. *Get a grip,* my inner voice instructed me. I did.

Since no one was talking, I had time to think. Who was lying in the alley? Was it Win Thorne? Is that why his wife was sitting there glassy-eyed, looking slightly sick? I'd seen Win downstairs, nose to nose with a local gallery owner, and idly wondered if they were arguing about something or if she was thinking of taking him on, notorious temper and all. Maybe she'd said no, and he'd decided to end it all?

What about Teeni? Had she seen what happened? I looked at her, sitting close to me on the couch. Her head was resting against the cushions, and her eyes were now squeezed shut. The silence meant I couldn't whisper to her, so I gave up and sank lower on my cushion. What a nightmare.

Just then, lots of things happened at once. A mechanical-sounding voice issuing commands through a bullhorn was audible from the open window. Cop number two's walkie-talkie, lodged among the paraphernalia on his utility belt, crackled to life. Teeni's policeman marched back in, looking as stone-faced as when he'd left. And Lisa fainted.

I was the first person to notice as she slid off her chair, and, as heads swiveled in her direction, I jumped up and went over to where she lay crumpled. The shock of seeing her husband fall from the window must have been delayed. If Dickie had fallen and if he was still my husband—which he is not, thankfully—I would have hit the floor a lot sooner.

"Uh-oh," said Teeni, coming to life and bounding off the sofa. "There's a restroom right down the hall," she said, waving at the cop. "Can I go get some wet paper towels or something?"

The policeman who had been standing guard over us looked bewildered by all the activity. He frowned and held his hand up to stop Teeni, either from talking or moving, but she was already on the move, managing to brush up against cop number one as he eased back into the room and she rushed out.

I sat down on the floor beside Lisa. Her face was white, and her fingers were freezing cold. She looked so fragile, lying there. I rubbed her hands for lack of anything more useful to do. Her eyelids fluttered, and she mumbled something I couldn't hear. Cop number one looked at me and said, "How is she, ma'am?"

"Well, she said something, so I know she's not dead," I said tentatively. I always meant to take one of those CPR courses to qualify as a good citizen, but until this moment, it had never seemed like something I might actually use. I was relieved when Dickie came over, pushing the errant hair off his forehead as he squatted beside me and reached for her hand.

"Her pulse is okay," he said after a few seconds. "Can someone get water for her?"

The first cop said, "Listen up, folks. There's an officer outside. He's going to escort you to the conference room down the hall. The inspector in charge will be taking your statements. Please do not talk to one another while you wait."

At that point, Teeni breezed back in, a dripping bunch of paper towels in one hand and a paper cup slopping water in the other. "Here we are," she said, making straight for Lisa but tossing her brown curls artfully as she passed the cop.

Lisa struggled to sit up, and Dickie and I helped. I took the towels and made a compress for her forehead. She accepted the cup from Teeni with a nod and gulped it down. "My husband," Lisa said weakly. "Winship Thorne. He's at the party somewhere. Can you get him for me?"

My mouth fell open. Teeni froze in midgesture with her dripping paper towels. Dickie turned to stare at her. Was she deluding herself, or was it possible that the person who lay five flights down was someone else?

To my surprise, the cop answered easily. "Mrs. Thorne, right? Your husband's outside at the elevators. He's been asking for you. We told him you'll be out as soon as you've given us your statement. We'll have you go first."

And so saying, he helped her up with Teeni's conspicuous assistance and led her out the door. She clutched her bag in one hand and leaned on the cop's arm with the other. Dickie's eyes met mine, and he raised his eyebrows. I shrugged. How should I know who the dead man was if he wasn't Thorne?

We straggled out and took our places around the oval conference table across the hall. As soon as we left my office, several men and women in windbreakers with SFPD written in large letters on the back tromped down the hall, pausing to pull on gloves and booties before hauling in lights, cameras, and a couple of suitcases. I watched through the glass wall of the conference room as they brushed white powder on the doorknob and frame. After taking some pictures of the door, a young woman with a ponytail pushed the door closed with her foot, and then there was nothing to look at.

The voice in my head reminded me somewhat hysterically that it was my doorknob, my office, and my window. Did I really have to go back in there on Monday? Ever? My temples began to throb.

While I freaked out, Dickie went to sleep, a skill that had impressed me during our travels, whether it was on a third-class train in Spain, a rush-hour subway in New York, or a twenty-four-hour airline trip to Delhi. That he also went to sleep when I wanted to talk about our fracturing relationship during the last year we were married was less attractive.

Our short-lived marriage, which had infuriated Mrs. Argetter II, aka Mother, was somewhat puzzling, even to me. After all, I was a mere junior staffer at the Devor, relegated to pouring wine, when Dickie ambled into a benefit party with his dazzling smile and his ratty sweater and his Paris pied-à-terre and his four hundred and fifty million dollars.

I know why I was attracted to him: the sparkling eyes, the nicely rumpled style, the quality of paying attention to whoever he was with—so unlike the others in his crowd, who always seemed to be looking over each other's shoulders for someone better. Mostly it was because he was so much smarter and funnier than he let people see and because— *let's face it,* my inner voice snickered—I let myself entertain the romantic notion that I could change him, help him settle down and become a grown-up.

For a while, we'd seemed to be on the same wavelength when it came to observing the theater of the ridiculous in society and the sublime in nature up close. But action, challenge, drama—that was Dickie's comfort zone. I, on the other hand, have all the socializing I want at work, enjoy a solitary hike more than the Bay to Breakers race, and relish time to read or watch TV. It got harder and harder for us to meet in the middle.

What he saw in me I'll never know for sure. He once said I was the antithesis of everything phony in his life, which sounded sweet. Whatever it was, though, it wasn't enough to keep him from getting restless after a few years. Enter Veronique, queen of the lingerie catalog, intrepid scuba diver, lover of fast cars and the men who drove them.

When Dickie called me from Cannes to say that he and Veronique, the underwear model, were really, really in love and his lawyer would be calling me, I cursed my impetuous decision to marry him in spite of his self-indulgence and worked hard to keep my broken heart to myself. After a summer spent hiding out at my sister's house far from San Francisco, eating M&Ms for breakfast, lunch, and dinner, I dried my tears and slipped back into my professional role, two dress sizes larger but with an insider's perspective on how rich people think. The top fund-raising spot at the Devor opened up right about then, and I went after it.

Everyone assumed I'd go for a big chunk of Dickie's fortune in revenge, and I bet most of the gossipers assumed that the pre-nup was the only thing that prevented a golden consolation prize. I know Mrs. A lost sleep over the possibility. But I was way too proud to be bought off. Dickie's father, a wonderful man who died soon after we married, had given me a kind of reverse dowry as a wedding present, so I wasn't starving. I could make it on my own, and, in fact, I have.

We do bump into each other, San Francisco being the small town it is. I admit, Dickie can still make me crazy. In fact, at the beginning of tonight's disastrous event, he had surprised me near the coatroom, appearing suddenly in front of me with two glasses of wine, one of which he held out.

"Hey," he'd said, grinning. "Thought you'd be glad to know I got back safely."

"Back? From where?" I asked, raising my glass to show him I didn't need a new one. "Any glamorous company this time?" The model is long gone, and Suzy insists Dickie is on a quest to earn back my affections. Like I'm going to give him another chance to humiliate me? I don't think so.

"I thought Mother might have told you about my trip, and you might have worried."

"Your mother and I do not talk if we can help it, as you know. And I do not worry about you. That's not my job anymore, remember?"

"Have it your way." Dickie shrugged, looking at me with that soulful smile I'd once fallen for. "But if you ever want advice on how to make yak butter or survive in a sandstorm, I'm your man."

"Sandstorm? Yak butter?" I reminded myself that I was not interested. "I have to mix and mingle. Bye, Dickie." *Who knew,* I said to myself as I waited in the stuffy conference room, *that we'd be spending the evening together?*

Teeni roused me with a nudge and started to whisper something. The policeman reminded her she was not supposed to talk with other witnesses.

"But I'm not a witness," I protested. "I only came in after . . ."

"Please, ma'am," he said, stopping me with a look. "Hold your story until Inspector Weiler sees you."

"My story?" I said. "I don't have a story. I haven't got a thing to do with this except that it was my office."

But he was not going to chat with me. He offered me a bottle of water—courtesy of the caterer, who had sent in some unappetizing-looking leftovers from the party spread—and reminded us that the inspector would prefer we not use our cell phones unless we had to notify someone we would be late.

I had no one to call. I live alone, unless you count Fever, the cat, and he doesn't worry if I'm not tucked in by midnight as long as there's food in his bowl. My mother's a continent away and disgusted at me for giving Dickie up without a fight. My sister lives in a small city in a red state, where she's a big shot in the PTA. She was great when I needed to retreat and lick my marital wounds, and I love her. Still, the most we have in common is our big-boned frames, the chestnut-colored hair we inherited from our Irish dad, and knowing that her kids are destined for greatness.

Teeni bounced around in her chair, combed her hair, put on fresh lipstick, and called her mother, sister, and brother in turn to tell them she was fine but was "in police hands," a whispered phrase that each time produced audible squawks over the cell phone.

She raised her hand several times to ask to go to the bathroom, which began to make even me suspicious. Teeni does not do drugs. Teeni does not smoke. But, to my knowledge, she does not have a bladder problem either. When I looked quizzically at her after her third trip in an hour, she stage-whispered to me, "Nerves," and nodded solemnly. But I noticed she had slipped her cell phone into her pocket, and it had traveled to the ladies' room each time with her.

Teeni was called in after Lisa. Lisa had been in there for ages, it seemed. Teeni was there for a long time too. By contrast, Dickie was out in five minutes, yawning and giving me a thumbs-up on the way out. I had a full-blown headache by the time I was ushered in, last of the lot.

Chapter Three

A short man in his fifties with gray, thinning hair and big ears looked up at me from behind our public relations director's desk. His skin was sallow, as if he rarely saw daylight, and it matched in spirit the tired tweed of his jacket. He wore a white button-down shirt that had seen better days and a narrow, knitted tie. His posture signaled resignation. He waved me to the chair opposite him, then sighed and consulted his notebook for a minute.

"Danielle O'Rourke Argetter? I'm SFPD Inspector Weiler. I'll be leading the investigation of this case with my partner. Can you start by telling me what your position is at the Devor?"

"Vice president. I'm in charge of fund-raising. And I'm no longer Argetter. We're divorced."

He nodded. "Your office was the one with the open window?"

"Yes, but—"

"Did you see what happened?" he said, interrupting me.

"No. I—"

He broke into my protestations again. "Is your office door normally locked?"

Silently, I fumed at not being able to tell my story, but I was too tired to keep arguing. "Yes. Do you know who fell? Was it someone who works here?" It had dawned on me that it could be someone who had an office in the same wing.

Weiler ignored my question. "Did you lend your keys to anyone tonight, or misplace them?"

"No." To be sure, I rummaged through my bag and pulled out my set. "I have a second set I keep at home in case I lose these." I held them up individually to show him. "Staff entrance downstairs, entrance to this wing, Teeni's office, my office. All here."

"Okay, we may want to double-check to make sure the other set is at your house." He clucked his tongue against the roof of his mouth absentmindedly as he consulted his notebook, then looked up at me. "Does anyone else have a key to your office?"

"The security office has all the master keys. My assistant. No one else, as far as I know."

"Where were you this evening before the alarm went off?"

"Everywhere," I said with a sigh. "That's my job. What, specifically, do you want to know?"

"We need to track the whereabouts of everyone involved. I need you to walk me through your movements from the time you arrived at the museum until the time our officers came up to your office."

"You're kidding, right? *A,* I was not 'involved,' as you put it. *B,* that's not possible," I protested. "I spent about a half hour in the European galleries on the third floor, talking to our board chairman and his wife. But the lobby floor is where the VIPs were, pretty much, so I spent most of the time there. I was up on this floor early to make sure the staff was in place to host guests, and again about an hour later to check on things."

"Did you go into your office at any time before the alarm began?"

"Yes, around five, but only for a minute to check my voice mail for late RSVPs to the party."

"Is this the only bag you had with you tonight?" Weiler tipped his head toward my folly of a purse.

"Yes."

"May I see it? Would it be okay with you if I look inside?"

"Sure, I guess. But why—"

"Thanks." Weiler had as much trouble as I did opening it, but when he managed to do it, he quickly saw that there was nothing in it except my cell phone, the too-red lipstick, a handkerchief, and the keys he had already asked me about. He handed it back.

"Okay, where were we?" Weiler had slightly protuberant eyes, and when he stared at me, the effect was to make him look incredulous at whatever I said. He was making me feel defensive, which was stupid. Just because it was my window? *Get a grip,* my inner voice said. I stifled the urge to keep talking. How had Dickie managed to get out of his questioning in five minutes? I wanted to go home, put my head under the covers, take a break from this, which, in addition to being a tragedy, would make my job a lot harder for the next couple of weeks.

"Can anyone vouch for your presence during any of that time?" he continued.

"Give me an alibi, you mean?" My voice went up an octave. "Are you kidding? If you start calling people, asking where I was when someone went out my office window, I'll be toast. The gossip will ruin my reputation, never mind hurting the museum."

His cell phone rang, and Weiler held up a finger to silence me. He turned away and listened to someone for several minutes, uh-huhh-ing every now and then, looking my way sharply at one point. Then he thanked whoever it was and flipped the phone closed.

He spun the chair back toward the room and sat still for what seemed like a full minute, his chin balanced on his hand, eyes closed.

Hello? There are other people here who could use some sleep. I cleared my throat, and he blinked. Resuming where we left off as if we hadn't been interrupted, Weiler said it might not be necessary but asked me to provide the names anyway. Reluctantly, I recalled my schmoozing as best I could. I didn't pass along every name, a few being so far above this sort of thing that they'd never respond to a policeman's call. Include in that number the collector of Oceanic art. *How embarrassing would that be?* my inner voice shrieked.

After about five names, Weiler seemed satisfied. He cleared his throat and changed gears. "Have you ever had reason to open your office window?"

"Of course not. It's an emergency exit window for the fifth floor. I've never even been around when they do the fire drill. It's got some kind of quick-release catch. There are some on every floor so people can summon help if there's a fire. I was told it triggers the alarm system. That's about all I know."

"Wouldn't everyone need access to your office in that case?" Weiler asked.

"No, there are two more in offices down the hall. They all

face the alley. Since mine faces the front sidewalk, it's only a backup. I think it predates the last building renovation."

"What can you tell me about Ms. Watson? Do you know why she was in your office?"

"She said something about hearing a noise."

"What's her job?"

"She's my executive assistant and an assistant curator."

"What do you know about her background?"

"Teeni has a BFA and a master of fine arts from UC Berkeley, a Ph.D. dissertation in progress, no problems I've heard about except the cost of designer shoes, and a reputation for hard work and loyalty to the museum." I know I sounded snappish, but really. Teeni, pushing someone out a window, if that was where this was leading? "She worked in other departments here before I hired her, and everyone likes her."

"And Mrs. Thorne? What can you tell me about her?"

This would be harder. Truth is, I didn't much like Lisa Thorne. She still had the remnants of her youthful appeal— large eyes, perfect little nose, gamine figure. But time and avarice had coarsened the charm of her student days. While Dickie and I were married, she had been after us relentlessly to buy Win's big, gloomy, abstract paintings. These days, she lobbied me without much subtlety to introduce Win to the Devor's curators.

"She and her husband were invited guests tonight. He's an artist. But she probably told you that."

"Any reason she'd be in your office?"

"No. I was surprised to see her there."

There had been plenty of time to think about that, sitting in the conference room. Win has a mean temper and few friends. With a few drinks, had he gotten belligerent? Could he have gotten into an argument on the main floor, where I'd seen him, and was it possible Teeni or another staffer had ushered them into the private area to avoid a scene? If something like that had happened, Weiler would find out soon enough.

"Let's switch gears for a second," Weiler said, stifling a yawn. It was late for him too. "If someone broke into your office, what's there to steal?"

"Nothing. The computer's locked down to the desk. The art on the wall is reproduction posters from museum shows. It's a rule that no original art graces offices except the director's, for fear of theft, accidental damage, or vandalism." Hightower would tell the cops the same thing.

Weiler scratched his head and paused. "Do you know someone named Clinton Maslow?"

"Yes," I answered, puzzled at the sudden change of subject. "He's a local artist."

"Know him well?"

"We're friends. We used to date."

"Have you seen him, talked with him on the phone, written to him, or had an e-mail exchange recently?"

"How is this connected to what happened?" I didn't see why my personal life was any of Weiler's business. In fact, because of my position with the Devor, Clint and I had downplayed our relationship, at least until that night after I broke up with him when he crashed a party and started yelling at me. Neither of us had wanted people to say the Devor gave him special attention because someone inside pulled strings, especially since Peter was negotiating to get some of Clint's most recent pieces into the collection, preferably as gifts from Rowland Reynold.

"Have you and he been in touch in the past week or so?" he asked again, ignoring my question.

"No."

"Was he here tonight?" Weiler asked.

"I didn't see him, but he was on the guest list."

"Any reason he might be in your office?"

"No, of course not. But why . . ."

Oh, wait a minute. I could think of two reasons a policeman would be asking me about someone who wasn't in my office when I arrived. One, the cops thought Clint was involved in whatever had happened in my office. Two, if that wasn't Win on the sidewalk, could it be Clint? My stomach lurched. Weiler waited and watched my face as I figured it out. No sympathy, just curiosity.

"Are you saying that's who fell?" I whispered, gulping.

"I'll ask again. Is there a reason why he might have been in your office?"

"N-No," I stammered. "No reason."

"Tell me about your meetings with him," Weiler pressed.

My stomach was rolling over and over, and I was trying not to think about how he might have exited my office. *Not Clint,* my brain kept repeating. I swallowed sour-tasting bile and told myself to get a grip.

"Ms. O'Rourke, you okay?"

No, not really. Not when you tell me a guy I once kissed is never again going to show up at my door with a bottle of wine, tease me about my cat, or argue over who pays for the pizza. Clint and I had had a short-lived but passionate romance last year, and we were cheerleaders for each other's successes.

"You want a tissue or something?" Weiler said, looking around the office.

I pulled one from my jacket pocket and wiped a trickling tear off my cheek. "I'm okay. It's only that I'm surprised. And it's so ironic, you know? Poor guy, for ten years he works like a dog to get noticed. Now, he makes it big, and . . . what terrible timing." My voice was wobbly, and my nose was running.

"Meaning what?" Weiler asked, giving me time to blow my nose.

"Two weeks ago, he delivered a half dozen paintings for a group show at MOMA—the Museum of Modern Art—in New York, and bought a plane ticket to go to Venice. La Biennale di Venezia is the highlight of the European contemporary shows. His paintings will be in it. It's a huge honor. He has a powerhouse New York gallery, and his paintings are selling like crazy. Are you sure it was Clint?"

"Identification, including a recent driver's license photo, in his wallet. Ms. O'Rourke, I'm going to ask you again," Weiler said, emphasizing his words. "Did you have plans to meet Mr. Maslow this evening?"

"No. I said that already."

"Then how do you explain the letter my team found in his pocket asking him to meet you there?"

"What letter? I didn't write any letter." I blew my nose again and looked up, wondering how the cops could make such a mistake.

"Your name is signed on the bottom. The letter instructed Mr. Maslow to meet you in your office tonight." Weiler cocked his eyebrows, and the bulging eyes were more accusatory than ever.

I shook my head. "No way." Fatigue and shock, on top of a miserable headache, were working on my temper. "Look, I didn't write to Clint, didn't see him tonight. We haven't seen each other in a couple of months, in fact. I need some Tylenol. Do we have to continue right now?" I sank back into my chair, feeling faint, although I didn't know if it was with weariness or fear.

"The letter was typed on Devor letterhead with your name at the bottom. If you didn't write it, who did?"

"How would I know? Look," I said, running my hands through my hair. "You've just given me horrible news. I feel sick, and it's beyond late. Do we really need to keep at this?"

Weiler glanced at his watch, made the clucking noise with his tongue again, and said, "Okay, Ms. O'Rourke. You say you didn't write a letter to Mr. Maslow. We'll let that go for now. By tomorrow, we'll have lifted any prints. I'll need you to supply a set, by the way. We'll get them as we leave. One more thing. Who else in that room knew Mr. Maslow?"

"Probably everyone to some degree. Teeni knows a lot of artists from her work here and from UC Berkeley. Lisa is married to an artist and moves in the same set. Dickie— Richard, I mean—maybe not."

"Any event recently—before tonight, I mean—where these folks might have met?"

Of course there were events like that, but when you do them month in and month out, they can blur. "Clint and two other painters had an alumni show at the Institute of the Arts a few months ago, if that's what you mean. Teeni and I went together."

"All right, thanks. I can see you're wiped out." *Well, duh.* I felt like sliding off the chair. I think that qualifies for *wiped out.*

"I'll need to talk with you tomorrow, Ms. O'Rourke. By then, I may know more." Weiler got up, put his notebook into his jacket pocket, and came around the desk as I stood up. "I'll have a squad car drive you home after we print you and request a swab for DNA. You can check to make sure the other keys are where they should be. Don't talk to anyone who was in your office about the case. And don't identify the victim to anyone else. We need time to get a formal ID and let his family know."

"Okay," I said as the reality of Clint's death crashed down on me again. "I think he has a brother somewhere in the Midwest."

Weiler nodded. The fifth floor was dark except for the normal low lighting in the corridors and near the exits. Weiler punched the Down button, and the elevator doors opened immediately.

"You can get back into your office in the morning," he said as the doors opened into the main lobby. *As if.* I couldn't think of anything I wanted less than to go back in there ever again.

Chapter Four

When we stepped out onto the ground floor, I saw that I wasn't the only one still being questioned. There were about a dozen people sitting in the brightly lit lobby, looking as exhausted as I felt.

I saw Peter hovering with a glass of white wine over a woman in a sequined suit whose thin lips were pursed in irritation. As I looked, she abruptly waved away the glass and said something through clenched teeth. Peter looked miserable, and I felt for him. I took a few steps toward him and made hand signals to let him know I'd come over if it would help, but he narrowed his eyes and shook his head. His expression said I was part of the problem, which struck me as grossly unfair. I was clueless. This whole evening had been like bits and pieces of a play I knew nothing about, with the pages all out of order and some missing.

An efficient and seemingly wide-awake uniformed cop rolled my fingertips in black ink and then rolled them again into little squares on a piece of paper. It took all of sixty seconds. Then, as he handed me a tissue to scrub at the ink stains, he asked me with super politeness if I would let him swab under my fingernails. I couldn't imagine why but didn't object.

As Weiler and I walked toward the massive lobby doors a minute later, a familiar, lanky man turned from looking out the window. Rowland Reynold? Why would he still be here?

He ambled over. "Dani. You still around?" His gray eyes glinted, and he summoned up what could pass for a smile. "Police keep you here for questioning?"

"Like a lot of people," I said, looking around the lobby. "Did Suzy go home?"

"Yup. Before all this happened. Said she had to get up early for a Pilates class."

"But why are you still here?"

"I want to help find whoever did this. Clint was a friend of mine. Of course, you knew him better, since you were his girlfriend."

Weiler had been quiet until now, merely signaling a woman officer to join us. But his head snapped around at Reynold's remark.

"Girlfriend? You didn't mention that, Ms. O'Rourke."

"That's because I'm not. I told you that we dated for a short while." If this meant I was in for more questions tonight, I'd push Reynold out of the nearest high window myself. "Wait a minute, Rowland. How do you know it's Clint?"

Weiler stepped in. "That's my question. Who interviewed you, for starters?"

"Hey, I don't want to get anyone into trouble," Reynold said. "I overheard it somewhere."

"Just the same, which officer took your statement?"

"Check with the man in charge, why don't you?" Reynold

said. His drawl was becoming more pronounced. His jaw tightened as he looked down at Weiler, ready to go *mano a mano*.

"Rowland, he is the man in charge," I said quickly. "Inspector Weiler, SFPD. Mr. Reynold is an art collector and a patron of Clint's," I explained to Weiler, who was staring up at Reynold with those bulging eyes. "He owns a lot of Clint's work."

"That right?" Weiler said. "Worth much, would you say?"

I didn't know if Weiler was talking to me or Reynold, but it occurred to me that it might be prudent to avoid saying anything that might point Weiler's suspicious mind in the direction of a powerful man like Reynold. Instead, I reminded Weiler he had agreed to let me go home.

Reynold, who had bristled at Weiler's comment, quickly offered to drive me, but I was relieved when Weiler insisted the SFPD do it. Maybe it was RR's canine teeth. Whatever, I excused myself and left, not even looking back to see how my boss was faring.

It wasn't until I got home, had shown the woman officer my spare keys, and locked the door behind her that I remembered something I hadn't told Weiler. Lisa's husband, Win, teaches in the MFA program at the Institute, and Clint was once a student and protégé of his. Win would be devastated by the news that it was Clint who died.

So who, my inner voice prompted me, *would* not *be devastated by Clint's death?*

Fever had started complaining about his empty dish the instant I opened the door to my apartment and was not impressed by my trauma. As I shook out the kibble, I tried to figure out who had opened the staff-wing door and my office in the first place. And, how about the window, which was no easy feat? Someone with a key, which meant a staffer. An accidental fall didn't compute, given the height of the window-sill and the fact that it was painted shut before tonight. Clint? I never gave him a key, and, anyway, an ambitious artist becoming a hot property wouldn't seem like a suicide candidate even if I didn't know firsthand that he was reveling in his sudden stardom and the money coming his way. No, someone had pushed him. That led to the next issue: who-ever wrote that letter knew that I would realize it was phony. Did that mean I was in some kind of danger too? Rats. I should have pointed that out to Weiler.

I didn't sleep well. I drifted off at one point but woke gargling out a warning about a crowd of strangers yelling at someone who was trying to climb into my office window. I was trying to pull him in, but someone kept hitting me over the head with a handbag.

The clock next to the bed said 5:00 A.M. It was still dark. I reached for the only sleeping medicine I have ever found use-ful: my college poetry anthology, four hundred pages of small type marching along from early Greek epics to Robert Frost. I fell in love with a guy once because he took this book off my bookshelf and read me a poem, then sat and held my hand without speaking for an hour. I used to be quite a romantic. But that was then, and this is now, and the book serves as a coaster for my coffee in the morning and a sleeping aid at night.

It worked, sort of. But when the clock jangled and I came to again, I had difficulty thinking of a good reason to get out of my nest and into what looked from my bedroom window like a gray, cold day suitable for mourning Clint's death. San Francisco fog comes in fast, stays for a few days, then disap-pears without explanation, leaving that trademark California blue sky as a reward for our patience. The long, gray-green leaves of a eucalyptus under my window fluttered, signaling a stiff breeze. The cat uncurled from his spot dead center on the bed and marched up my legs, stopping when he got to my chest to stare meaningfully (the meaning always being the same) into my face.

"Coffee first," I said.

I dragged myself into the kitchen and went through the morning motions, feeling worse and worse as the fact of Clint's death sank in. I shuddered, thinking about walking into that office on Monday, dealing with all the unanswered questions. Had Clint walked in on a burglar? Was Lisa already in the staff wing when all hell broke loose? If so, how did she get in, and why would she want to? Maybe she knew Clint from his MFA days. It would make sense, since her husband was Clint's MFA faculty advisor. What if Lisa and Clint were having an affair? Suzy taught at the Institute and might know. I had no intention of giving Suzy's name to the cops, however.

I looked at the kitchen clock. Speaking of Suzy, under ordinary circumstances it was too early to call my social-butterfly pal, but this was the most unordinary morning I could remember since the roller coaster years I'd spent with Dickie. The only problem was, I couldn't tell her who fell out of the window. Grabbing my mug, I went searching for the cordless phone as it began to ring. A Mozart melody trilled from under the current issue of *Town & Country* on my desk.

"Ms. O'Rourke?" a man's voice said.

"Yes?"

"Inspector Weiler here. I wonder if I might come by."

"Here? Can it wait an hour? I'm pretty groggy and was just headed out for a walk." If that fake letter meant someone was trying to involve me, I needed time to think.

"Sure. I've got a few things to do first, anyway. Say, eleven?"

We agreed, and I decided to call Suzy after the inspector had left. Maybe he would lift his ban, and I could tell her who fell. I knew I'd feel awkward otherwise. Meanwhile, my regular exercise routine would help me organize my thoughts.

Five minutes later, in cross trainers, shorts, and a Cal Bears sweatshirt, I began a fast walk through Presidio Heights and down through the Presidio National Park, a former military base with million-dollar views and nineteenth-century wood-frame houses sprinkled on streets that wound through cypress and eucalyptus groves. Wind ruffled the Bay, so it sparkled against blue skies as the fog dissolved into wisps. I puffed partway up Broderick Street, then, by prior agreement with my heart, lungs, and calf muscles, slowed to a stately pace to finish the steep hill and turn back to my upstairs apartment in the white-painted mansion on Washington Street that had been turned into three floor-through condominiums a few years ago during one of San Francisco's frenzied housing booms.

Some days, that trip leaves me overloaded with those feel-good hormones scientists have discovered. Today, it couldn't overcome my sorrow or sense of unease about last night's events. I wasn't sure if it was good or bad that a cop was coming to interview me at my home. Was I a suspect or a respected bystander? As I climbed the stairs and let myself in my apartment door, I vowed to be as much interviewer as interviewee this morning. I had a right to know what the police were thinking. After all, it was my office, my name on the mysterious letter, my friend. *And let's not forget,* said my helpful inner voice, *your window.*

Drapes, I decided as I stripped and stepped into the shower. Thick, opaque drapes were what I'd need if I were going to open that door every morning and sit at that desk with that window behind me. I'd shop for them early next week and bill the museum.

The doorbell rang as I gave my hair one last swipe of the brush. Inspector Weiler and I swapped comments about the weather while I ground more coffee beans. His eyes had bags under them, and he radiated glumness in the morning light. I tried to be fair. I had not spent much time in front of the mirror this morning, but from what I'd seen, I didn't look much fresher.

He slurped his coffee. "Ms. O'Rourke," he said, eying not me but my kitchen. A shiny red wall behind the big gas range, windows looking out over a backyard decorated with red and white impatiens, a tall bookcase full of vintage and specialty cookbooks. Most of the time, it cheered me up to sit in here. "I'd like to go over what you told me and ask you a few questions about the people I met last night," he said, the eyes coming back to rest on me.

"I have some questions too. For one thing, I would really like to know what you think happened."

"We're pretty sure Mr. Maslow was pushed out of your window," he replied flatly, looking intently at me as he spoke.

"Pushed? You mean deliberately? You know, I've been trying to relate what happened to the fact that this was an art show, for pete's sake. The people who come to these things are not stone-cold killers, you know. I keep wondering if he fell somehow. Oh, I know, I know. It's unlikely. But I can't get my head around the idea of such violence."

"I'm a homicide inspector, Ms. O'Rourke. I'm investigating the possibility, not proven, that Mr. Maslow was helped to his death by a person or persons unknown." He closed his mouth with an almost audible snap. When I didn't say anything, he continued. "I'm here to ask you to help in the investigation. Let's start with the letter you say you didn't send to Mr. Maslow. It was found in his pocket. I've examined it, and it appears to be genuine. We'd like permission to check your home and office computer files to see if it was written on either one, for starters. We can," he added as I hesitated, "get a warrant."

"Hear me, Inspector. I didn't send a letter to Clint. No one but me uses my laptop, which is here. You're welcome to check it out anytime. But whoever stole the stationery could have taken it from my desk. Heck, they could even have written and printed the letter right there, so finding a file on the desktop computer wouldn't prove anything."

"You have password protection to keep other people from using your account, don't you?" Weiler asked.

"Sure, but like most people, I don't log out or shut down every night. I do that only on weekends, and not even then if I get busy and forget."

"If you were his girlfriend, or had been, you might have asked Mr. Maslow to meet you last night, maybe to see if the spark was still there? Were you planning on getting together after the party?"

"No, definitely not. And there was no 'spark,' as you put it. Mr. Reynold is a wonderful supporter of Clint's, but he didn't know much about Clint's personal life, or he would have known we had stopped dating long ago."

"How long ago?"

"Five, maybe six months ago."

"Why 'definitely'?" Weiler asked, squinting again as he picked up my quote. "You have an argument or something?"

"We've both been busy," I said, skirting the facts. "He's

been working frantically to get ready for the shows I told you about last night. They could make or break him with the international dealers."

"Did that bother you? Having him put an art show before you?"

"Are you kidding? This is—was—his shot at the big time. I was thrilled for him. Even now, it breaks my heart to think he won't be here to reap the rewards."

"Doesn't his death pretty much end all of that?"

"Hah. His death may increase the value of his work, if the critics like it. Think about Basquiat, for example."

"And he would be?"

"Jean-Michel Basquiat was a young guy who had barely hit his stride on the international scene when he died of a drug overdose. When his paintings come up for sale these days, they're grabbed at exorbitant prices because there aren't going to be any more. Clint was right on the edge of that kind of success, and I'm sure the paintings in his estate will be worth a lot more than they were before Friday, as horrible as that sounds."

"Do you own any of his artwork, Ms. O'Rourke?"

"No, and I don't like the suggestion that I might benefit from Clint's death. I'm beginning to wonder if I need to get a lawyer to make that clear." Weiler was creeping me out with this constant pushing at the idea that I had some reason to want poor Clint dead.

"I'm only asking questions. By all means, get an attorney if you think it's necessary, although that seems like a waste of money if you're as innocent as you say. I'm still interested in the letter, which seems to be what got Mr. Maslow to your office Friday night. If you didn't send it, who did?"

"Good question. In fact, I'm worried that whoever killed Clint might decide to come after me, since I know the letter was fake."

"Could be," Weiler said, fixing those eyes on me, seeming to signal his doubts about my innocence. "If it wasn't from you, someone might be trying to implicate you in a crime. You have any enemies? What about the people in your office last night, beginning with your ex-husband?"

"Dickie? You can't be serious. Dickie's harmless. Well, I suppose not completely harmless in my case, but not an enemy," I amended. My divorce had received some breathless coverage on the society pages, probably because of the fame of the underwear model. If Inspector Weiler had done some research already, he might actually know about it. But sinister?

"Dickie couldn't stay angry long enough to kill anyone. He's just a . . . a . . . well, kind of a puppy, if you know what I mean. Short attention span. Anyway, why on earth would he push someone he's hardly met out of a window?"

"Jealousy?" Weiler said, looking over his coffee mug.

"Jealous of what? Dickie has never wanted to be an artist. And since he always gets what he does want, he'd hardly have a reason to be jealous about money or women."

"Would he be jealous if he thought you and Mr. Maslow were having a romance?"

"Are you kidding? He left me, Inspector."

"You didn't love Maslow? He didn't love you? No lovers' quarrel?" Weiler's voice had hardened. Not third-degree hard but a couple of points up the scale. I didn't think he could have found anyone yet who had witnessed Clint's outburst, but if he dug around, he would. Sooner or later, I was going to have to explain Clint's scene to Inspector Weiler. But not right now, I decided.

"Wait a minute. I'm an innocent bystander in all of this." I jumped up and began pacing. "I'm an executive at the Devor Museum. I was out on the floor talking to people all evening, which you can easily confirm. I didn't see Clint last night, didn't know he was in my office, much less that he had gone out the window." I shuddered, in part at the callous way I was beginning to treat Clint's death. Nothing like self-interest to strip away compassion in a hurry.

"If the police need my help with background or Devor Museum business, I'm glad to do my civic duty. And because I liked Clint and am shocked at the loss of an exceptionally talented artist"—and here my voice began to wobble in spite of my efforts to sound detached—"I'm willing to cooperate. But if you're going to keep implying that I had some role in what happened, forget it."

I ran out of steam and sat down in a straight-backed chair near the kitchen door, shaking so hard that coffee splashed out of my mug and onto my fingers.

"I'm just asking," Weiler said, running a hand absent-mindedly over his thinning hair. "My job. How well did Mr. Argetter know Mr. Maslow?"

I was tempted not to answer, but the small voice of reason that lived somewhere inside my skull reminded me that silence might be mistaken for holding back something. "I don't know. We didn't know Clint when we were married. It's probable they were both at some museum event, but you could be at the Devor with your entire high school graduating class and not know it on a really big night."

"Okay, we'll let it go at that," Weiler said, flipping to

a different page in the notebook he'd pulled out of his jacket pocket. "How about Mrs. Thorne? Did she know Mr. Maslow?"

"Why ask me? Why don't you ask her?" I tried to sound polite. I looked him in the eye. But, I admitted to myself, I was not telling him the whole truth, because I'd just remembered some gossip I had heard about Clint and Lisa.

Before Clint and I started dating, Suzy told me that she had overheard Win and Clint having a shouting argument in Clint's studio at the Institute. It was part of her normal gossip download, our habit over lattes, and I hadn't been paying a lot of attention. But Suzy had laughed and said maybe Lisa and Clint were sleeping together. It would serve Win right, she said, if Lisa chose this way to strike back at the husband who treated her in public like a cross between a business manager and a domestic servant.

I'd forgotten that until Weiler's question prompted me. Now I wondered if that was why Win and Clint weren't on good terms the last couple of years.

I didn't tell Weiler. Having worked myself into a state of righteous indignation about his harping, I was afraid it would look like I did have information he could pry out of me if he kept pounding away. Anyway, it seemed unfair to pass along gossip about someone who could no longer defend himself.

"And Ms. Watson? You said you think she knew Mr. Maslow?"

The more interesting question was how well she knew him. Teeni attracts men like a candle does moths. She had worked in the curatorial and education departments of the Devor before moving into a staff position in the fund-raising office when her grant ended. Clint had been on the summer school faculty one year. Putting two and two together, it was possible they had dated, although she had not mentioned that to me when I started seeing Clint. He hadn't said anything about that either. What if she didn't know we had broken up and was pissed off that he was dating me? Teeni pissed off would be a formidable threat. Come to think of, Clint pissed off was kind of threatening too.

All I said was, "It's her job to know a great many people. She's worked at the Devor for about five years. If she knows him, it doesn't necessarily mean anything."

"How about the museum's director, Mr. Lindsey? Did he know Maslow?"

Weiler's cell phone rang. After a few terse words, he got up and told me we would have to continue later in the day. I breathed a sigh of relief as I closed the apartment door behind him. Of course Peter knew Clint. You don't get to be the leader of a prestigious art museum unless you know who the best talent is, who has influential patrons, and who has the attention of the dealers and your rival directors. Two weeks ago, Peter had invited Clint to one of the VIP dinners he periodically hosted in his sixth-floor suite. He'd told me a dozen or so trustees, local artists, and prospective donors from his and my "cultivation" lists had attended. I mentally noted that Clint was there and that I had missed what turned out to be my last chance to repair our friendship when I begged off the event.

A headache descended, fed by the dark cloud of Clint's horrible end. I refused to consider that Peter had anything to do with it. There was no reason he would push Clint out a window, and Weiler's questions were making me uneasy. Peter was on my case already, if his nasty looks at me the night before meant what I thought they did. Did Weiler seriously think I would point my finger at my boss in a murder investigation?

I watched the inspector from my living room window as he got into his car, parked in front of the fire hydrant next to the driveway—now, there's a perk—and then went to grab my phone. I had to find Suzy.

Chapter Five

Suzy's answering machine was on. "Hi. This is Suzy. You know the drill. If you're a telephone solicitor, take my word for it, the answer's no. If you're a buddy, leave a message or try my cell phone. *Ciao!*"

I had left a brief, probably incoherent message last night. As I listened to Suzy's message, I flipped through a stack of art gallery opening postcards perched on the edge of the desk. There are maybe twenty galleries in the city that show serious contemporary art. That's not counting the tourist traps selling dubious original prints by the most famous artists of the twentieth century. ("Hey, Mary, look at this. A real Picasso, and only five thousand dollars!")

Slick chain galleries at Fisherman's Wharf and on Sausalito's main drag deal in bronze, Deco-style sculptures of women in slinky evening gowns, pseudo-primitive animal paintings, and misty landscapes. Not that they don't have a place in someone's living room, mind you, and I bless anyone who is moved to shell out big bucks for beauty.

Many of the artists I meet don't do such easy-on-the-eye work, however, and they would kill to get into one of the score of local galleries that are respected by their peers. Getting your own show at one of these galleries is a big deal, because people who are willing to buy something without the Picasso guarantee trust the tastes of the gallery owners. The galleries invite the buyers, and the artists whose work will be on display make sure everyone else gets the four-color postcards advertising these exhibits. I'm on the lists partly, I know, because I was once married to money and also because the artists and gallerists think I might slip the information under Peter Lindsey's nose.

I grabbed at a stack that was threatening to slide off the edge of the table and remembered why I had particularly noticed Win Thorne deep in conversation with a San Francisco gallery owner during the disastrous gala. WINSHIP THORNE. NEW WORK, EXCLUSIVELY AT MILTON DOLLAR GALLERY, SANTA FE. I turned it over. On the back was scribbled, *Friend of yours, I think? Time to visit,* cherie!

The seed of a very attractive idea started to germinate. The handwriting was Vera Argetter's. She must have touched down in Santa Fe recently. The card was different from most in that it didn't display artwork. Instead, it featured a brooding photo of Win in a black turtleneck sweater in front of a canvas that was mostly obscured by his head. Very arty, especially if you didn't know that that was his normal expression. Flipping it over again, I saw that it was opening in about ten days.

The phone rang. I let it go to voice mail, so I could ignore it if it was Weiler.

"It's me. My God, what happened? I tried—"

"Hey, Suzy," I said, snatching up the phone. "I was afraid it was the cops again."

"Cops? Jeez, what's up? I couldn't make sense of your message, but it sounded like something awful happened last night after I left. It's not about Dickie, is it?"

I opened my mouth, but not to speak. I've learned not to try to interrupt Suzy when she gets going. She is a tiny bit melodramatic, and her thoughts tend to burst forth in a river of words. Only when she runs out of breath is there a break into which I or anyone else can interject a word or two. So I let her wind down. Six or seven questions later, she paused.

"I'm fine, but someone fell out of a window at the museum," I jumped in. "It was a zoo. And, no, it wasn't Dickie who fell. I can't talk about it too much—the police specifically asked me not to—but he fell from my office window."

Exclamations. More questions. I waited for the big one. "Uh-uh, sorry. For one thing, I don't actually, one hundred percent, know myself who it was."

Mentally apologizing for my untruth, and so wishing I could tell her everything, I filled her in as best I could and then floated the idea that had been forming in my mind as I idly played with the card for Win's show. Dropping onto a dining room chair and stretching out my stiff legs, I said, "Why don't we go to Santa Fe for a few days? I really need to get away from all of this. It's depressing and strange, you know?"

With Clint dead and me possibly next, and with Weiler making it sound like I was a suspect, Vera's invitation was the answer to a prayer. I'd have to clear it with Peter, do some damage control with my donors, and figure out how someone had faked the letter, so Weiler would get off my back. If the cops hadn't found out who pushed Clint by the time I left town, I could arrange to meet with Rowland Reynold in Santa Fe. I might learn something about who would benefit from Clint's murder, or at least why Reynold was nearby when the alarm in my office went off, a small fact that kept whispering to me. As a matter of fact, Lisa might be more willing to talk to me or Suzy than to the police if she and Clint had some history. It was better than hanging around and becoming the default suspect.

"We can stay at Vera's house," I said to Suzy. "She's Dickie's aunt and has invited me to come down."

Vera, Dickie's deceased father's sister, liked me, or at least disliked her sister-in-law enough to know that taking me to her malnourished bosom would be annoying to Mrs. A. The first time I met Vera, she insisted I visit her in Santa Fe, where she grilled me nonstop for two days about my background, my family, my career. I realized I had passed when she pronounced me strong enough to drag Dickie away from Mama. Alas, she didn't factor in underwear models.

She dismisses the divorce as a "silly thing he didn't mean at all. It was that horrible Veronique, aided and abetted by my sister-in-law. You could have him back in an instant if you'd send the tiniest signal."

Vera spends most of her time en route to Paris from Venice or to Palm Springs from New York, wherever her overly groomed and tanned boyfriend of the moment desires. I doubt she's wired into my ex's emotions, since she never lands anywhere long enough to make real-time connections, but since having him back is the last thing I am contemplating, I make very sure I'm not sending signals. One marital adventure with Richie Rich was plenty for me.

Still, I keep getting postcards and notes, all of which end the same way: *The Santa Fe house is empty. Elana keeps asking after you.*

Elana, Vera's housekeeper, was the best interpreter of

Mexican food I'd ever had the pleasure of dining with. The promise of a few days of her cooking was tempting, and what better time than now? If my boss complained, I could remind him that I hadn't had a whole week off in two years, if you didn't count the Napa Valley wine tour for six high-maintenance couples with lots of luggage, which I definitely do not. It had cemented a half-million gift for the acquisitions program but left me feeling like a sherpa.

Teeni—assuming she wasn't arrested for murder or for soliciting an officer, which was more likely—could hold down the fort.

"If we fly down next Friday, we could spend a few days hiking and shopping. In fact, Win's having a show there, and I'm curious to know more about his relationship to Clint. What do you say? We can stay at Aunt Vera's *casa*. It's quite luxe in a low-key way."

"It's a thought. Rowland wants me to come down and visit him—did I tell you?"

I wasn't sure how I felt about my best friend getting too involved with the wolf man, especially since he was on my personal list of suspicious people.

"Santa Fe is spa central these days," Suzy added, "and you know I don't do hikes, so I think I'll stay downtown. Promise we'll make time to go to the Indian market at the Governor's Palace and eat at Café Pasqual every day?"

"Sure. Whatever you want."

"I'll call the Red Desert Inn and see if they have space. They take such good care of me, and I can roll out of bed and into a yoga class early in the morning with no hassle."

We said good-bye, and I raced to Perfect Pasta a couple of blocks away to order a small basil, pine nut, and goat cheese pizza for lunch, picked up my dry cleaning nearby while the pizza baked in their oven, and got home in time to hear the answering machine click in to the sound of Inspector Weiler's voice.

"Ms. O'Rourke? My partner is in your office with me right now. We'd appreciate your coming in to the museum when you get this message. We've got something we'd like you to see."

Shoot. The aroma from the pizza box was making my stomach growl, reminding me I hadn't eaten anything since a canapé or two at the Devor last night. Woman cannot live on wine and coffee alone. At least not this woman.

What did he mean, something in my office? It was embarrassing to think of someone poking around in my dump drawer—everyone who works at a desk all day has one— through half-eaten energy bars, old laundry slips, little packets of soy sauce, cruise brochures, discount coupons.

I gobbled my lunch, checked that Fever wasn't feeling lonely (probably not—he was asleep), and headed out to my car, only to realize with a start that it was still at the Devor. Swearing profusely, I ran down to California Street and snagged a bus that was ambling slowly downtown.

On weekends, there's more of a crowd at the museum, families and out-of-towners. They're good for business, since they invariably stop at the museum shop. Heck, some people don't even come past the lobby but head right for the shopping experience, which is okay with us, since all that lovely merchandise helps balance the budget.

I made my way to the elevators, got off at five, and headed for the now closed and locked STAFF ONLY door. My office door was open, and there was a jumble of yellow crime-scene tape hanging off the knob. Inspector Weiler was sitting in my chair with his back to the now-closed window, talking on his cell phone. Another man was slouching on the couch, flipping the pages of a small notebook. He smiled up at me, slowly rose to a hunky six-foot-two, and held out a big hand.

"Inspector Sugerman. Inspector Weiler will be off the phone in a minute. We appreciate your coming in."

"Yes, well, I wasn't aware I had much choice." There were dirty smudges on the windowsill and the frame. It was going to be impossible to work here without drapes. I shivered.

"It'll come off," Sugerman said, mistaking my revulsion for a tidy housewife's complaint. "While we wait, do you mind filling in a few things for me?" I noticed he had nice eyes. Greenish, soft looking. Unusual. "Let's start with the window." Wouldn't you know he'd go right to the grisly heart of the thing?

"Did you have any reason to open the window in the last week or so?"

"No. As I told Inspector Weiler, I've never opened the window in all the time I've been in this office. The whole building's air-conditioned. In fact, because of the art and objects, and the buildup of heat from lights and people, the building's kept colder than most places."

"Ever unlock it?" Sugerman asked.

"No. Why would I, if I wasn't going to open it?" He was kind of cute looking, but maybe he wasn't terribly smart, which would be too bad. I haven't done much looking around since Dickie. Bruised ego, buried in work, fussy—I'm not even sure why. Then, there was the public flameout with Clint when I did get involved with someone. But this guy was tickling my pheromones.

"Can we sit?" he asked. Polite too. I glanced unobtrusively at his left hand. No ring. When I looked back up at him, I caught the smallest upturn at the corner of his mouth.

"Please," I said, hoping my face wasn't getting red but feeling hot. *Enough of that,* I warned myself. *I'm no good at flirting, and, anyway, this is a police investigation. Get a grip, girl.*

"The reason I asked," Sugerman said, settling back on the couch as I sat on the same chair Lisa had occupied—after turning it as far away from the window as possible—"is that there are fingerprints on the bottom edge."

"Of what?" I asked, having lost the thread of the conversation.

"The window frame."

"Not mine."

"We're checking," he said in a neutral voice. "There don't seem to be any on the doorknob, though. You didn't do some housekeeping late Friday, by any chance?"

"You're kidding, right? Of course I didn't clean the doorknob. Or anything else, for that matter."

"Okay, let's leave it at that for now."

For now? Did he seriously think I was going to say something different if he asked me again?

"Tell me what you can about Ms. Watson."

"I already told the inspector."

"I know, but tell me again, please." He smiled, green eyes giving off a little glow.

Oh, well. "She's published several important articles on California funk art—"

"Funk art? You have to be kidding." Inspector Weiler was off the phone and had wandered around the desk to sit on the arm of the couch.

"Not at all," I explained. "It's highly prized today."

"What the hell is funk art, some kind of Summer of Love stuff?" Weiler asked.

"Not quite. It thrived in the Bay Area in the sixties and seventies. Large scale, sense of humor, playful use of materials. Robert Arneson, Roy DeForest, and Lois Anderson, who created wild furniture out of scavenged costume jewelry, are some of my favorites. I know collectors who will spend several hundred thousand dollars for a really good work, although that can be dicey." Weiler raised his eyebrows, a trick I was coming to know. It encouraged me to talk more. "One problem is that the materials sometimes are, well, funky, and are crumbling, or discoloring, or generally falling apart."

Weiler's mouth turned down at the corners. "You are kidding me," he said flatly.

"Actually, Andy, I don't think she is," Mr. Good Cop said. So Weiler had a first name. Now, if Weiler would return the favor, I might know what Superman, er, Sugerman, was called when he wasn't on duty.

"Never mind," Weiler said, standing up and waving his arm. "I'm one of those people you experts stick their noses up at. I know what I like, and I like it to look like something I know."

All this talk about art was going nowhere. If I don't, in fact, act like a snob about art, it's only because that would make me too much like Dickie's mother and her friends. I love art. Old paintings, new media, and darn near everything in between. So I let it go and waited.

"Mrs. Argetter—"

"Not Argetter," I said to Green Eyes. "O'Rourke." He had a nice jawline, strong but not obstinate. "I went back to my maiden name when Richard and I divorced."

"And that was when?" he asked.

"Two years ago."

He scribbled something in his book.

"Could you tell me why you wanted to see me?" I asked, focusing my attention on Weiler. "I have to change and meet someone downtown. Work related." Teeni and I had planned earlier in the week to drop into an opening at a Grant Avenue gallery to try to interest a new couple in town in the Devor. It wasn't urgent, but between Sugerman's green eyes and Weiler's hectoring style of questioning, I was getting itchy. I was also getting over my squeamishness and wanted an opening to fish for some information while Weiler and I were in the same room.

"Let's start with this," Weiler said, holding up a plastic bag. "Can you tell me anything about it?"

The "it" in question was a crumpled business envelope. Weiler held the plastic bag up so I could see it better. The envelope had the distinctive Devor logo on the address label, and an address was computer-printed on it.

"Well, it looks like our stationery," I said. "But I'm not sure what else I could tell you. Did you find it here?"

"Nope," Weiler said, almost cheerfully. "Mr. Maslow's apartment. My question is, did you send this? It's addressed to him, mailed to his home address."

"I'm not sure what you're driving at, but Clint's on several mailing lists at the museum. And, if it's from me or my office, since we were friends, it's quite possible I sent him something in the mail over the past year."

"Did you write to him last week?"

"No. He might have received a mass mailing for contributions to the annual fund sometime in the last month, although those letters actually are packaged from a fulfillment house, an outside operation that handles our bulk mail after we provide computer-generated lists and a master letter."

"This was hand stamped and mailed from a substation near your home. We think the letter telling him to meet you in your office came in this envelope, although we can't be sure."

"It wasn't from me. That's all I know," I said, fighting off a sense of panic. Was someone trying to frame me? If so, Weiler seemed to be buying it. "Look, do I need a lawyer? I'm trying to be helpful, but this is spooking me out. Can't you check for fingerprints or something? That would prove I didn't mail it myself, right?"

"No prints except Mr. Maslow's—surprise, surprise. Do you want a lawyer? I'm just asking a few questions to clear things up. But it's up to you."

I debated with myself. Getting a lawyer involved now might make it look as if I had something to hide, which I emphatically didn't. Being led off to jail with my hands cuffed behind my back didn't exactly appeal either.

"I'll think about the lawyer," I said. "I want justice for Clint, and anything that will help find the person who did this is my highest priority, Inspector, whether you believe that or not. If you still think I had something to do with this . . . this horrible thing after tomorrow, I will call someone. For now, let's keep talking."

"All right, then," Weiler said, smoothing his sparse hair back over his scalp. "We found something in your office you can help us identify. But first, let's get back to Ms. Watson. How long has she worked for you?"

Concentrate, I told myself. *You don't want to give the cops the wrong impression.* "She's worked for me for about two years. But she worked at the museum before that—first in the education department while she finished her master's thesis, and then with the curatorial staff while she had a research grant to write a paper on Alexander Calder. The mobile artist?" I added, getting a blank look from Weiler. Sugerman, from the couch, nodded that he, at least, knew who Alexander Calder was.

"As I said before, everyone loves Teeni." It sounded a little defensive to my ears, but I hoped Weiler didn't think so.

"Anyone in particular?" he said, in the same suspicious voice with which he asked every question. I pitied his kids, if he had any. God forbid they came home twenty minutes late some Saturday night. He'd probably grill the unlucky date under a bare lightbulb.

"I meant that platonically," I sighed. "You'd have to ask her about her romances."

Which might have included Clint. Or might not, I reminded myself. By now, it was nagging at me.

"Okay, let me ask you about this," Weiler said. He got up and moved behind my desk again, reached into a cardboard box, and pulled out another clear plastic evidence envelope.

"Recognize this?"

And here we were in trouble. I reached into my tote bag for a tissue and blew my nose. "Well, I can't be sure exactly," I said, squinting at the envelope, as if I couldn't see that it contained a rainbow-hued acrylic fingernail, complete with sparkles.

Weiler sighed, got up, and came around the desk, waving the envelope slightly. "Here, maybe you can see it better, Ms. O'Rourke," he said heavily.

"Um, well, it's obviously one of those fake fingernails," I said. "I don't have nails like that myself." I held out my short, unpolished fingers, wishing, as Sugerman raised his head to look at them over Weiler's outstretched arm, that I had taken a half hour for a manicure during the week.

"So, does it look like anyone's you know?" Weiler asked with exaggerated patience.

"Well, I guess it could be Teeni's," I began, "but, you know, a lot of women have that stuff done, and I really couldn't say this was, you know, her nail specifically."

Actually, I could, since I had complimented her on her nails' in-your-face style the day before the gala. But who knew if the manicurist had given someone else the same design, someone who happened to be in my office Friday night? Did these things fall off? Didn't they only come off if you sawed them, or dissolved them in acid, or something?

Weiler's cell phone rang again, and he turned away, tossing the envelope to Sugerman, whose reflexes were so good, he had it before I even saw his arm move.

Now was my chance to get some information. "Has Mrs. Thorne told you how she got in?"

"It's probably best," Green Eyes said, "if I don't discuss other witnesses' statements with you."

"Yes, but don't you think it's important? I mean, the door to the wing swings shut automatically. My office, you have to pull it shut, but people can't simply wander into our executive suite."

"We're checking on it," was all Sugerman would say. "I don't think we'll have to keep the office taped as a crime scene after today. The crew has pretty much vacuumed it clean. I told a janitor earlier how to get off the fingerprinting-powder stains. By the time you come in Monday, you won't even know anything happened."

"I will always know something awful happened here," I mumbled, my throat suddenly closing and my eyes stinging.

"In fact, starting Monday, I'm going to be on a crusade to get my office moved. It's gruesome."

Weiler snapped his cell shut, tucked it into his belt, and picked up the box. We left single file, the younger cop waving me before him and pausing in the doorway.

"We finished here?" he asked.

"Yeah, Charlie, the team did all they could," Weiler said. Aha, successful detective work, finally, even though I wasn't in the mood for pursuing Charles Sugerman, aka Green Eyes right now. He gathered up the crime-scene tape and dumped it into my wastebasket before pulling the door shut. The elevator door slid open, and we descended to the lobby along with three chubby teenage girls in ill-advised, low-cut jeans and midriff-baring tops, who were complaining about a homework assignment.

I decided to practice my interviewing skills on a more familiar target, one who was probably at the manicurist's right now. Teeni had some questions to answer, and I was determined to get to her before Weiler did.

Chapter Six

I'm not a rigid person, but I do operate on a schedule, and last night and today had really screwed it up. I drove back to my apartment and changed into a not-so-little black dress, put on some big silver earrings to distract anyone who might notice the bags under my eyes, added a pair of ridiculously high heels in case the earrings didn't do the job, and raced back downtown.

Irma Golden's second-floor gallery on Grant Avenue was humming, packed so tightly, you couldn't step back to see the art on the walls if you wanted to. But no one wanted to, it seemed. It was party time. Goldie herself, all five-feet-two, two hundred pounds of her, came over to give me a hug and shoved a glass of Champagne into my hands. "Sweetie, you're a doll for coming. I know you'll love Rusher's work and, my God, is he handsome or what?" Goldie turned me around by the shoulders to see the artist. Surrounded by women of all ages who cooed and indulged in girlish laughter, he smiled knowingly, showing off his sparkling almond

59

eyes and achingly white teeth. Goldie didn't need my assur-
ance. But he was so handsome that I immediately thought:
gay? Single women in San Francisco know all too well that
the city is full to bursting with athletic blonds, smoldering
Latins, and buff African-Americans who leave the party with
guys as cute as they are.

After assuring Goldie that he was, in fact, a god among
men and thanking her for the bubbly, I scanned the crowd
for Teeni. Before death had shocked us out of our routines,
Teeni and I had agreed to check this opening out, to see if
we could connect with the wife of a new CEO in the city, a
woman who might be interested in the museum as her way
into the social life of the town. If I could get her on an advi-
sory committee, and if Teeni could do some research on her
husband's salary and perks, we might be on the way to a
new donor. I didn't have the heart for the chase today, but a
job's a job.

Goldie squeezed her way through the masses to welcome
someone else, and I started circling the room discreetly, now
and then lifting my glass and mouthing hellos to people I
knew. Goldie had been at the Devor last night—I had seen
her with Win Thorne—but she must have left before all hell
broke loose. Otherwise, she would have wanted to hear what
I knew. In fact, I wasn't picking up any overheard comments
here, so the news must not have hit the art community yet.

The god's paintings were going for fifteen to twenty-five
thousand dollars a pop, which explained why this was a
pretty uptown group. No Teeni so far, but I did see the
prospect and her husband. He stood out, poor guy, in a camel
sports coat that marked him as overdressed and a tight-
lipped smile that suggested he was in pain. She wore a pink
suit and matching pink shoes and looked lost. I maneuvered

my way over to them. "Hi, Paula. I'm Dani O'Rourke. We
met at the Blakes' a couple of weeks ago."

Confused by this so-San Francisco crowd, she greeted me
like her new best friend. We quickly did the dance of new
acquaintances. Yes, Wichita. Summer house on Lake Michi-
gan. Two kids in private college. Looking for a McMansion
in Marin, although the prices were hard to swallow.

"I'd love to give you both a private tour of the Devor sometime," I said, following my script to the *T*. "Maybe arrange
lunch with the museum director and the chair of the docent
committee? You'll like her, and I think she's from the Midwest too."

Paula said she would love that. Mr. Important squinted
and explained that he was too busy, CEO duties and all, "but
Paula will represent us." She beamed at him in apparent gratitude for allowing her to carry the family flag, scribbled her
phone number on the back of his business card, and all but
begged me to call her in a few days. Assignment completed,
I could leave, except that I wanted to corner Teeni and look
at her fingernails.

I spotted Win Thorne in a corner, clutching a plastic wineglass and looking morose. I wove my way through the crowd
until I was right in front of him.

"Hi, Win. I'm surprised to see you here. Didn't think
openings were your thing."

He looked at me as if I was a ghost.

"Dani, from the Devor?" I said. It didn't seem likely he
had forgotten who I was, but his expression indicated I could
have dropped in from another planet. Much as I hate to admit
it, I am not the most memorable person in the world now that
I don't have four hundred and fifty million dollars backing
me up.

"Sorry, my mind was somewhere else," he said, attempting to smile. He looked as tired as I did and didn't have the advantage of accessories to disguise it. "So, how are you doing?"

"Not great, to tell the truth. Who would be? When did you and Lisa get home?"

"Midnight, I guess. But neither of us knows anything about what happened. What did the cops tell you?"

"Not much. I think they still don't know a lot. Is Lisa here?" I looked around.

"Too upset. But I promised Goldie I'd stop by."

"Were you upstairs with Lisa when he, um, the person, fell?" I asked.

He ran a hand through his thick mane of dark hair. "I was talking to Goldie down in the lobby."

That didn't make sense, if Goldie really had left by then, but he could have gotten the times mixed up in the confusion. "How did you know Lisa was in my office?"

"She told me she was headed up to the fifth floor to look for someone. When I got up there, a friend told me she'd gone in that direction, looking for a ladies' room. I waited near the elevators for her and figured she must have gone down the hallway when she didn't come out of the restroom. The guard didn't know or wouldn't say, so I just hung around."

Win shifted his feet and drained his glass, signaling he was ready to go. Poor guy was going to be shocked when he found out the dead man was a protégé of his. I felt bad, not being able to tell people like Suzy and Win, but I didn't dare test Weiler's patience.

I waited another fifteen minutes, but the stress of the last twenty-four hours had worn me out. I was depressed and cross-eyed with fatigue. Teeni would have to wait. Mr. and Mrs. CEO left, and none of the donors I am charged with befriending were in the room. I pushed myself off the wall and snuck out.

Fever had gotten tired of waiting for me to come home and had gone to sleep, or, perhaps, had not woken up from when I saw him last. Step out of shoes, brush teeth, drop dress over chair, turn phone ringer off.

Murder, mystery, mayhem—it mattered not to me. My brain was fried. I couldn't juggle all the bits and pieces of information and innuendo that were swimming around in my mind. As I fell asleep, I remembered Teeni flirting with the first officers who came to my office. That was quintessential Teeni, and I didn't see how anyone could be like that right after pushing someone out a window. So, then, if not her, who? Why on earth had anyone pushed a brilliant young artist out of my window in the middle of a party?

Chapter Seven

I woke up with a cat sitting on my chest, staring intensely at my face, willing me to open my eyes. The sun was shining, and the sounds of traffic that usually drift in from the street were muted, signaling a Sunday morning.

"Okay, okay, I know it's breakfast time," I sighed. His tail shot straight up in the air, and he marched down the hall.

Thirty minutes later, the phone rang, and I knew why. MYSTERIOUS FALL AT DEVOR MUSEUM, MAN DIES IN PLUNGE. The front-page newspaper article didn't offer much: fifth floor, "jumped, fell, or was pushed," man's name not being released until next of kin were notified, etc. Peter was quoted to the effect that it could have happened anywhere and wasn't the museum's fault. Weiler was not quoted directly, but the police department spokeswoman said they were interviewing a number of people who were nearby when it happened and had no suspects yet. I could hear Weiler in the *yet*. Our handsome, silver-haired mayor, who was at the gala but downstairs swilling Champagne as he did whenever free booze was within reach, was quoted as being grateful for the speed and skill of his police department. There was a photo of the front doors of the Devor, closed, with a worried-looking museum guard peering out from behind the glass. Peter would be groaning. Board members would be freaking out and calling one another. Damage control would be the order of the day, Sunday or not.

The phone rang again. I refilled my mug, pulled up the blinds so Fever could sit on the sunny kitchen windowsill and lust after the finches in the yard, and picked up the phone.

"Dani, you must feel awful about all this." It was Suzy.

"Yes, I feel hungover from the shock."

"Why would anyone pick the museum to murder someone in? Well, I say leave it to the police, sweetie—that's their job. I've been thinking. Why don't you have lunch tomorrow with RR and me? I want to hear what's going on, and the newspaper doesn't tell you anything. Plus, when I told RR we might go to Santa Fe, he said he's headed back there and that we should plan on being his guests for dinner while we're in town. I know you warned me that he's got a bad rep as a developer in New Mexico, but he genuinely loves art."

Power is sexy. My research for the Devor on Reynold had turned up a handful of nasty lawsuits involving his super high-end, gated residential developments. But Reynold has an impressive painting collection, and if some of Suzy's paintings might wind up in said collection, I can understand her interest in him. And, since she is cute, dimpled, and has a trust fund that keeps her warm and dry without having to lean on a man, the fact that Reynold enjoys her company doesn't surprise me either. What did surprise me is that Reynold had apparently not told her who had died at the Devor. What surprised me more, and was creeping me out, in fact, was that he seemed to know it was Clint. He had implied that one of the cops let it out, but I was still bothered. Reynold had been pissed off at Clint, and I hadn't liked the look in his eyes when he said as much.

Suzy was suggesting a trendy, raw food restaurant for lunch. *Raw* translates to carrots and radishes carved up to look like Japanese brush paintings, cold soup, and zucchini slices pretending to be lasagna noodles. Just thinking about it made me crave a juicy hamburger.

"I had a thought," she added. "Why don't you call Clint and invite him too? I think he and Rowland are angry at each other. With all the shows coming up, they need to get over it. I know Clint behaved badly to you too. But I'd like to see you two be friends again."

I choked on my coffee. I couldn't tell Suzy that Clint was dead. If Reynold hadn't told her, and if Weiler wasn't ready to tell the world, I didn't dare leak it. Weiler would be all over me. And telling Suzy would definitely qualify as a leak. Within a couple of hours, everyone at the Institute, not to mention her hairdresser and her mother in Chicago, would be in on the secret.

Suzy was still talking. "You know, Clint drives himself too hard, and it sometimes spills over to the people close to him."

I jumped in as she paused for breath. "Why don't we two have lunch with Rowland this time? But not raw. I vote for Le Charm and some real French onion soup."

"Okay, I guess. French bistros are romantic, and there's a great gallery across the street."

That reminded me of Lisa and her possible flirtation with Clint.

"I've been trying to remember. Was it you who told me Lisa and Clint had a thing last year?"

"I don't remember saying that, but if I did, it was because Lisa was hanging around the Institute's studio building a lot last year. I'm sure he's not interested in her, if that's what's worrying you."

Poor Clint wouldn't be interested in anyone anymore. I felt like scum, pretending he was still alive. Suzy chatted for a few minutes more, but she didn't have more to say about Lisa and Clint. As soon as I hung up, the phone rang again.

It was Cecilia Rodriguez, the Devor's PR director, asking me to come in for an emergency senior staff meeting in a couple of hours. Not surprising. Rumors flying, she said. Reporters bugging her for information. Peter panicking about the coverage in the paper and on television.

"It's a nightmare," she said. "The police department spokesperson is telling me I can't say anything related to the fall or the victim. Of course, the reporters are mad at me for not giving them what the SFPD won't. It's frustrating, and I'm a bit ragged. Thank heavens Teeni's here."

"Teeni's there? At the museum?" She's a front-row regular at Glide Memorial Church on Sundays, so what was she doing at the museum this morning?

"She was here when I arrived. Asked if she could help me, for which I am grateful. I think she's doing what she can to get our offices back into shape. There's still crime-scene tape up on your office door, did you know?"

"The police asked me to come in yesterday to fill in some blanks in their investigation, but I got the idea they were finished."

"We're stationing the regular security staff at every staff door throughout the building. It'll be a nightmare with overtime, Peter says, but with so many visitors, we need to make sure nothing even remotely unusual happens today. Of course, the local TV channels sent crews and reporters to do stand-ups in the lobby."

I commiserated. We work so hard to get reporters and editors interested in the museum's art and historical exhibits, and the only time they come with their cameramen and remote trucks is when disaster strikes. As they say, "If it bleeds, it leads."

I wasn't looking forward to dealing with Peter, who tends to be a bit high-strung at the best of times. I have a soft spot for Peter. He's arrogant at times, smart, ambitious, does his homework, and takes risks when he believes in something. In the art world, he's considered someone to watch. The buzz is that his next move will be to the Guggenheim, the LA County Museum of Art, or some other high-profile job. I've always thought he might surprise everyone by taking on something unusual, though. He does love to shake things up. At times of stress, however, it's best to speak slowly to Peter in the tone of voice one would use when trying to calm a runaway horse. If today wasn't a time of stress, I did not know when we might expect one, so I was pretty sure he would be freaking out.

Teeni's being at the museum early was a puzzle. I wanted to get there before she left, to look at her hands. If Clint's identity was still under wraps, I'd have to think of some clever way to find out how she felt about him. She had what the police called opportunity, in the form of keys. She was in my office when I got there. She knew the building well and could move around the stairwells and in and out of the staff wing.

I admitted that part of my desire to know was curiosity and the sense that I was in a good position to figure all of this out, since I knew the players and the place. But I also felt responsible. My name was apparently what had brought Clint up to my office and into danger. I had to hope he didn't die thinking I was part of a horrible plot.

The red light on the answering machine was blinking. Turning up the volume and pushing the Play button as I headed to the kitchen, I listened first to Dickie, who wanted to make sure I was all right, then to my sister, recognizing the name of the Devor in the wire story her local paper published but probably not imagining that it was my office, and a couple of friends and co-workers, all of whom were curious.

The last message caused me to pause with my knife over a tub of cream cheese. It wasn't a message, or was it? Silence, the kind that screams that someone is on the other end of the line. It went on for what seemed like a minute, followed by a firm click. I replayed it, but there weren't any jabbering telemarketers' voices in the background. Maybe a crank call, maybe a mistake. I decided to return calls later, ate breakfast, and left Fever to his routine, after-breakfast nap curled up in my comforter, the morning sun dappling his stripes.

The museum lobby was humming. Most visitors were there for the art, or perhaps the weekly children's "Draw like Picasso" program. There were enough high, screeching voices in the meeting room off the main lobby to suggest that the future of abstract art was assured.

I got off the elevator at five, entered the staff wing, and started looking for Teeni. She wasn't in her office, my office, the women's restroom, or the coffee room. No one else was there. Cecilia was right: there was still a strip of crime scene tape across my door, but I had no more time to look for Teeni. The meeting upstairs was about to start.

On the sixth floor, folks were gathering. Peter's glass-doored suite of offices opens directly off the elevator, which won't go to the sixth floor without a key inserted into a special lock. About half of the Devor administrators have keys. Peter's executive digs cover what amounts to half of the floor. The rest is taken up by the financial VP's staff and the senior curators.

The director's suite includes an elegant reception hall, offices for two assistants, a small kitchen, and his own L-shaped work space complete with a sitting area built around classic leather Le Corbusier couches and chairs, glass tables, a built-in bar, and sweeping views of San Francisco's steadily rising downtown skyline. He even has his own executive washroom.

Cecilia and Peter were huddling with the president of the board of trustees and the security chief. A handful of managers carrying notebooks were settling into straight-backed chairs pulled up on the fringes of the couch area. Several trustees were helping themselves to coffee and rolls from the sideboard, and I headed for this group.

Peter waited until we had settled down, and he moved to a spot in front of the windows. He raked his hair off his forehead with long fingers, then shoved his hands deep into his pockets.

"Well, friends," Peter began, his normal tenor voice tight with stress and his eyes flicking from one face to another. "I appreciate your coming. This has been a most distressing weekend."

"And it isn't over yet," murmured the vice president for human resources, sitting next to me.

Peter heard, looked at me, and frowned. I smiled warmly at Peter and nodded my support, horse-whisperer that I am. He relaxed his frown slightly.

"There isn't much we know for sure," he continued, concentrating on the tassels of his polished loafers. "Apparently, a visitor—an artist, not a donor," he added quickly, looking around, the relief in his voice audible, "fell from a window in the fifth-floor staff wing. From Dani's window, in fact."

I winced as every head turned toward me.

"I wasn't there at the time," I said weakly.

"True," Peter said, sounding wistful. Did he think it would have been better if I had been identified as the murderer and hauled away in handcuffs? "The police have no idea who might have been involved, if anyone but the victim was. It is possible," he said hopefully, "this was a suicide."

Suicide. Why hadn't I thought of that? That would be perfect—well, not exactly perfect, since it still meant Clint was dead, but at least I could stop looking suspiciously at people I knew.

"What do the police say?" asked one of the trustees.

"They aren't sure yet," said Johnson, the board chair, clearing his throat and turning around to include us all in his answer. "I talked to the mayor again this morning. He says the chief of police is not ready to call this murder yet but that, even so, they are beginning to construct a list of people they think might have had a reason to dislike the unfortunate young man."

"Excuse me, Peter," piped up the HR head next to me. "Do we know for sure who it was? Can you tell us?"

"I guess it's official," Peter said, his brow furrowing. He looked down at his shoes again. When he looked up, his eyes were darting from face to face. He was actually mumbling, a first in my experience. "He was a graduate of the master of fine arts program at the Institute, winner of several juried awards for early-career painters, and taught three years ago in our summer program. Clinton Maslow. Some of you may know him."

I didn't hear any gasps of recognition or pain.

"Will this affect the museum's activities?" someone asked.

Peter straightened his tie. His hand trembled, but the tactical question seemed to settle him down, and the group began discussing media coverage, insurance, the cost of extra security, and other practical matters.

"Dani? What can you tell us?"

"Hmm?" I'd lost the thread of the conversation.

"Have you gotten any calls from Patrons Society members?"

"Only one. My plan is to brief them individually, after we agree on what we can say."

"We can assure everyone that this has nothing to do with the Devor, can't we, Peter?" asked a woman trustee anxiously.

Peter nodded, but his tentatively reassuring smile was pasted on.

"I'm not sure we can say that quite yet," said another, familiar voice.

We all turned to look behind us. Inspectors Weiler and Sugerman had come in quietly and were standing at the back of the room.

Chapter Eight

Weiler was frowning, of course. My buddy Charlie Sugerman's expression was neutral until he noticed me. Then he smiled cheerfully and lifted his arm in a truncated wave. Several heads swiveled in my direction.

"Ah, hello, Inspectors," Peter said too loudly. "Please join us."

Since they already had, this was hardly necessary. But neither cop remarked on that, and they made their way into the room, Weiler to one of the sofas and Sugerman to a chair in the rear.

"We were talking about the impact this, er, event, might have on the running of the museum," Peter said. "Perhaps you could bring us up to date."

"I'd like to know what the policeman meant, Peter, by saying the incident might be connected to the Devor," piped up the woman trustee.

"I'm sure Inspector Weiler meant only the coincidence of its happening on the premises," Peter said, wringing his

73

hands. This meeting had gotten away from him, and he knew it.

"I agree with Agnes," said Johnson, which was significant because, in matters concerning the Devor, Johnson had the deciding vote, maybe two votes. Should anyone envy that power, all he or she has to do is pony up twenty million dollars for a new building, raise an equal amount from his golfing buddies, and make sure his good pal, the mayor, persuades the planning commission to sign off on the expansion with dispatch. Johnson's desire to hear from Weiler directly caused Peter to close his mouth with a snap and sit down without ceremony.

Weiler sat forward on the sofa, scrubbed at his eyes with balled-up fists, then dropped his hands onto his thighs and sat back into as comfortable a slouch as the squared-off furniture permitted. He might have been a famous actor about to declaim Hamlet's famous "to be or not to be . . ." speech, we were so attentive.

"I'm not prepared to go into detail, mostly because we don't really know a lot yet," Weiler said, looking directly at Johnson. "But I think it's fair to say that even if no one who works for the Devor was involved in the death, someone who had keys let the victim into the locked area. I don't think Inspector Sugerman or I talked with everyone here. Maybe, Mr. Lindsey," he suggested, looking over at Peter, "you'd be good enough to let these folks introduce themselves to us?"

Peter waved to someone up front, and we went around the room. When it was my turn, Weiler broke in to say, "That's okay, Ms. O'Rourke. We know who you are." It didn't sound friendly. I slid down in my chair.

"Well?" demanded Geoff Johnson when we had finished. "Let's hear what you have to tell us, Inspector. We're busy people, and I know everyone here has work to do in connection with this unfortunate accident. Or was it suicide, in which case, I hardly think the Devor could be to blame?"

"Suicide?" Weiler said, as if it were a novel idea. "I don't think suicide is likely. Did any of you know Mr. Maslow well enough to think he was depressed, unhappy, or in bad health?"

Much shaking of heads, murmurs, but no one spoke up.

"Excuse me," said Sugerman from the back of the room. "Did any of you know Mr. Maslow?"

"You knew him pretty well, didn't you?" the board chairman asked Peter.

My boss opened his mouth, closed it, cleared his throat, and opened his mouth again.

"Isn't he the guy you said would make your fortune, or something?"

All fidgeting and whispering stopped. The room was silent as we waited to hear how Peter would respond to such an interesting question. His mouth was still open, as if he were about to speak. He looked at the ceiling, then at the floor. His ears were getting red. Finally, he cleared his throat and spoke.

"Oh, sure, I knew him. A real comer in the art world. We wanted to get a few of his paintings for the Devor while they were still affordable. I had hopes that Rowland Reynold would donate something from his collection. I think what I said, or at least what I meant to say, was that having his work here would help the Devor's fortunes."

So not convincing. What was Peter worried about? I waited for Weiler to follow up, but all he did was rub his hand over his head once or twice and turn back to the group. "Anyone else?" he said. The tension broke. Our human resources VP raised her hand, and Sugerman confirmed she was on the list of people he planned to talk to on Monday. No one else seemed to know Clint.

Johnson pushed for information for a few more minutes, Weiler danced around, and then the meeting seemed to lose its momentum. When Cecilia's cell phone rang, she peeked at the screen, jumped up, and excused herself, explaining in a rush that another TV news team was downstairs. With that, we all stood up, and I joined the others moving to the elevator.

Teeni stepped out as the doors opened.

"Hey," I said, catching her eye. To my shock, she ducked back inside when she saw me and pushed the button.

The waiting crowd squawked in protest, and someone tried to jam his arm into the closing door, to no avail. The elevator light went to five and stopped, then continued down to the lobby. I edged around the group and took off for the stairs. Teeni's office is several doors down from mine, and I made straight for it, noticing as I marched past that the crime-scene tape was finally gone from my door.

Teeni's door was closed. I knocked, then turned the doorknob. It was locked. I called out her name and rattled the knob, but nothing happened. I put my ear to the door to listen for movement.

"I always knew you were nosy, but this is over the top."

I jumped at Teeni's voice right behind me.

"Jeez, you scared me!" I yelled, jerking away from the door. "Where have you been?"

"In the ladies' room," she said dryly, cocking her head to one side, hands on hips.

"For two days?" I countered. "Since Friday night?"

"What are you talking about? I haven't been anywhere, or at least not anywhere I have to report to you," she said. "What gives?" There was hesitation behind the aggressive tone in her voice and an unusual reserve in her deep brown eyes. Okay, now I knew something was wrong.

I let out my breath in a loud puff of frustration. "For one thing, this is hardly a normal weekend, with detectives prowling around and everyone here a suspect in a murder. For another, you were supposed to meet me at Goldie's, remember?"

"So I didn't make the party," Teeni said, her voice rising. "Big deal. I had something better to do." She jutted one hip out, her pencil skirt pulling tightly across her thighs, pushed her head forward, and stared at me. When Teeni wants to signal indignation, she does it better than most people, but I wasn't buying today.

"Well, what was that up on the sixth floor, then?" I asked.

Teeni reached past me with her key, slipped it into the lock, and pushed open the door to her office. It's smaller than mine and has no sofa—a bureaucratic triumph on someone's part, reflecting the fact that she's lower down the administrative food chain, since she works for me. The truth is, she reports to me much the way a cat reports to its owner, which is to say I'm well trained to let her do what she wants as long as she brings me my share of the hunt.

My office is at the corner made by the front and side of the building. Teeni's is on the side of the building, and her window faces onto a blank wall and alley. She would not be able to see my window from her office. In fact, no one could, since all the offices are off that hall. The corridor runs along the inside wall, with men's and women's washrooms and a water fountain in a recessed area halfway down its length.

Teeni motioned me in, closed the door, sat down hard on a chair, and kicked off her shoes. For a minute she stared at me, her lips compressed and her eyes kind of squinty. One hand played with her brown-black curls. The hand appeared to have five sparkly, rainbow-hued talons attached. The other was balled in a fist.

"It was Clint Maslow who went out of the window, wasn't it?" she finally said.

"Yes, it was," I answered. "How did you know?"

"Peter's assistant told me a little while ago. Why did it happen? He was such a talented guy." She reached over to the tissue box and pulled out a couple, wiping her eyes and blowing her nose. *Aha,* my inner detective observed. *Five identical, seriously flashy nails.* "May he rest in peace," she said, punctuating it with a sniff.

Her response hit me hard. With all the stress, the interviews with Weiler, and my uneasiness about my connections to his death, I hadn't had the good cry I owed Clint and myself. A lump formed in my throat, and I swallowed it. Not now. I've never liked being vulnerable in public, and the experience when Dickie and I split made me even more determined. *Later, at home, when you're alone and only Fever can see you,* the get-tough part of me insisted.

I took a deep if somewhat ragged breath. "Yes, it's a bummer and totally mysterious. But I need you to tell me what's going on. You're acting, well, flaky, and I want to know why."

Teeni nodded several times, slowly, as if she was convincing herself of something.

"Okay," she said finally. "I gotta tell you. But you have to promise me you won't tell anyone else what I say. My brother said I should keep it to myself."

"I can't promise if it has to do with the . . . with Clint's death. Is that what this is about?"

"I don't know," Teeni said, and she began to sniff. "I've been worrying about this ever since Friday night. Arnie says to shut up and mind my own business."

Through a nasty trick of the gene pool, Arnie, her big brother, is a convicted felon. He spent most of Teeni's formative years in juvenile hall before graduating to Soledad. I wasn't surprised at Arnie's advice, although I did wonder why Teeni would consult Arnie on anything to do with the law.

"So why were you in my office Friday night? Not that you can't go in whenever you want, but in light of what happened, I'd sure like to know." *And to know why the police showed me a baggie with your fingernail in it,* I added silently. But one thing at a time.

"I was in my office working on a paper. A phone was ringing somewhere, and at first it was only background noise. But it got annoying, so I went out into the hall to listen. It was your phone. Your door was open, but no lights were on. I flipped the switch and went in. I thought it might be important—maybe a personal call from Dickie or something."

I grimaced.

"Well, you know, why does anyone keep calling unless it's urgent?" she continued, sailing right past my irritation at her assumption that my ex might still have an emergency involving me. "Anyway, I picked up the phone and said it was your office. No one spoke, but I'm sure there was someone there. I said hello a couple of times. Whoever it was hung up."

"Was the window open?"

"No. I would have noticed."

"What are you worried about? You told Weiler, right? Now it's his job."

"No, I didn't tell the detective. It's not so simple," she said, looking up at me. She fell silent.

I waited. I was pretty sure I wasn't going to like the complication.

"Okay, here's the deal. The phone call? Your console showed it was coming from Peter's personal line, from his office. At the time, no big deal. Later on, I thought it might have something to do with the accident. I wanted to ask Peter in person, so I could see his face. But I can't get to him privately in all this mess."

"But why on earth would Peter be tied into Clint's death?"

"I didn't know it was Clint, did I? I didn't know anything. And to make it worse, I hit my hand on the edge of your desk, and my stupid fake fingernail came off. I'm scared the police will find it and build some kind of story around it."

"Too late," I told her. "They found the nail. I think they know it's yours. Have the police asked you about the fingernail or a letter?"

"What letter? No, they only asked me about what I saw and heard. Are the police asking questions about me?" she asked, her voice rising an octave.

"Sure, but I told them you're the last person they should suspect. I'll tell you about the phony letter in a minute. But I'm confused," I admitted. "When I came into my office, the alarm was on, the window was open, and you were there."

Teeni seemed less interested in the train of events than in circling back to her own situation. Lifting her shoulders impatiently, she said, "I knew I had to mix and mingle, so I went out to the party."

"Did you leave the lights on and the door open when you left my office?"

"No, I'm sure not."

"And then?"

"I came back later to use the bathroom. It was easier than waiting in line for the public one."

"Was my door still closed?"

"I think so. I would have noticed if it was open, wouldn't I? The alarm started ringing while I was in the john. When I came out, your door was definitely open, and the light was on. No one was there, but the window was open.

"I went over to shut it, then looked out. This thing, like a bundle of rags, was down there. It was near a streetlight, and I realized it was a body." She shuddered.

"I could see people running up to it and hear them yelling. The rest is a blur. I know I called security. Then you and everybody else came in. . . ." She put her elbows on the desk and lowered her head into her hands.

"Did you see Lisa?"

"Not right away. She showed up fast, though." Teeni raised her head. "I wish I knew why Peter called you that night. He didn't say anything to you, did he?"

"Nothing, but we haven't had time to talk. I can see he's worried sick about this whole thing."

"Well, yeah," she said, drawing out the word and giving me a look that suggested only an idiot wouldn't be. "So, what's this about a letter?"

Briefly, I told her what the cops had told me and how spooked I was.

"Didn't you guys call it off awhile back? I heard you had a huge fight."

"Not a fight. Well, not huge. Actually, Clint got out of line when I told him I didn't want to date him anymore—made a scene when we both showed up at the same party. He'd had way too much to drink. It was embarrassing, but I told everyone he was just under stress from the demands his success was making on him. And it was ages ago."

"Okay, but who in hell would try to set you up? And if you weren't angry enough to push him, who was?"

"I have no idea yet, although I promise you I'm not going

to sit by and let someone frame me. But nothing you've told me explains why you've been avoiding me. Is there something else?"

Teeni sat up straighter and started fiddling with a stack of art books on her desk. Then she looked up sharply at me. "All right, but this has to stay between us. You'll understand why," she said as I opened my mouth to protest. "Yesterday morning Peter called me at home to ask a favor."

Odd but not unprecedented. We're not too hierarchical in the fund-raising office, and Teeni is a fount of useful information about artists and rising corporate players.

"He told me he had misplaced his keys a week before and asked me to check around in the development offices. But he didn't want anyone else to know. He was afraid they'd mention it to the cops or the board members and, in the light of everything that had happened, it might raise eyebrows."

"Oh, there's a concept. What did you tell him?"

"I said I would. After all, he's the boss. What did you expect me to do?"

"And then?"

"Um, he especially asked me to look in your office. When I asked why, he got snippy, said it was none of my business."

"Not cool. So, did you search?"

"Yeah, I came in Saturday afternoon and looked everywhere."

"How did you get into my office, since there was crime tape up?"

"There wasn't when I got there. I found it in your wastepaper basket, which was handy, because just as I got started looking, I heard voices. Some of the staff had come in to see if they could help. I put the tape up on your door to keep everyone out, chatted for a while, and left.

"I came in really early this morning, hoping I might find my missing acrylic nail too. Believe me, I looked everywhere, but the keys and the nail weren't in your office. I went upstairs to try to get to Peter to tell him, but then I saw you and . . ."

"Bolted, I know, probably hoping to avoid this conversation. That explains the tape, anyway. I wonder why Peter would think his keys were in my office. Did he give you a clue?"

"Nope. As I said, he was in no mood to tell me anything."

"And now you need to let him know you didn't find the keys. You also want to ask him why he apparently called my office right before things went crazy. I appreciate your loyalty, but has it occurred to you that the police may need to know about this?"

Teeni's shoulders rose as she frowned. "I'm not sure. At least not yet. Anyway, that's his decision, not mine. I'd hate to see him dragged into something ugly right now. He has a lot on his mind. Clint's death, I mean," she added.

Her eyes left my face, and she pushed back her chair, spreading the fingers of the hand I hadn't seen. All five nails glittered. I had a feeling she was holding something back, but if Teeni didn't want to tell me, I wasn't going to find out.

"One last thing. That fingernail. You've got ten fake ones now."

"You didn't think I was gonna walk around with my hands in mittens, did you? That's what I was doing Saturday afternoon. I had to beg to get on my manicurist's schedule, but I couldn't take a chance someone would notice. Anyway," she said, "nothing looks worse than one stubby finger when you go in for this flash." She held up her brilliant talons as evidence.

What next? I asked myself ten minutes later, sitting at my desk. I booted up the computer but couldn't find any recent documents I didn't recognize. The Trash icon indicated it held content—not surprising, since I hardly ever remember to empty it. Drafts of letters and reports, outdated budget memos, PDF files, backups of files . . . Wait a minute, what was this? I hadn't seen a file with this name in my Recent Documents. *Tuesday.doc,* it read. Double clicking, I opened a document I definitely hadn't written.

Tuesday
Dear Clint,
I have to talk with you. It's urgent. I'll meet you in my office at 7 during the party on Friday. It's private. I don't want to discuss it at all before then, so don't even mention it. It's not a problem, though.

Till then D.

I looked in Preferences. *Created by D. O'Rourke.* Well, sure, since it was on my logged-in hard drive. Even though the letter said it was written on a Tuesday, it had been created on a Friday, two weeks ago. Strange. I was at work all day, even though I'd begged off the dinner upstairs.

Not Modified, said my computer's records. I looked again. Even stranger. The letter was created and printed around nine at night on an evening when we close at eight. There was no Saved Envelope file, which didn't mean anything. Had Weiler's team found the backup when they looked through these files? If I called Weiler, would he think I was trying to cover up my own tracks, that I had realized the incriminating file was still on my hard drive and was pretending to have seen it for the first time?

My phone message light was blinking, and I postponed dealing with the problem of the computer evidence by listening to a handful of messages. A staffer trying to get ahead of

Monday's meetings wanted to know if we should cancel our slide show for Patrons Society donors. A newspaper reporter I know slightly, hoping to get information about Friday's happenings through me. Lisa Thorne, probably wanting details. Given what Suzy had said, maybe I should call her back first. I could fish for information as well as she could.

My stomach craved dim sum and hot and sour soup, a sure sign of stress. It had been a standing joke between Dickie and me and something of a custom in the days when I did logistics for events and worried myself into craziness over things like name tags, working microphones, properly chilled wine, and the like. The day after something major, I always wanted Chinese comfort food, and Dickie's courtship rites included bringing box upon box of steamed shrimp dumplings, pot stickers, and a large cardboard container of hot and sour soup, so tantalizing that my mouth watered now, almost tasting it.

There was no sign of reporters and no TV trucks in the Staff Only parking area next to the Devor. By now, I was so locked into the idea of Chinese food that I could smell it even in the alley. Chinatown is far too crowded, but maybe I'd get lucky and find a parking place somewhere near the bustling Clement Street Asian markets, farther out on the avenues and less tourist-clogged.

A car horn beeped, and I looked around. Dickie stepped out of a silver Porsche. Nice. I'd never seen it before. In one hand he held one of those ubiquitous white plastic bags, knotted at the top. Take-out food.

"Hey, kiddo," he said, coming up to my car. "Thought this might be a good idea."

He opened the bag and held it out to me. My nostrils quivered. Shrimp dumplings? Barbeque sauce? Without saying anything, I took the bag and peeked.

"Hot and sour soup?" I said hopefully.

"Of course. Did you think I would forget?"

For no good reason, my eyes began to smart. It was fatigue, and uncertainty, and the proximity of death. I kept my head down for a second or two before looking up at my ex. *Careful,* said my inner voice. "I was thinking about a visit to Clement Street. How did you manage the parking on a busy Sunday afternoon?"

"With this car?" he asked. "Are you kidding?" His lips curled up in a trademark smile.

Ah, yes. I never get used to the ways of the rich. Dickie simply parked the Porsche—and the Porsche before that—wherever there was space. Bus stop, red zone, fire hydrant—it made no difference. What's the worst they can do, he used to say, shrugging. Give me a parking ticket? Tow it away? My own law-abiding, middle-class upbringing made me squirm, but for him it was a non-issue. I remember my embarrassment climbing out of the car when he did it, trying not to see the hostile glances of people walking by. Strangely, he almost never got a ticket, perhaps because of the vanity plate message: FAV4DSN.

"There's enough for two, if you want company." Dickie's middle name is *impulsive,* his typical mode of operation is *why wait,* his ability for introspection almost nonexistent. It explains a lot about him—both what makes him so romantic and appealing and also what makes him insufferable at times. He coasts through life, apparently not understanding the damage his impulsive behavior does to people. Well, to me. I opened the door and got into my car.

"Dani, I want to talk to you seriously," he said, the cheer gone from his voice. He leaned down so his head was only a foot away from mine. I could see the gold flecks in his eyes and the tiny scar that separated the line of one eyebrow into two parts. I looked away.

"I've been told the police have you on their list of suspects."

I opened my mouth to protest, but he kept talking. "Your office, which you keep locked. Your violent boyfriend."

"Violent?" I said. "All he did was yank my arm once."

"In public, I heard."

"Yes, well, it wasn't violent. Take my word for it. He was only trying to keep me from walking away, and it was just that once. Who told you, anyway?"

He shrugged. "A friend who was there at the time. I thought it was unlikely. You're not the type to put up with that."

I mentally slapped him. What did he know? Hadn't I put up with a lot from him?

"I think they have some other reason. Weiler's partner called me Saturday. Wanted to know if I had something with your signature on it. I said no. I do, of course, but I'm not into sharing. Want me to call the lawyers and get you someone? I don't much like the idea of you dealing with these guys on your own. They want to solve it quickly. Pressure from the mayor's office and your board chair. I don't want to see you dragged any further into this than coincidence takes you."

Dickie was scaring me, making me look at precisely what I was trying not to think about. And he didn't even know about the letter or that it was written on my computer. But, truth was, if I leaned on him now, he might get the wrong idea—*i.e.,* that he was forgiven—or flake out on me when something else caught his attention. I had learned my lesson, and I sure as hell wasn't about to forget it in return for a carton of soup.

"Thanks for the warning and the offer of legal help," I said, shaking my head and pushing the bag back toward him. "I really can't. I'm meeting someone."

The only meeting I had was with Fever and my backed-up e-mail, but I wasn't in the mood for Chinese anymore.

Dickie's eyebrows rose, but then he smiled again. "Ah, company for your Clement Street visit. Oh, well, if you can't, you can't. But"—eyebrows up again—"if you want to take this home for later . . . ?"

"Afraid it would go to waste," I said with a chirpiness that sounded totally fake even to me. "But thanks for the thought."

Dickie stood there for an instant, the quizzical smile still on his face. Then, pivoting, he headed for a trash can at the alley entrance. Before he reached it, an unshaven man in a ratty green parka and a knitted cap, pushing a Safeway shopping cart from which hung at least a dozen black plastic garbage bags, shambled over to it, no doubt looking for aluminum cans and bottles.

Thrusting the bag of food into the man's hands, Dickie sauntered back to the Porsche, grin in place. "Some other time, then. Take care of yourself," he called to me as he sank into the car. "Let me know if you want to call in the lawyers." With a roar of the engine, he was off, leaving the man slack-jawed and me feeling worse than when he'd arrived.

"Damn him, anyway," I said out loud, hearing the self-pity in my voice. The street guy was holding the open container of soup in one hand, the lid in the other. As I edged past, he started pouring it out onto the ground, splashing the side of my car. I'd wanted sweet and sour; I got sweet and sour. Chinese proverb: *Beware of getting what you wish for.*

Chapter Nine

That night, Fever and I went to bed cranky. Neither of us slept well, he mostly because I tossed and turned, pulling the covers out from under him and forcing him to sit up and wash himself completely all over again.

Cats are lucky; they don't get bags under their eyes from nights like this. Cold water helped but not much. At thirty, the little shadows under my eyes spoke of romantic tragedies. At thirty-five, they spoke of stress. This morning, my thirty-six-year-old face told me I had better stop at Nordstrom's for some concealer to hide the dark circles that seemed to be spreading on my pale Irish skin. Another year at this rate and people would be asking me what door I'd walked into.

I read the front page of the newspaper to Fever, who ignored me and strolled to the window to commune with the birds.

When I turned the page, my heart did a little skip. There was my hero, Charlie Sugerman, standing next to Homicide Inspector Weiler, both of them in front of the Devor. The story didn't say much but confirmed Clint's name. No relatives, no leads at this time, police determined to solve this puzzling death quickly. Board of trustees of Devor very cooperative.

Sugerman appeared to be smiling faintly and looking off to one side. Weiler looked as if he suspected the photographer of having pushed Clint out the window. In the blurry background, through the glass doors, I could just make out Cecilia peering out anxiously, cell phone to her ear. I used my knife to cut out the picture. After I wiped off the jam, I looked at it for a while. Cute, definitely cute. Calm in a storm. Polite. Good listener. But married? Divorced? Knowing his first name and where he worked was a start, but not really much to go on. If I picked up a murder clue in Santa Fe, I decided, I would bring it back to Inspector Sugerman and only to him. *Good puppy,* my inner voice sneered.

"Like a dog with a stick," I said to Fever, who gave me the look I deserved before turning back to glare out the window at a white-crowned sparrow sitting on a eucalyptus limb and singing like an opera diva.

In the office, things were reassuringly normal. It was Monday. We had standing meetings to confirm what was on the calendar for the week and to debrief about last week's work. My team met in the conference room, where, by mutual consent, we skirted the really big thing.

"Okay, people. Give me the good news first. Any excitement from our Patrons Society about underwriting the German new-media exhibit?" A few thumbs-ups and one maybe sign meant we had something to work with. A couple of years from now, visitors would be arguing about the meaning of Oliver Boberg's mysterious videos of rainy night roads, or Ulrike Rosenbach's multiple, overlapping video narratives. They probably wouldn't notice the handsome sign on the entrance wall thanking our faithful donors for the money to pay for the outrageously high insurance premiums, transportation, illustrated catalog, iPod tours, and wall texts. My job would be to make sure the donors were thanked in as many ways and as often as possible.

"Outstanding. Parents happy with the kids' painting workshop?"

"Not enough to open their wallets," a younger fund-raiser said. "I know I was all for it, but I have a hunch it was more like a very expensive babysitting experiment. I'll call some of the people I know who came and get back to you with suggestions."

"Good idea, Nick. Looking forward, brilliant thoughts on what we can do to profit from the new Egyptian tomb exhibit coming up? I'd like to bring a few winners into the meeting with the finance VP next month. We're talking about private tours, a lecture series, whatever would book the space after hours." These megashows are huge opportunities for museums to raise money through benefit parties, bring in new museum members and visitors, sell stuff, get media attention, and stoke the pride of the board members and other heavy hitters. They're lots of fun for the staff. It's a trip to be at the center of the excitement. It's also an incredible amount of work piled on top of what people already have to do. We had actually begun planning four years ago, while the Devor was still in negotiations with the show's prickly producers, the Egyptian ministry of culture and antiquities.

When I got back to my office, there was a stack of messages in the in-box. It reminded me Lisa Thorne had left a message, and I decided to call her first. "Sorry I couldn't get back to you sooner. It's been more than the normal zoo here since . . . well, you know."

A pause, then Lisa answered. "I can imagine. Is there any

more news? I mean, I saw this morning's paper, but it didn't say much. Dani?" she said when I was silent. "Were you with him before it happened?"

"No. But you were in my office. You know more than I do."

"Not really. I went to the bar near the elevator to get a glass of wine. Win was downstairs. The door was open, and I thought I might find a bathroom without the usual line, so I went into the hall. All of a sudden, I heard someone yelling from an open office door, so I went in. That woman you work with was there, and she was screaming. She said someone fell out the window."

"You didn't see . . . the . . . the body? Was the window open?"

"Yes, it was, and, no, I didn't look out. My legs got weak. I had to sit down."

"I guess you knew Clint pretty well?" I asked, fishing for anything that would turn Weiler's attention away from me, although seeing her flat out on my office floor Friday had persuaded me that not even fear of Win's jealous rage could give her the strength to push a grown man out a window that hadn't been opened in twenty years.

"When he was an MFA candidate, he and Win spent lots of time together, of course. I didn't see him much."

Interesting. Suzy saw Lisa and Clint having lunch more than once at the Institute last year. Clint's star was rising, and Win was going nowhere. Given the chance, would Lisa ditch Win in favor of Clint? Had Clint threatened to tell Win what she was up to?

"You saw him Friday night before the accident, didn't you?" I said, persevering.

"It was so crowded, I can't remember."

Lisa and I fenced for another couple of minutes, but she was firm. I told her I would be in Santa Fe the following week and might come to Win's opening.

"Why will you be in Santa Fe? I didn't realize . . ." She trailed off, waiting for me to fill in the blanks.

"My aunt by marriage invited me. She sent me the announcement for Win's show. Suzy Byrnstein's coming too."

"Suzy will be in Santa Fe?" She didn't sound thrilled, probably because if Suzy didn't like the show, she wouldn't hesitate to tell people back in San Francisco. "Maybe she won't come now. She was close to Clint, you know."

"Close, as in friends?" I asked.

"Close as in close," Lisa answered tartly.

There was no way Suzy and Clint were involved. It never happened. If I hadn't quite trusted Lisa before this, I sure wouldn't now. "Is Win showing new work?" I asked to change the subject.

"He painted most of them several years ago," Lisa said, "but wanted to hold off showing them until he had a complete body of work."

"Sounds good," I said, wanting to end the call before Lisa wound up for the pitch. Even if I had money to spend, I wouldn't buy a Win Thorne painting. He communicated a kind of arrogance in his work, as if the viewer was being discouraged from adding meaning to what the artist had dictated. Which would be fine, except that his huge, flat canvases never seemed to have much meaning of their own beyond Abstract Expressionism's general angst.

Cecilia poked her head in the door and silently mouthed something at me. I waved her in as Lisa and I said our good-byes.

"Whew," I said, swiveling away from the phone and toward the doorway. "I think everyone I know wants the real story. That happening to you too?"

Cecilia leaned against the wall, made a face, and tugged at the mass of red-gold hair that framed her face like a courtesan's in a Venetian painting. "Every local reporter who never returned my calls, every critic who ever panned a Devor show, every city VIP who didn't bother to RSVP when I invited them to an event? They're all my new best friends. The worst is, they assume I know something I don't. I know about as much as anyone who opened up this morning's paper. Peter's going bonkers. I honestly think he might have a breakdown before this is over."

"Why? It's not his fault someone was pushed out the window."

"You know how boards are. It could be bad PR for the museum, which means the board might look around for a scapegoat. I think that's what has him worried."

"The board eats out of his hand," I protested. "They brought him here, paid him the big bucks, and have been giving money to the museum at record levels to support his projects. And why would they need a scapegoat? For all we know, it was a crazy person who slipped in during the party."

Cecilia shook her head. "I get the impression the police think it was someone who knew Clint pretty well. I'm not trying to imply anything here, but you knew him, didn't you? Didn't you put him on Peter's VIP dinner list?"

"Thanks a lot. Clint was one of about twenty local artists I recommended to Peter this year as people who have some success, can carry on a decent conversation, and don't drool over their food, not necessarily in that order."

"At any rate," she continued, "I couldn't find any connections to the museum other than a summer teaching stipend. So far, we don't know why him, why here. But," she said, turning her eyes to me and tugging at her hair, "he went out your window. It seems like, if anyone had a connection to him, it might be you."

Her cell phone rang, and with a groan she pushed herself off the wall, snapped the phone open, and rolled her eyes, all the while chirping brightly to the person on the line, "Don't know anything, Rona, really. No one tells me anything." Wiggling her fingers over her shoulder to me, she disappeared into the hall and toward her office, still talking.

Teeni was nowhere to be found. She might be meeting an artist for lunch to keep an eye open for emerging talent, visiting a local school that was bidding to host a Devor-sponsored artist-in-residence, doing biographical research in the library, or sitting in the office of an art auctioneer, conducting due diligence on a painting someone had offered the Devor.

She'd learned how to gather intelligence from a brilliant art history professor at Berkeley. He'd taught her not to accept anything as fact until it could be "triangulated"—confirmed from three different and unconnected sources. It occurred to me to triangulate Lisa Thorne's possible romantic relationship with Clint. I'd ask Suzy to help.

First things first. I called Vera's resident housekeeper, Elana Ortega. No, Vera wasn't expected. She was still in Rome, or was it Aruba? Yes, the house was more than ready for company, and for me in particular. She would lay in some food.

Plans in place, I picked up my stack of message slips, walked to the conference room, and started returning calls from that phone, grateful to be out of my own office.

Chapter Ten

The secret was out. Suzy had left three messages on my voice mail while I was on the phone. She was in tears when she answered my call.

"I don't know which is more horrible, that he died so violently or that he didn't get to bask in the success he worked so hard for," she said, weeping.

Reynold was on his way to her house to share the misery. She didn't feel up to lunch any more than I did but wanted to get together, so we agreed to meet at her place after work. She'd invite Reynold and get takeout.

The rest of my day was unproductive, with Devor people dropping in to gossip or ask questions. In my increasingly black mood, I privately wondered how many of them came to peek at the crime scene. I pestered Peter's assistant to get me thirty minutes on his calendar, but she couldn't promise anything. Around four-thirty, I gave up trying to get anything accomplished and called Peter's assistant again.

"Hey, Dani. I was about to call you. Peter says he's sorry

he's been so swamped. He wonders if you can meet him at his place in an hour. It's the only way to get a chance to talk in peace."

"Awesome. Remind me how to get there, Dorie, would you? I've only been there for the senior staff party last year. I'll be there, and tell him I'll bring a bottle of wine. We need it." Suzy would understand why I had to be a little late.

Peter lives alone in a showcase late-Victorian house on Scott Street. His neighbors include a consular general, a movie star and his brood, a couple of CEOs much admired for their ability to fleece their own companies legally, and some of the city's finest old families.

A shiny black SUV was parked in the narrow driveway. A small white decal bearing the Devor's logo marred the perfect gloss of the rear bumper. Peter answered the door, loosening his tie as he invited me in. I followed him into a small den off the front hall, where he flopped into a worn leather chair and gestured for me to take the sofa. Caramel painted walls, floor-to-ceiling bookcases, and low lamps made the space feel warm and intimate.

I was feeling my way on this, given the impression I had that my boss was pissed at me about the crisis for some reason. I held the wine bottle up by its neck, a peace offering if ever there was one.

"Great, if you have the energy to pour," he said, grimacing. I looked around and saw a drinks table in a corner. In a minute, I had two glasses of Cabernet in hand. Peter raised his in a salute, then took a swallow. "Perfect, thanks. Don't know about you, but I spent all day around this Maslow thing."

"Of course I did, and it's hardly a 'thing,'" I chided. "Murder, most likely. And you liked Clint, or at least his work."

"Love his work, although he could be a pain in the neck at times. Now that he's dead, the collectors will be in a feeding frenzy, which will make it tough for the Devor to add more than a couple of pieces."

"What about Reynold? If Clint's work spikes in price, and he donates a batch to the museum while there's still a hot market, he'll be set up with tax breaks for years. A friend of his told me his construction business is booming, so I'm guessing he could use the write-offs."

Peter shrugged, slid down in his chair, and stared at his polished loafers. "I'm not so sure the Devor's going to get much from Reynold. The market's overheated, and people seem willing to buy anything, at insane prices. But it's a crapshoot. The people with the most money and the least experience or knowledge are shelling out massive amounts for name brands. If you're not already famous, it takes the blessing of the big-time collectors and dealers to drive up your prices. Who knows? Maybe Maslow will become the hot new dead genius."

I had a hard time seeing Clint in this new way. It was enough to realize with a sudden thump in my chest that he was dead. But a dead celebrity? Kind of icky, actually.

Peter took a gulp of wine and twirled the glass, looking up at me. "I really wanted to ask you what you know about the police investigation. I'm getting frustrated at how aimless it seems. Do you know anything that would explain why they keep coming back to talk with me? With all of us, I mean? They don't suspect one of us, do they?"

"Who knows? They ask a lot of questions but don't exactly explain themselves."

"I keep wondering why it happened in your office. Have you thought about that?"

Was that why Peter had been giving me the evil eye? Could he possibly think I killed Clint?

"Jeez, Peter, of course I've thought of that. So have the cops. The police interviewed everyone who was there when all hell broke loose. I didn't kill him, by the way, and I don't know who did."

"Hey, don't get excited. I didn't mean to imply that."

"So why do I get the feeling you were mad at me Friday night?"

Peter frowned. "Sorry if I looked that way. I was mad at everything—the whole mess. Embarrassing with the donors there, bad for the Devor."

"Did they tell you about the letter?" I asked, only slightly mollified.

"The guy in charge, Weiler, asked me something about letters you send on Devor stationery, but he clammed up when I asked why he wanted to know. What's up?"

I summarized what I knew while Peter stared into his wineglass, sipping occasionally. When I finished, he jumped up and went over to get the bottle. After he topped mine off and poured himself another glass, he sat down again and raised his glass in my direction.

"I know you didn't do it. Sorry if I was too upset to say that clearly the night it happened. It was such a frigging disaster in real time.

"Anyway, don't worry on that score. I knew you dated Clint, but I knew him well enough to know he was too focused on his career to be serious about anybody right now. And you're not the murdering type. If you were, you would have murdered your ex a long time ago."

I took a big gulp of the Cabernet. "Thanks. I think. I'm ignoring the part about Dickie. Unfortunately, the cops are making a big deal about its being my office, and the bogus letter isn't helping any more than the fact that Clint went ballistic in public awhile ago about my decision not to go out with him anymore."

"Yeah, I think I heard something about that. Do the police have any idea how your door was opened?" he asked.

Aha. A leading question if ever I heard one. "Nope, or if they do, they haven't told me."

There was a long pause as Peter examined his shoes, then pulled himself out of the chair and began to walk around the margins of the room, turning on his heel and retracing his steps every time he got to the end of the sofa. At one point, his hand went up to his mouth, and I saw a small tremor. I didn't help him. I was curious to hear if he told me the same thing he'd told Teeni. Downing the rest of his wine and plunking the glass onto the table, he looked tentatively at me.

"I need to tell you something, but I don't want you to mention it to the cops, okay?"

"Why not?" I hedged.

"I'm afraid they'll make a big deal of it."

"You're my boss, Peter. I won't deliberately make trouble for you. What's all the mystery about?"

"I misplaced my museum keys about two weeks ago," Peter explained. "I didn't think anything of it at first. I figured I left them in the men's room or the conference room. Dorie has a set for emergencies, and I borrowed those. I asked her not to tell Hightower. He's such a stickler for procedure, and I didn't want to hear one of his lectures on the need to take security more seriously."

"You haven't told the police? For heaven's sake, Peter, you have to. This could be important."

"I'm sure it isn't. And, anyway, I found them this afternoon.

They were still on the sixth floor, in the bathroom off my office, in the cabinet. I bet someone saw them on the counter and put them there for safekeeping, thinking they were helping, you know? I missed them when I looked around, I guess."

"Has it occurred to you this might be significant?" I persisted. "What if someone took them and then put them back? That might explain how someone opened up the staff wing and then got into my office on Friday night."

The phone on his desk rang at that moment. He apologized as he reached for it. I whispered that I wanted to visit the facilities, and he nodded and pointed me toward the living room as he said hello to whoever was on the line.

The mantel over the living room fireplace was dominated by a modern oil portrait of two young women lounging on a long sofa. Smaller pieces adorned the walls, and one corner of the room was occupied by a large, painted mobile that moved lazily in a circle as I stirred the air in passing.

I ventured down a hall off the living room, vaguely familiar from my prior visit, with several doors. The first was open and led into an obvious guest room. The second turned out to be wine storage. Very impressive. I figured the third was the guest bathroom, but when I opened the door, I froze. It was a large storage closet, and it was filled with paintings standing on the floor and leaning against one another. The canvas I could see was by Clint Maslow. I'd know the style anywhere.

I could hear Peter talking to whoever was on the phone. Quietly, I began to push the paintings far enough apart to see what each was. They were all Clint's—I was sure of it. There had to be almost two dozen in the closet. At his new price level, these would be worth at least two million dollars in today's sizzling market, maybe much more.

The last time we had dinner, two weeks before his death,

Clint told me he was exhausted, having worked day and night to meet the shipping deadline for the New York show. He said he had barely finished several other large canvases for the Biennale in time for the shipper to pick them up for crating. This cache could represent a whole year's work. It made no sense.

From the tone of his voice, Peter was finishing up the call. I closed the closet door carefully and darted into the guest room, my heart pounding, hoping there was a bathroom there. There was, and as I washed my hands, I debated what to do. Admit I saw them and ask him why the paintings were there? Keep quiet but tell Weiler and Sugerman? If only I could think of a reasonable explanation for a closet in the museum director's house full of a murdered man's art, I'd confront Peter. But what if it wasn't a good reason? What if Peter didn't want me to know?

I told myself to get a grip. It would look strange if I didn't come out of the bathroom soon. I had no choice but to keep quiet about it and figure out some way to bring up the subject of Clint's remaining paintings. Not tonight, though. Peter might guess why I was asking. Better to wait until tomorrow.

Now mine was the shaky hand as I poured a little Cabernet into my glass. Peter was too preoccupied to notice. After explaining it was a call from the president of a local foundation wanting to assure him that the recent grant to the Devor wouldn't be affected by all this bad publicity, Peter brought the conversation back to the missing keys.

"Telling the cops would not be smart, since they never were actually gone."

I argued for telling them, in part because it would convince them they had to cast their net a lot wider than me, but Peter wasn't buying. Perhaps he was still trying to put as much distance as possible between the Devor and anything criminal. Maybe he felt guilty about not confessing having lost the keys earlier and didn't want to have to explain that to Inspector Weiler. *Perhaps he wants to keep the spotlight on you,* observed my inner voice.

Before I could follow that troubling line of thought, Peter spoke. "One other thing. You should know, I asked Teeni to look around but not to tell anyone. I was afraid it would look bad for . . . for the museum. She understood."

"Um," I said, not ready to admit she had broken her promise to him. "That reminds me. Teeni told me that shortly before all hell broke loose that night, my office phone was ringing, and she picked it up. No one was on the line, but the display showed the call came from your office. Teeni told the police too," I lied, hoping that would keep us both safe if, in fact, Peter had been checking to see if the coast was clear. But he seemed genuinely puzzled.

"I was out on the floor all night, as you know. I didn't even go up to drop off my coat, since I didn't have my keys and Dorie wasn't there. Is Teeni sure? Why didn't she ask me?"

"She tried yesterday, but you had your hands full."

"Ah, I wondered why I saw her hovering before the meeting. Well, it wasn't me. Seems odd that anyone would bother to open my door when there's a phone out in the reception hall." He stood up, signaling me that it was time to leave.

"Is there anything else you and Teeni haven't told me?" I asked, remembering Teeni's evasiveness, as I shrugged on my jacket.

Peter's body stiffened. "Like what?" he said, trying to keep his voice light.

Oh, I don't know. Like a freaking closet full of stolen paintings, I wanted to yell.

I bit my lip. "Nothing specific. But I feel I'm not entirely in the loop here."

"Not true. There's nothing else," he said firmly, setting his empty wineglass down on the table with a clink.

Peter kissed me European style on both cheeks at his front door, the effect of the wine or having unburdened himself about the keys, or both. As I unlocked my car, I looked back at his house briefly and did a small double take. Peter was peering at me out of his living room window, silhouetted by a lamp behind him and apparently talking on his cell phone. As I raised my hand to wave, he disappeared from view. Was he checking to make sure I got to my car safely? Or had I rattled his cage unknowingly, alerting him to something he thought might put him in danger?

I drove west toward Suzy's house in the Sunset District, which seldom lived up to its name, working overtime to come up with a reason Peter would have so much of Clint's recent work stored in a closet in his house and why, if there was a good reason, he hadn't mentioned it to me.

I cruised for parking and got superlucky after only five minutes, jamming my car into a minuscule space only a block away from Suzy's. As I hurried up the darkening street toward her house, head down against a chill wind, I heard my name and looked around. Reynold was walking behind me, the collar of his jacket turned up against the cold, carrying a full plastic bag in each hand. Dinner, I deduced. I stopped until he caught up.

"*Phô,*" he explained. "Can't get it in Santa Fe, so I have it as often as I can up here." The hot Vietnamese broth, into which you stir fresh chopped vegetables, silky noodles, and a choice of meat or fish, is delicious and cheap. The city is fortunate to have a population that demands it.

"How is Suzy?" I asked as we trudged up the block toward the next corner, hunching against the cold ocean breeze. "You knew she and Clint were both on the Institute's faculty, right?"

"Oh, sure. In fact, we all had lunch down there one time. She's pretty down. Dani," he said, turning to look at me, frowning slightly, "I wonder if Clint ever told you about some missing paintings."

My heart stopped for a minute, as did my legs. "Missing paintings?" I repeated, my voice sounding squeaky in my ears. As in the ones in Peter's closet?

"That sounds more dramatic than I meant it to," Reynold said, gesturing me forward with a laden arm. We continued walking, ignoring the steady homebound traffic whizzing past us. "A couple of years ago, I tried to commission a series of triptychs from him. He had started thinking about structurally tying pieces together, and I liked the idea. A month later, he told me that he had given up on the idea. He felt it was too ambitious for him, at least for a few years."

"Uncharacteristically modest for Clint, don't you think?" I said.

"I don't know. He was very smart about his career. Anyway, when I visited him some time later, I asked if I could look at what he had done on the triptychs. He said they were gone, maybe painted over or tossed into the Dumpster behind his studio. The only thing I saw was a couple of oil sketches. Frankly, I had the feeling he was being evasive."

We had reached the corner, and, after waiting for a break in the flow of cars turning in front of us, Reynold motioned me to cross. I was silent, preoccupied with the images I'd seen in Peter's closet.

Reynold shifted the plastic bags as he glanced at the traffic again. "Now, I'm wondering if they're around the studio in some form or another." Raising his voice slightly to be heard over the traffic and putting his hand on my elbow to move me forward, he said "Did he mention them to you?"

My answer was lost in a sudden scream of tires, an accelerating engine roar, and a horn blaring in my ear. Something nudged me, and I lost my balance, whipping my head around in time to see a dark SUV careering around the corner from behind us. Fighting for balance, I jumped backward onto the curb, knocking into Reynold. A bag fell, its contents flying everywhere as we lurched backward onto the sidewalk. The SUV's tires scraped the curb, and the body of the car rocked as the driver fought to straighten the wheel. Then, to my further shock, it shot forward and away, down the block, and through the green light at the next corner, gleaming in the headlights of other cars.

I looked at Reynold. He was bent forward, breathing hard through his mouth.

"Are you okay?" I asked. "I can't believe that driver."

"Yeah, I'm all right," he answered. But his voice was wheezy, and he looked as if he might fall down.

"He didn't hit you, did he?" I asked. Adrenaline was making my heart pump like a drum.

He shook his head. "No, thanks to you. But the front bumper came as close to my leg as it could have without ripping it off. I was afraid that when I stumbled, I would knock you into the path. Are you okay?"

"I think so, if you don't count the fact that my pulse is sky high and my legs feel like jelly."

"I know what you mean. And it looks like we've got only half of our dinner left."

"No big deal. After I get you to Suzy's and we're both

breathing normally again, I'll run back for more veggies and stuff."

The traffic hadn't even registered our close call. San Francisco drivers share a belief that stop signs mean *look straight ahead, and keep going.* Pedestrian crosswalks are laughable as safe zones.

We got to Suzy's without more drama, and she fussed over us, settling her admirer in a copper-colored leather chair and me on the love seat in front of the fireplace. Reynold was gray-faced and silent.

Suzy prescribed brandy. "Omigod," Suzy said suddenly, pointing to my slacks. "You did get hit."

Strangely, I hadn't felt it until this moment. The black fabric on my pant leg was stained and frayed. "Oh, no," I groaned. The trousers were part of a favorite Armani suit, and it didn't take a genius to see that they were toast. If that wasn't bad enough, I was going to have a large bruise.

Suzy insisted I sit with my leg up while she and Reynold went to get ice. As they bundled ice cubes into a towel, I realized with a shiver that the car might have hit more of me if Reynold had motioned me off the curb an instant sooner or if his own near fall had taken me with him like a domino. But there was something else that was creeping me out. Even in the dark and confusion, the SUV had looked familiar. I closed my eyes and tried unsuccessfully to remember if there had been a white sticker on the bumper.

Chapter Eleven

"**I** can't believe it. Wouldn't you think she would know better by now?"

It was Wednesday, and I was standing on the outskirts of a cocktail party in the huge, gloomy living room of one of Pacific Heights' most immodest houses, nursing a martini so dry it made me cough and trying not to peek at my watch more than once a minute. The hostess, whose husband was a trustee of the Devor, had finished her umpteenth redecoration project and was holding a party to show it off.

An elderly lady who lived a couple blocks away had asked me to come with her, ostensibly to drive but more to help extricate her "when you see me falling asleep from boredom." She owned a staggeringly good Picasso given to her by her grandfather, a notorious silver baron, as a wedding present. She knew we longed for it, and we knew she intended to give it to the Devor, but one never, ever takes things like this for granted. It would be unfair to say she uses the Picasso to keep us dancing attendance, but it wouldn't be totally wrong. If my husband had died of influenza six months into our marriage, leaving me without children but with two great, merged fortunes and surrounded by sharks who had designs on said fortunes, I'd probably be as lonely as she was.

The critical speaker was a woman standing with her back to me. She and her friend were discussing the hostess, who was as slender as a whippet and whose nose was about as long as one's. Her husband, leaning against the massive and darkly Gothic stone mantelpiece, was equally thin. He affected a small mustache and bow tie and had a mean mouth. Over the years, I had come to see that he had the habit of holding his chin up so he could look down his nose at everyone.

The hostess darted from group to group, telling everyone who would listen about George, her current decorator, and his "genius," which was nowhere to be seen. The house was a monstrosity, built in the 1920s for the sole purpose of intimidating the neighbors. George had rid it of the overstuffed chintzes the last genius had installed. The new look was Addams Family to the max. Dense, dark, brocade drapery dripping to the floor blocked the bright California sunlight and the stunning ocean views. Dark carpets absorbed the light from a pitifully few overwrought table lamps, making walking treacherous. Huge antique tables and cabinets crowded the walls. An elk head hovered over the living room doorway, its glass eyes staring thoughtfully at a murky nineteenth-century oil painting over the mantel.

"I swear, every time he has an affair, she finds a new decorator and spends another million." The ladies wandered off to find some food. It occurred to me, not for the first time, that I probably got a lot of verbal abuse when Dickie left me. *I'm better off now,* I reminded myself, *especially not having to deal with Mrs. A.*

Speaking of the devil, she loomed in front of me in an unsuitable pink Chanel suit with black piping and swags of gilt chain, taking me by surprise. I smiled noncommittally.

"Well, Danielle, I hardly expected to see you at dear Julia's," she hissed, glaring at me. I seemed to recall "dear Julia" being criticized pretty severely when I last took tea and cookies in my mother-in-law's drawing room, but I said nothing.

"I suppose you're here on business," she continued, not waiting for an answer and pronouncing *business* as if it made me a server or coat check girl. In her eyes, I was always on the lookout for money, and it made little difference if I was raising funds for a nonprofit museum or to feather my own nest.

Mrs. A was not noted for her charitable instincts. Her late husband had dutifully sponsored hospital wings, libraries, and a city park. But when he died, the well dried up in a hurry, to the sorrow of a score of local project directors who thought the widow would honor her husband's informal pledges of support. Dickie tries to remedy it, but he only got part of the Argetter largess right away. When "Mother" passes away, the rest will be his. Richie Rich, playboy extraordinaire, will have no brakes at all. It's scary. He's not cut out for moderation.

"Well, why are you here?" Mrs. A snapped, not letting up for a moment.

"Jane Martingale asked me to come with her. She doesn't like to drive anymore."

"I should say not. She's almost blind, for heaven's sake. But why you? Doesn't she have a driver?"

Note insult. Grind teeth. "Yes, but he's off today. Ah, here's Jane now."

Jane was no fool, and I had a hunch her showing up to rescue me was no coincidence. But Mrs. A wasn't ready to let me go yet.

"What's this I hear about a murder in your office? Richard Junior says you were there when it happened."

Jane's mouth dropped open.

"I'm sure Dickie didn't say that. Dickie was with me—"

Mrs. A's mouth clamped shut, and her firm jaw got firmer.

"That is, we were all in the museum when it happened. It's just that it happened in, uh, my office."

"Why on earth would it happen in your office, and what does it mean? Who was this person? I didn't recognize his name."

Tuesday's paper had carried Clint's name and the details Cecilia couldn't share on Monday. The police were calling it a homicide now. His next of kin, a brother from Omaha whom I had never met, had arrived to take charge on behalf of the family.

"What on earth are you talking about?" said Jane in confusion, looking first at me, then at Mrs. A. "Who's dead, and why does it concern us?" That's why they call it high society. If it didn't happen in Pacific Heights, Presidio Heights, or at Lake Tahoe in the summer, it might as well not have happened.

"It's no one you know, Jane," I said quickly. "An artist. And how it happened is a mystery. I'm sure the police will figure it out and let us know. But everything's fine at the museum."

"Richard Junior says," Mrs. A jumped in, her voice rising, "that he got the third degree, which is ridiculous. Those policemen obviously didn't know who he was." She was still glaring at me through pale, watery eyes.

"Oh, he must have been joking," I protested, taking Jane's arm to steer her toward the doorway the elk was guarding. "They spent all of five minutes with him. We have to go now, don't we, Jane?"

Jane had little choice. I was in motion, navigating past the waiters with trays of sushi and the starving guests who leaned toward them with outstretched fingers. I guess it's all that Pilates and calorie counting, but the people in this room looked and acted a lot like the subjects of direct-mail fund-raising pleas for help feeding starving citizens of parched Third World countries.

The butler handed us our coats and signaled the valet parking crew to bring our car around. Jane and I stopped on the steps to catch our collective breath.

"Well, Dani," she said, chuckling. "I have no idea what that was about, but I'm sure it was none of my business, as long as the Devor isn't having problems. One wants to be sure, of course, when one has a decision to make."

As we proceeded to the car, I hastened to assure her all was well at the future home of her Picasso. Ten minutes later, after agreeing the redecorated mansion was still awful, I declined her offer of a glass of wine and drove my own car back to the adjacent neighborhood, where my rather more sparsely furnished apartment welcomed me.

Something Jane had said as I left had set off a small alarm, however, and I wasn't sure what it meant. As she pecked me on the cheek at her front door, she'd said, "One does hear things, my dear. Is young Peter doing well? One hears that he rather extends himself financially and that he might be pushing for the modern work a bit too much for the comfort of the Devor's closest friends."

Startled, I said only that he was building a strong collection and that gifts to the Devor were up every year. I wanted to know more but was caught off guard. It didn't seem loyal to ask what she meant, but I needed to know. So now I had to add that to my list of unanswered questions.

In my kitchen, I pulled together a tray with a glass of Zinfandel, a local Portuguese-style cheese, fresh sourdough bread, and a crunchy apple. In the peace and quiet of my living room, I plopped down on my sofa, wiggled out of my high heels, put my feet up on the coffee table, and tried to put out of my mind for a few minutes everything that had happened since Friday night.

Fever, seeing that I was wearing a black dress, leaped into my lap, purring mightily. Shedding is his sport of choice, and black is the arena in which he shines competitively. Sweatpants and jeans do not merit a glance. He's happy when I put on my Rive Gauche tweed suit, but nothing gets his juices going like expensive black slacks or a black dress. As he stretched out to bobcat length on my legs and lowered his head contentedly onto crossed paws, I gave up trying to distract myself and tried to make sense of the events surrounding Clint's death.

A mysterious letter supposedly sent by me. Teeni's wariness. Lisa Thorne's fainting. Peter's lost keys and the paintings in his closet. The suggestions that Lisa or Teeni had had an affair with Clint.

None of this went anywhere. The police had fingerprints and DNA samples, the forensics team's results, statements from scores of people from all over the museum. What made me nervous was that, with all that, they had asked me to come to the police station for another interview tomorrow. I was dreading it, experiencing again that irrational guilty feeling and wondering if that added to Weiler's speculations about me as a murderer.

Fever yawned, which made me yawn, which apparently inspired him to yawn again. This was my quietest moment since Clint had died, and I was enjoying it.

The phone rang, jarring me out of my recollections. Dumping Fever off my lap, I answered on the third ring, said hello, and waited. Silence. Well, almost silence. Breathing.

"Who is this?" I said, suddenly remembering the similar call here and the one Teeni had told me about at the office. "Don't bother me again," I said into the continuing silence, and I slammed the phone down. If it wasn't a pair of eleven-year-old boys now convulsed with laughter, or a telemarketer juggling multiple speed-dial lines, did it have something to do with Clint s death? I hadn't bothered to sign up for caller ID, so I was in the dark. But a dangerous caller? It didn't compute. Who would be trying to intimidate someone who had no special knowledge?

The phone rang again as I settled onto the couch. I let the machine pick it up. "Hi, Dani? It's Peter. I know it's a bit late, but would you call me when you get this? I'm in the office. You can call my private line."

It was after nine, not too late for a workaholic like Peter. I hadn't seen him since the night at his house and my brush with the mysterious SUV. Shaking off my hesitation, I refilled my wineglass and dialed.

"You haven't talked to Weiler about my keys, have you?" Peter asked when the preliminaries were over.

I explained I hadn't spoken with the police since he had told me about the keys but that I was uneasy about tomorrow's meeting with Weiler and might feel I had to. I reminded him that having the Devor's VP for fund-raising cleared of a murder charge would be good for the museum.

I could hear a chill developing in his voice. So much for the European kiss-kiss of the other night. "Is there anything else you intend to tell the police that I should know about?"

"Peter, why don't you tell the police about the keys? It

would look better." Truth was, I was uneasy about mentioning them. Reynold's talk about lost paintings and Jane's talk about Peter's finances worried me. Did I really want to point the finger at my boss?

I decided I'd better tell him at least part of what Jane Martingale had said. It was critical that she had confidence in Peter. If something had happened to damage that trust, the Picasso could go elsewhere, and Peter would be crushed.

I replayed Jane's comments about the tastes of the Devor's core donors verbatim to Peter. He grunted once while I was relaying the conversation and, when I finished, said, "What did you tell her?"

"Tell her? I didn't have a clue what she was talking about, Peter."

"I can't imagine why she's griping about our efforts to improve the contemporary collection. The board is fully behind that. I hate saying it, but maybe someone else is after the Picasso and is putting ideas into her head."

I hadn't thought of that, but he was right. I wouldn't put it past an influential person with ties to another museum to court her behind our backs. We'd have to ramp up the lobbying to get Jane to designate the Picasso in some irrevocable trust agreement. *Note to myself: lunch with our trust attorney ASAP.*

"Okay, that's a fair guess. But I'm nervous. If an opinion leader like Jane defects, the loyalties of the in-crowd can shift pretty quickly to the symphony or the opera. We need to respond to her concerns."

"Got it. I'll make nice with Jane right away."

That wasn't my point, but Peter was obviously not going to tell me if anything Jane had hinted about his finances or the solid support of his board had hit home with him.

"Don't worry, boss. The Picasso's safe," I said, forcing a laugh to take the sting out of my words. "I have to get off the phone now. The memorial for Clint is in the morning at the Institute, and then I'm off to Santa Fe Friday with Suzy. Teeni will have my aunt's number, and my cell operates there. I'm sure I'll see Rowland Reynold. Should I start vetting him as a potential board member or see if I can interest him in donating his Georgia O'Keeffe still life?"

Peter was silent for a long minute. Then he chuckled. "Sure, give it a try. You know the mantra: You never get if you don't ask."

"I'll do my best. But, remember, this is primarily R & R time for me. I intend to do what I can to relax and put the terrible events of the last week behind me." I thought it might be best if I didn't mention to my boss that I was also checking out Reynold as a potential murder suspect.

Chapter Twelve

I glanced at my watch as I waited for a delivery truck to edge its way through the crowded crosswalk at Broadway and onto Stockton. I needed to make this light if I was going to park in the garage next to the police station and get up to Weiler's office in five minutes.

San Francisco's Chinatown is busy day and night, awash with tourists, deliverymen, and neighborhood residents on a mission for the crispiest duck, the greenest beans, and any of a thousand souvenirs. I love the experience of slipping into what could be a small city in China, bobbing and weaving my way down the sidewalk, overhearing the sharp give and take of bargaining between customers and merchants. The smell of steamed shrimp dumplings and ginger wafted into the car window, and I promised myself a dim sum bag lunch.

Ten minutes later, presenting myself at the information desk, I was surprised to learn that Inspector Sugerman would be meeting with me. I felt better immediately, although my stress level was still high, due in part to the old man in handcuffs being dragged, yelling, into the reception area by two bored, uniformed cops.

It was a lot quieter in the office two flights up that Sugerman shared with three other detectives. A man and a woman occupied two of the metal desks. Dingy maroon modules separated one workstation from another, file cabinets and boxes covered every inch of available floor and wall space, and a bulletin board thick with notices dominated the wall next to the door. Somehow, the planners had carved a tiny, glass-walled conference room out of the cramped space, and Sugerman ushered me into it, closing the door behind him.

"Thanks for coming in," he said as we settled ourselves on a couple of chairs. "We want to review some of what you told us, check on a few other things that have come up, and see if you have anything more that might help the investigation. Let's start with the letter you say you didn't write."

"I found the backup of the file on my computer," I said, eager to prove I was cooperating. "Someone wrote it two weeks ago, after I'd gone home for the day."

"Yes, we know. The crime scene team copied the file and its information when they searched your office." So much for my clever detecting. "Can you prove you were somewhere else at"—he flicked open his notebook "nine P.M. the night the file was created?"

"Not unless my cat learns to talk. I was at home. Alone." I almost added that I was home alone most nights but didn't think that would send the right message about me as a potential date, not that Sugerman was telegraphing interest.

"How long had you and Mr. Maslow been dating?" he asked.

"We dated for about six months, but that was over some time ago," I said.

Sugerman's eyebrows notched upward.

"We were both too focused on our work, I guess."

"So you wouldn't have been jealous if you knew he was seeing someone else—romantically, I mean?"

"No, but he wasn't. Clint was freaking out about the amount of work he had to do once the New York dealers started taking an interest in him. But, no, I wouldn't have been jealous."

Sugerman looked at me speculatively, then smiled and nodded. "Okay, let's try something else. Would your ex have been jealous of Maslow, say, if he knew you were dating?"

"Dickie isn't violent, doesn't lose his temper, and couldn't care less about me in that way."

Sugerman was looking at his notebook, seeming to listen and nod his head as I spoke. When I finished, he looked up at me, his green eyes especially bright, and smiled ever so slightly. "So you and your ex are really an ex-couple?"

"Yes," I said, trying to sound light and casual. Unfortunately, it was getting hot in the little room, and I was sure my upper lip was damp with sweat. "Could I have some water?" I asked.

While he fetched a paper cup filled from the water cooler wedged along a wall, I blew my nose, blotted my lip, and shrugged off my coat, wishing I had worn something more interesting than my black cashmere twin set.

"Okay," he said as he sat down again and pushed the cup across the table. "Let's get back to the night of Maslow's death. You can't account for your time when the letter was written on your computer, and you aren't missing any keys that would account for someone getting in. Your assistant says she was at the movies with a friend on the night the letter was created, and Mrs. Thorne didn't have a key unless she got it from someone else, and she says she didn't. You didn't lend your keys to your ex, by any chance?"

"Of course not."

"Or to Mrs. Thorne?"

"No, never."

"Mr. Thorne?"

"Certainly not. Why in the world would I?"

"Did Mr. Thorne visit you in your office sometime before the night of the murder, even earlier that day?"

"No, I'm sure not."

"It would help if you could think back. Can you recall any time when Mr. Thorne was visiting the Devor and you brought him into your office?"

"Really, no, unless maybe he was with a group, or another staffer brought him by. Why are you asking?"

"We have to check lots of things out. Did any of those people I asked about visit your apartment, where you kept the spare keys, during the past several months?"

"No."

"Not even your ex?" The green eyes were teasing.

"Not even my ex," I said, blushing.

"I know you've done this before, but I'd like you to tell me as precisely as you can what happened when you first entered your office."

I closed my eyes and ran through it again, remembering when Sugerman prompted me that Len had banged his head on the window, that Dickie might have touched something on my desk, and that Reynold had poked his head in the door. None of that seemed to excite my detective, and I didn't have much more to offer.

Sugerman confirmed that Teeni had admitted the fingernail was hers. I was relieved to hear that a couple of young artists had given her a firm alibi for the time period in which the police thought Clint had been killed. Teeni's phone call to Hightower's office was on record too.

Lisa had been talking to a newspaper critic near the elevator until shortly before the scene got wild, and the police had found several people who saw Dickie following me from the elevator bank into the office suite.

The police were looking at phone records to and from my office around the time Clint was pushed. They had a court order, he explained. Fine by me, especially since Sugerman said the records would only show calls coming from outside the Devor.

"One last question, and we'll be finished for today. Do you know who stands to benefit from Mr. Maslow's death?"

"I don't know if he had a will, if that's what you mean. I read that you tracked down his brother. He's here for the memorial gathering, I know. Will you be there? Isn't that the kind of thing murderers do? Come to see people grieve?"

He chuckled. "Watch a lot of TV, Ms. O'Rourke? Actually, we probably will have someone there, not looking for a killer as much as making sure we've identified people who were close enough to him to be helpful in our investigation."

His cell phone rang, and he looked briefly at the screen before turning it off. Raising his head again and shifting in his chair, he changed the subject. "What about Maslow's artwork? Where is it all, and who gets it now?"

"It's pretty standard to consign work to galleries and lend it to museums. A lot of his work is with dealers right now, but it should come back to his brother if it doesn't sell, assuming his brother inherits, and unless the dealers and curators want to buy it outright."

"Did he lend any paintings to you, or to the Devor?"

"I don't have any. The Devor has been negotiating for a painting to be acquired in a combination purchase and gift."

I didn't mention that Peter had a small fortune stashed in a closet.

"What about Mr. Reynold?"

"He owns a lot of Clint's work. But there's nothing suspicious about that. He's a patron and has been investing in Clint's paintings for many years, long before they were fetching big prices."

"Would that entitle him to any of Maslow's surviving work?"

"You'd have to ask him or a lawyer. If he has an agreement, he might get first right of refusal, I guess."

"Okay, I guess that's it," Sugerman said, snapping his notebook closed and smiling at me. "I appreciate your coming in. We'll be in touch."

"I'm headed to Santa Fe for a few days. I hope that's all right."

"How about leaving me your contact information?" he said, flipping open his book again. "As long as we can reach you, that's fine. Going with anyone we know?" he asked, those green eyes sweeping up from the notebook and locking me into their beams.

I was pretty sure *we* meant *I* and, in the spirit of sparking some interest, was tempted to invent a tall, handsome boyfriend. But, I reminded myself, Charlie Sugerman was a cop, and it would take him all of a minute to find out I was fibbing. "A girlfriend," I admitted.

"Aha," he said, grinning at me for just a second, those green eyes sparkling. It wasn't much, but it was enough to tempt me into an extra order of barbeque pork buns in recognition of the nicest few minutes I'd had since poor Clint went out the window a week ago.

Chapter Thirteen

Fever is too fat for in-cabin airline carriers. On the one cross-country round-trip from hell I dragged him on, he'd resembled a furry waffle in the tiny cage the airline provided. His protests at 37,000 feet did nothing for goodwill between his species and ours. Now, as I gathered my computer, office reading, and warm clothes for Santa Fe, I tried to explain to Yvette, my downstairs neighbor and occasional cat sitter, whose English is almost nonexistent when it comes to doing something she does not enjoy, what and when to feed the cat. In a weird personality disorder, my laid-back pet undergoes a radical change when I am about to leave him. He hates strangers, my vet says. Brilliant deduction.

"Don't let him nag you into too much food, Yvette."

"Two cans of food?" Yvette replied, her eyes darting from my face to that of the cat.

Yvette's mother tongue is French, as in Montreal, and I think she throws in cute personality stuff she picks up from television sitcoms in the belief it will add a little *je ne sais quoi* to her personality. It must work. She has one cute boyfriend after another.

"Dry food, Yvette. Dry food once a day . . ." Fever jumped up onto the counter to let her know who was in charge. Yvette made scolding noises in French, flapping her hands unconvincingly in his general direction. He squinted at her.

"Oh, for heaven's sake," I said in irritation, sweeping him off the counter in a single movement, "quit the posturing." Tail swishing, ears flat, Fever stomped away, toenails clicking.

"Yvette, I truly appreciate this," I said soothingly. "I'll bring you back something wonderful, I promise. Maybe a cowgirl skirt? And you know he sleeps all the time."

Yvette loves cowboy stuff. She's small-boned and trim, with wavy black hair and dimples, and sports a kind of retro fifties look. The Stetson with the curled brim I got her last time knocked her out. I pecked her on both cheeks and handed her the spare keys.

Before I had packed, plagued by my worry about Peter's possible involvement, I had gone looking for some discreet help in pursuing a nasty train of thought. Reynold, the collector. Peter, the museum director. Clint, the artist of the moment. Add a closet full of valuable paintings tucked away. I needed to talk to someone who knew more than I did about the superheated art market and the scams it might trigger, and I knew precisely the right person.

Two years ago, at the Devor's annual New York fundraising dinner, I met a dashing young man with a wicked sense of humor and a sharp eye for the fads and fashions of what he called "the trade." Kendall Wolff was the bratty editor of the most powerful, must-read magazine on the business side of the fine-art market. He knew everyone and everything and didn't hesitate to publish the details of any scandal he and his reporters sniffed out, so I had to be careful.

"Hey, girl, whassup?" he said in a pathetic, prep school imitation of street talk.

"Hey, yourself, Kendall. I need a lesson about the art market. Can you give me twenty minutes?" I heard him shoo someone out of his office and yell after them to close the door.

"I'm yours, girl. What do you want to know?"

"I'm having a hard time figuring out how much money to ask donors for when the Devor wants to purchase something at auction. The prices seem to be inflating faster than I can multiply."

"It's wild right now, isn't it? I've got curators crying into their Champagne because they came to Sotheby's or Christie's with a fat wallet and got shoved aside by *nouveau riche* private collectors in the first round of bidding. They're in my office asking what the hell happened to reality."

"Is it only Old Masters that feed the frenzy? What about the current crop of painters?"

"People who haven't developed an eye will buy anything old because they're terrified of never having a Dutch or a French painting to brag about. Lots of third-rate work has spiraled out of sight, and I think the owners are going to wake up with massive hangovers someday. But the same is true right now with contemporary painters, living and dead, my dear. People are buying stuff I would sell at a garage sale if I had a garage, and they're doing it sight unseen, in many cases, phoning in or e-mailing commitments for totally un-proven work. It's sad, really."

"So what happens when one of these artists dies? Do his prices keep going up?"

"Right now? If the artist was on an upward trajectory in

the market, probably up, up, and away. Uneducated collectors, trendy curators, speculators who plan to turn around and sell in a year grab everything in sight."

"So being dead might actually help sell someone's work?"

"Well, if you put it that way. Why? Don't tell me you're visiting elderly artists, looking for signs of decrepitude?"

"Don't be silly. No, just trying to get a better picture. One last question and I'll let you go until the next time I'm in the city. I promise you dinner at Vong to thank you for the tutorial."

"That's so last year, love. I'll pick the place, but thanks."

"Who understands this market best? Who knows how and what to play?"

"It's like wine. Some people have developed their senses by looking at art for decades. They study, they read, they talk to other passionate art lovers. Find collectors, long-time gallerists. They'll keep you out of the mosh pit, sweetie."

"First time I've heard Sotheby's auction room referred to as a mosh pit, but, okay, I get the message."

It was a lot to think about, and, unfortunately, it didn't eliminate my ugly speculations.

As the plane began its descent into Albuquerque, I pressed my nose to the window and scanned the landscape below. New Mexico's immense plateaus, ancient rock formations, and burned-out volcanic cones fascinate me. I was born and raised in a city. We don't have landscape this big. There is something about it that makes me feel insignificant in a nice way. Time is so long, and we are mere short-term renters. My problems? Not worth a cosmic yawn.

The jet touched down, and twenty minutes later, I scooped up my bag from the luggage carousel and picked up my rental car keys. As the terminal's automatic doors slid open, I heard a familiar voice.

"Hey, Dani, wait up. Can I hitch a ride? The car rental place screwed up, and if I don't get up to Santa Fe by check-in time, I'm sure my room will be given away too."

Suzy descended on me in a rush of words, soft luggage, big jewelry, scarves, shopping bags, and assorted paraphernalia. Her breath formed clouds in the crisp air outside Albuquerque's terminal.

"I thought you came down yesterday," I said as she caught up.

"Well, I was going to. I actually sold a big painting to someone yesterday, so it was worth waiting around. And RR couldn't come sooner, anyway. In fact, he's due later this evening."

In ten minutes, we were on the highway driving north past outcroppings of one-and-a-half-billion-year-old pre-Cambrian rock, old before the dinosaurs roamed. Suzy chattered on. She knew how much money other artists had made in recent gallery shows (not much, it seemed), the dope on marital breakups and reconciliations within the art community, who had been turned down for what juried show.

"Win is supposedly on the verge of signing on with a big New York gallery. But for reasons known only to his holiness, he seems almost annoyed about it." Suzy paused for breath, peering at me for a reaction.

"Well, maybe he's superstitious," I said. "Maybe the deal isn't signed yet, and he doesn't want the world to know if the deal goes south."

Forty minutes later, having deposited Suzy at the Red Desert Inn and determining that they were, in fact, expecting her, I wound my way up into softly contoured hills studded with low, flat-roofed houses almost hidden from view. The landscape was nearly barren, decorated with twiggy shrubs and low-growing, sweetly fragrant piñon trees. The curving roadway was bordered on one side by red earth falling off into deep ravines, called arroyos. A side street eventually led to Vera's house, a deceptively large place with two wings balancing either side of the central adobe facade.

One wing was home to the caretaker couple, Elana and Manuel Ortega. Vera had hired Manuel first, as a gardener. When Victor, Vera's then-gentleman friend, noticed that Manuel was dropped off and picked up by a large woman who seemed always to be pointing out something he had missed, he inquired. Mrs. Ortega, it seemed, was the general of the family and had grand ambitions for her children, ambitions Mr. Ortega's salary was to make possible.

It hadn't taken Victor long to realize that he had found the ideal housekeeper for Dickie's absent aunt. Victor was long since out of the picture, but Mr. and Mrs. Ortega are still fixtures.

I rang the doorbell and surveyed the tidy courtyard while I waited. The door swung open, and Mrs. Ortega burst out, grabbing what luggage she could reach and sweeping me into the hallway. "Manuel," she called. "Come here. There are bags. Hurry."

Manuel, who was probably immune by now to the note of urgency that punctuated most of his wife's commands, came out of the back hall. He was as silent as Mrs. Ortega was voluble and only murmured hello as he picked up my bag and various odds and ends and headed toward one of the two guest suites. Leaving the bags on the bedroom floor, he left as quietly as he had come, while Mrs. Ortega carried on an effusive, welcoming conversation.

My Spanish was barely good enough to encourage her to speak about five times as fast as I could comprehend, so she soon switched to English. After inquiring about my health and any possibilities of my getting back with "that sweet boy," she turned her attention to food while I unpacked.

"Whoops, what's this?" I mumbled, as an unfamiliar, cloth tote bag slumped to the floor between my two larger suitcases. It was colorful, tied at the top with a scarf, and definitely not mine. It had to be Suzy's, shoved into the trunk with everything else at the airport and overlooked when she grabbed her things and handed them to the bellman at the inn. When I put it on the table next to the bed, it slipped, and some of the contents fell onto the floor. Lipstick, dry cleaners receipts, an address book, and scraps of paper tumbled out.

One was a small pastel sketch, folded into quarters. The artwork was probably hers, the page, a little ragged and smeared, salvaged for the phone number jotted in one corner. I tucked it back into the bag, retied the scarf, and promised myself I would bring it to Suzy the next morning. Just in case she hadn't figured out where she left it, I called the inn. She was out, but the receptionist took the message and promised to relay it to her when Suzy returned.

Changing quickly and grabbing some binoculars from Vera's hospitable guest closet, I headed out for a walk along the nearby ridge road to clear the airplane buzz from my head and the cramped muscles in my legs. Mrs. Ortega promised one of her special treats, blue-corn chicken enchiladas, for dinner. I set off at a quick pace, reveling in the crisp, late-fall air and the deep blue skies. Even the shadow of Clint's death couldn't keep my spirits from rising like the hawk way out in front of me riding a thermal up the face of a red rock cliff.

Chapter Fourteen

My improved outlook stayed with me the next morning. Declining breakfast because I was meeting Suzy, I had coffee with Mrs. Ortega and caught up on her kids' activities. It sounded as if they had their mother's temperament and their father's capacity for hard work. Since my biological clock was ticking faster than my love life, I might need godmother status to at least one of the Ortegas' daughters to get some bragging rights.

When I looked at my watch, it was almost ten. I grabbed my jacket and keys and Suzy's tote bag and told Mrs. Ortega I'd be out all day. Suzy was waiting for me in front of the inn, and we drove the short distance to Café Pasqual, one of Santa Fe's best and most popular cafés. Reynold was meeting us there.

"Development around here is booming," she told me happily. "His firm has commercial and residential deals all over the place. Makes money hand over fist."

From the sidewalk, we could see Reynold seated with his

back to us at a table by the window. When Suzy and I made our way over, he rose from his chair. He was wearing a silver and turquoise belt and cowboy boots, which looked natural on him.

He gave me that wolfish smile, seeming to assess me as a source of protein, as we squeezed into high-backed wooden chairs around the little table. To each her own, I guess. I didn't get what Suzy saw in him. *Besides the money and the influence in the art world?* my inner self asked.

The restaurant packed 'em in from morning to night, and to ease the wait time as much as possible, every available square inch was in use. You'd know why if you stood inside the door for all of a minute, sniffing the smoky salsas, fresh coffee, melted cheese, and signature southwestern sausages that emerged in a steady stream from the kitchen.

The waitress arrived with thick mugs of black coffee and her order pad. We ordered more food than we could possibly eat and settled back to talk. Suzy and I had avoided mentioning Clint on the drive up to Santa Fe by unspoken agreement, but Reynold had no such self-imposed restrictions.

"Do the police have any better idea what happened?"

"They're not exactly into sharing," I responded.

"Have you talked to Clint's brother?" he persisted. "Does he inherit?"

I could understand why he would ask, but it bothered me nevertheless.

"Actually, Rowland, it's funny you should ask. The police may want to ask you the same question."

"Hah," Reynold barked. At that moment, our waitress returned, balancing an armload of dishes. We sorted out who got which omelet, where the bowls of jalapeño jam and fresh salsa belonged, and who needed more coffee.

I said, as I forked a mouthful of crispy, spicy hash to my mouth, "You own a lot of Clint's work, don't you?"

"Yup. I think he is, or was, one of the best painters coming out of California nowadays. Not sure he would have held up for a hundred years—most don't, do they?—but he might have, and that's the point."

"You're obviously a serious collector. And maybe a bit of a gambler?" I asked.

"I don't think of it as gambling, more like investing. I was keeping him in paints and canvas, you might say, so I'd get first shot at the work he did later on. Poor guy. Makes me damn mad, if you'll excuse my French."

I wasn't sure exactly what made him mad, Clint's murder or the missed opportunity to make money off Clint's future success. Before I could figure out how to push it diplomatically, Suzy chimed in. "RR, what are you going to do with the paintings by Clint that you already have?"

Reynold took his time chewing a mouthful of chorizo, washing it down with coffee and wiping his lips on a large napkin. "Well, that's an interesting question," he said slowly, frowning at his mug.

Someone called my name, and I turned around in my chair. There by the door stood Lisa Thorne and a short, reed-thin man I didn't know. In this light, she looked tired.

"Oh, no," said Suzy with a groan. "I'm not up to Lisa this morning. I'm sure she's obsessing about some imaginary problem with the show, or the percentage of the commission, or whatever."

Lisa headed over to our table with the man in tow. He was running a bony hand over his bald head as if he had forgotten he had no hair to smooth down.

Reynold looked up, then rose, hand out. The man's long

face lit up. "RR," he said, sounding surprised. "I had no idea you were in town this weekend."

"Ladies, this is Milton Dollar, owner of the best painting gallery in Santa Fe."

There were quick introductions all around. Reynold said, "Mrs. Thorne and I met a couple of weeks ago at the Devor. A friend, now tragically deceased, introduced us." For Dollar's benefit, he expanded. "You heard about Clint Maslow being murdered in San Fran last weekend? A real shock."

Turning to Lisa, he said, "It must have been a blow to your husband. I understand Maslow was a student of his. Clint mentioned it to me the last time I visited his studio."

Lisa frowned slightly. "You visited Clint's studio? You must be quite a patron, then," she said with a tight smile. "Win was a great influence on Clint. A number of Clint's themes were inspired by Win's own vision."

Suzy looked skeptical, and Reynold's expression was bland. He only said, "It's interesting how mentors and students can actually influence each other's work, isn't it?"

Lisa stared at Reynold as if she were trying to interpret his meaning. Dollar filled the small silence by mentioning a couple of famous instances, one of which wound up in court a few years ago when the mentor accused his former student of pirating his technique. The teacher failed to persuade the judge that his brushstrokes or his subject matter were unique, or that he had lost income or reputation because his student did similar work. In the process, it created a small firestorm of debate about the ethical line between influence and outright mimicking.

The waiter had been squeezing past our group, coming and going to other tables. Lisa turned to the gallery owner. "I don't think we're going to get a table anytime soon, and Win expects us back to hang the show. I think we should try somewhere else."

I exchanged questioning looks with Suzy. Lisa voluntarily abandoning a possible patron in return for mere food? However, it was true that there was no room to sit with us, and the crowd outside was getting bigger.

Dollar agreed. "You're right. I love that Pasqual's is only a block from the gallery, but it's packed pretty much all the time. Hope you can come to the opening on Tuesday, RR. This is the first time I've had Thorne's work, and I'm sure you'll like it."

"I regret to say I haven't seen Mr. Thorne's work before, but I wouldn't miss it. We'll definitely be there."

Lisa and Dollar backed out of the dining space, Dollar looking more relaxed, Lisa more preoccupied. If I was hoping to pry information from her about Clint and her connection with him, I was going to have to wait.

Chapter Fifteen

I groaned as I slid back from the table thirty minutes later. Never mind getting back into my size tens. At this rate, everything I currently owned would be sharing space with them in the dark recesses of my Wishful Thinking closet.

Suzy and Rowland Reynold planned to visit galleries. I begged off so I could head to the antique store I always visit when I'm in Santa Fe, to see if they still have the stunningly beautiful Navajo rug I'll never be able to afford.

Dickie wasn't a shopper. If you needed something, you bought it. End of subject. That probably accounted for the two Porsches and the barely-driven Harley-Davidson that had sat in our Pacific Heights garage during our marriage. On the other hand, while I am totally comfortable asking others to consider spending small fortunes on behalf of the Devor, I have been known to think circles around even a small personal purchase, weighing its possible future role in my life until even the people closest to me are ready to abandon me to my indecision.

135

The saleswoman recognized me, and the rug still looked terrific. After paying my respects to both, I drifted up one street and down another.

Something happens to all but the most disciplined shoppers here. Who knew they needed punched-leather chaps, painted ceramic gourds, turquoise-and-silver earrings, or oversized suede floor pillows until said items called to them from purple and sage-draped shop windows? And that's saying nothing about the mother-of-pearl hunting knives, Native American drums, cowboy boots, and nineteenth-century Russian icons that cover the walls and the display areas in scores of galleries around Governor's Square and the old-town streets of the city.

After about an hour, I had circled back to Pasqual's and saw the sign for Dollar's gallery a block away. Out of curiosity, I wandered in that direction. Through the window, I could see that half of the large space was blocked with screens in preparation for a new show. There was no one in sight when I opened the door, but I heard voices from somewhere in the gallery and thought I recognized Dollar's. I wondered if Milton Dollar knew Peter, perhaps through Reynold. I would have to tread lightly with my questions, given that I was still harboring vague ideas of some conspiracy, which I couldn't seem to shake.

In the art world, we all know about cases in which a rich collector purchases the majority of some unknown genius' paintings from a hard-sell art dealer at bargain prices. The tricky part comes when the collector makes a big cash gift to his favorite museum and throws in a few of those paintings, with the stipulation the museum display the work as a condition of getting the gift.

An artist's work begins to appreciate once it's been included in a credible museum exhibition. Sometimes, the museum is too hungry to turn the deal down even though they think the artist's work sucks and they know they're being used.

As the prices spiral, Kendall had told me, the collector and the art dealer can make out like bandits if they start selling work bit by bit, keeping the market tight. If Reynold wanted to make a market for Clint's paintings, Milton Dollar might be a good middleman. Reynold's mentioning Clint's death as if Dollar didn't know could have been an act. In the worst case scenario, they could have arranged to have Clint pushed out of my window. *Hey, don't go there,* my inner voice said.

Then what about Peter? Jane had dropped a hint about Peter's personal finances. Museum directors can make a lot of money, but Peter was pretty young, and I doubted he was one of the highest paid. And people in his position had to spend money. Nice clothes, travel, the ability to wine and dine and be seen all over town—not all of it paid for by the museum. If Peter had been part of a scam, or even created one by himself, it would explain the closet full of paintings. How far would he go for some very big bucks? I shivered and shook my head to banish the dark thoughts even as I promised myself to get on the phone with friends in the business to see if I could unearth any rumors.

As I opened my mouth to announce my presence, I was stopped by a roar of fury.

"Dammit!" a familiar voice yelled. "Like hell I will, Dollar. We do it like we agreed. You can't go changing the agreement at the last minute. I tell you, I won't."

Another voice chimed in, urgent but quiet enough that I couldn't make out the words. Dollar, no doubt.

I recognized Win Thorne's voice as the angry one. He

138 — Susan C. Shea

broke into the murmuring, not shouting now but still loud. "I hate these things. It's your job to make nice to the jerks who come to openings, not mine. I just paint."

Then Win himself came stomping around the screen closest to where I was standing, going so fast, he almost collided with me. He stopped in his tracks. "What do you want?" he said in greeting.

"Hello, Win," I warbled, smiling sweetly. "Nice to see you too."

"You surprised me."

"Sorry you're not looking forward to the opening," I said. "I guess I should be flattered that you were at ours last week, since you feel this way about them."

Dollar emerged from the screened area at this moment, saving Win from a reply, and bustled over, smiling and exclaiming how pleased he was I had stopped by. Win turned away, ran his hands through his unruly mane of hair, and stomped back into the screened area without another word.

"I'm glad you stopped by," Dollar said hurriedly. "Lisa's gone, and I didn't know how to reach you. I wanted to invite you to a party tomorrow. I already checked with the host," he added as I opened my mouth to object. "They know RR, so he and your friend have been invited. You really must come," he continued. "They have a gorgeous home up in the hills and a fabulous collection of paintings and sculpture. *Architectural Design* did a huge feature on them last year.

"The Thornes will be there too," Dollar said before I could speak.

I paused. I would like to get to the bottom of Lisa's possible interest in Clint. I might even find out from Reynold what he intended to do with all the paintings of Clint's he owned.

"Thanks. Sounds fabulous. But I overheard Win say he wasn't going."

Dollar rolled his eyes. "Oh, that? That was about the opening. But don't pay any attention. I assure you"—and here Dollar's voice took on a hard edge in spite of the broad smile—"he will be here for that. The competition"—he answered my raised eyebrows—"is fierce, and there are only so many buyers in town at any one time. The artist simply must be here to help them relate to the work. I wouldn't take on a new artist who didn't commit to that. He'll be here," he repeated firmly.

While Dollar and I had been talking, thumping and scraping noises were coming from the work area behind the main room. It sounded as though Win was moving canvases around.

"As long as I'm here, could I take a peek at the work?" I asked Dollar.

The light was not great, because the track lights that would be pointed at specific pieces weren't aimed yet. About a half dozen large canvases were up on the walls, and others leaned up against the walls, some overlapping each other. Win had grasped one by its frame and was peering around its edge as he lugged it across the space. He frowned when he saw me.

"No visitors, Dollar," he growled as he set the piece on edge at the base of an open spot on the wall.

"Oh, Win," Dollar said, exasperation in his voice. "Dani is only looking around for a second. She likes your work—for heaven's sake, she came to Santa Fe to see it. Didn't you?" He turned to me with mild entreaty in his eyes.

I was already tired of Win's behavior and saw no reason to baby him. How did Lisa put up with it? Maybe Dickie, with all his faults, was not the worst example of a bad-boy husband walking the earth.

"Well, it was nice that my trip overlapped with the opening, at any rate. This is really good, Win."

He was using more color and less black, and there was more texture in his brushstrokes than in the self-consciously academic, muted, gray-on-black palette and flat finish I remembered. The shift might explain his nerves. There are lots of examples of better-known artists who had trouble bringing their collectors along when their vision changed.

Win was still moving pieces around. He stopped for a minute and looked at me. "You like them?" he said.

"Yup, what I can see. I'm looking forward to seeing the whole series. How long have you been doing these?"

"For about three or four years," Win said. "You know how it goes. Start and stop, go away from it, and come back months later. I wasn't sure. . . ." He paused, looking over at them and pursing his mouth. Dollar chose that moment to come back, handing me directions to the party on a slip of paper.

I made my excuses and left. On the sidewalk, I checked my cell phone. I had turned the ringer off when I got to Pasqual's and, as usual, forgot to turn it back on. The icon was blinking with a message from his assistant to call Peter and another from Teeni about someone who wanted to time a big gift for year-end tax credit. Would I please check my e-mail?

The last was a message from Yvette. I enjoy her offbeat style and appreciate her help when I'm out of town. Fever would be at a kennel, forced to share psychic space with other felines, if not for Yvette. But Yvette is a drama queen, and she is always the star of the play. Even so, as her words tumbled out, I stopped in my tracks, breaking the flow of window shoppers.

Someone, the voice mail message said, had broken into my apartment.

"What do you want I do, Dani?" Yvette wailed. "Please, please call."

I speed-dialed Yvette from where I stood on the sidewalk. "Yvette, it's Dani. What happened? Are you okay?"

"Dani, thank heavens. *Oui,* we are fine. Don't worry about the cat. A robber would have to crawl under your bed, you know, to capture him. But I was so scared. The person who got into your apartment? I was worried he might still be there, you know, so I called 911 first thing."

"911? Got into my apartment? When was this? Have the police come yet?" I stopped dead in my tracks, stumbling over my words, imagining the worst kind of TV crime scenes and knowing that San Francisco's police are, alas, all too frequently chasing down more serious offenders.

"Early this morning I found the door lock broken when I go in to feed the cat. First, a man came who was the uniform cop, yes? Then he calls, and another man comes, very handsome. Green eyes. I think he knows you."

How many SF cops do I know? Handsome cops with green eyes who would be likely to say they know me? "It sounds like Inspector Sugerman," I said. "That's good. So, what did he say? Can you tell if anything's missing or broken or when it happened?"

"He says the lock is broken, and so the police did the powder for fingerprints. It must have happened when I was out with Adrian last night, because I heard nothing later. But I couldn't see anything missing, just some papers on the floor. The policeman said you have to call him. Until then, I can't go in, he said. Don't worry, though. The cat is under the bed. I left plenty of food and water this morning. 'Ave you found me cowgirl skirt yet?"

You have to admire someone who keeps her eye on the

ball. She repeated Sugerman's phone number, assured me Fever couldn't get out of the apartment, and that if it was otherwise perfect, a size four would be okay, since she was planning on losing five pounds.

I told her not to worry about the break-in, but I was spooked. I've lived in that apartment since Dickie and I split, and I know what a safe neighborhood it is. It's probably as closely watched as a military installation, if military guards wore spandex shorts, sipped lattes, and patrolled with one or more yellow Labs on leashes.

Sugerman answered on the first ring.

"It's Dani O'Rourke. Yvette says someone burgled my apartment, and you came over to check it out."

"Ah, hello, Ms. O'Rourke—"

"Dani, please."

"Um. Well, your place has been visited, for sure. Your neighbor, the cute French girl—"

Great. Five minutes with Yvette, and Mr. Cool as a Cucumber is smitten. Forget the cowgirl skirt. Maybe a baggy sweatshirt for "the cute French girl"

"—didn't hear anything during the night. Neither did the other neighbors. The lobby lock was forced too. But the locks in your building aren't that hot, so it probably didn't take much to jimmy them open. The place looks undisturbed except for some stuff that could have fallen off a desk. Is there anything small and valuable that someone might know about—jewelry, precious stones, maybe?"

"Not that I keep around the house. No stock certificates or T-bills lying around. I'm wearing my watch, and I keep my good jewelry in a safety deposit box."

"Good thinking. Actually, Weiler and I are pretty sure it wasn't theft. The person who broke in was looking for something on paper—something you wrote, maybe? Can you think of what he was after?"

"No. Should I come back?" I was torn. Part of me wanted to leap back to San Francisco in a single bound and put new locks on everything. But the round-trip would take forever, much of it spent waiting barefoot in airport lines, half undressed, having my chest wanded because my bra has metal hooks.

"Not unless you tell me you suspect it's something dangerous. I dropped by because I heard it was your place. The cops on the Pacific Heights patrol say robbers who hit your neighborhood generally come in for quick grabs—jewelry, laptop computers, TVs—stuff they can sell fast. Your friend says you took your laptop, and the TV's too big. She also told me she can get a locksmith out there today."

"My important papers are all locked away," I said, "and no one in their right mind is going to snatch my cat. I'd prefer to wait until my scheduled return. It's only a couple more days."

"Sounds reasonable. I'll leave a message for the officers on patrol to check the door," he said. "Call us when you get back, though. Oh, and one last thing—have you gotten any odd phone calls recently? You know, silence on the line, hang-ups? Especially at home? Sometimes someone casing a house checks to see if you're around."

"Uh-oh," I said, putting two and two together slowly. "I got one just before I left."

"Was the number visible?"

"No, I don't think it was."

"Too bad. I'll see if we can find out where the call came from."

"Can you do that?" I wondered.

"We can pretty much track everything."

Normally, that would get up my ACLU dander, but in this case, I didn't object. He suggested I keep a time record of any other hang-up calls I got and to contact him as soon as I got back to San Francisco. I thanked him for his help and told him I'd take care of the door and call Yvette. Then I went into the nearest café and ordered a large latte.

These things don't happen to me. It had to have something to do with Clint's death. But what the connection was, I had no clue. *One more mystery,* I thought bitterly. I kept adding mysteries but didn't seem to be making progress solving any of them.

Chapter Sixteen

It was getting late by the time I finished my latte. The cloud-streaked sky was that peculiar orange and purple mix that inspires painters in Santa Fe and ends up hanging, in one form or another, on virtually every gallery wall in town. Braving the displeasure of the other patrons in the café, I pulled my cell phone from my bag and called Suzy's hotel. She still wasn't back, so I left a message asking her to call me. I wanted her to know I was going to the party tomorrow and why. I figured she could help. I also wanted to tell someone about the break-in at my apartment.

The phone rang as I hit the sidewalk.

"Suzy?" I said eagerly.

"Nope, my lovely. Only me. How're you doing, and where the heck are you?"

Dickie. It must have been my vulnerable state of mind, but I was actually glad to hear his voice.

"Hi, Dickie. I just left a message for Suzy, so I thought it

145

was her. Sorry. I'm staying at your Aunt Vera's house in Santa Fe for a few days. Why?"

"Ah. Say hello for me, will you? And tell me, confidentially, does she still have that freshly stretched face she wore the last time I saw her, the one that scared me half to death?"

"Don't be mean. You know it always settles down after a while. Anyway, she's not here. She lent me the house and the companionship of the Ortegas, of course. Who, by the way, send you their love, or at least Mrs. Ortega does. Now, why did you call?"

He chuckled. "The day Manuel Ortega sends his love is the day I know Earth's magnetic pole has suddenly shifted. Why Santa Fe? Getting away from the murder scene?"

"Actually, I'm here because of the murder, in a way, although I'm hoping to get some rest and relaxation. But I'm really pissed because my downstairs neighbor, who's taking care of Fever, said my apartment was broken into last night. And there are all these bits and pieces of things I can't quite make sense of. Dickie, I have a hunch. . . . Look, can I call you back from Aunt Vera's?"

It suddenly dawned on me that until the police arrested someone, I needed to be more discreet in public.

"I'm not sure you ought to be down there on your own. You could get in over your head. Tell me about your hunch."

"I'll call you, okay? As soon as I get back to the house."

"I've got a better idea. Why don't I drop by your apartment and see if I can coax Fever out from under the bed?"

"How did you know he was under the bed?" I asked.

"You don't remember Figaro?"

Figaro was a large, shaggy Bouvier with more charm than brains. One winter night while we were married, Dickie opened the front door, and a bundle of wiggling black fur came bounding into the house, yelping in excitement and leaping all over the room. Figaro was to be in our care while a friend of Dickie's was away on business—laundering money or whatever he does—in Dubai. Fever streaked for the bedroom, dove under the bed, and refused to budge.

"I think Yvette has it under control, and Inspector Sugerman promised to have a patrol officer stop by and check the doors at night."

"Is Sugerman the tall, dumb one or the short, snarling one? I can't remember. All I remember is how tired I was by the time they let us go."

"Let *you* go, you mean. But," I said as I unlocked the car and climbed in, "why did you call me?"

"Huh? Oh, yeah. I stopped by your office on my way from a meeting with the trustee committee, and Teeni said you were on vacation. You never go on vacation, so I figured I'd better make sure you hadn't been kidnapped or anything. You aren't being held for ransom, are you?"

When we started dating, Dickie and I had hung out in his living room night after night watching *The Thin Man* movies, shouting out our favorite lines. At moments like this I think he's channeling William Powell.

"No, and if there's nothing else, I really have to go. I'm meeting Suzy and her new best friend, Rowland Reynold, for dinner. But wait. First tell me why you were at a trustee meeting. You're not joining the board, are you?"

That would be too much. As it is, I can't seem to stay entirely out of my ex-husband's orbit. Only Suzy knows that my stomach still churns when he sails into an event with a tall, thin blonde on his arm. San Francisco being a small town, word gets back to me whether or not I want it. Often they're not real dates but friends needing an escort to go trolling for

Mr. Right. But no way do I want to sit in meetings with Dickie every other month at the museum.

"Nope. The acquisition committee's making noises about the Henry Moore sculpture that's parked in Mother's rose garden. I think they'd like it, but Mother's holding firm. So tell me what you suspect and why you're skulking around Santa Fe when you could be picking people's pockets right here in San Francisco?"

"Later. I gotta run." I have no objection to driving while talking, but the police get touchy about these things, so I snapped the phone shut and put the rental car into gear. The cell rang again, but I figured it was Dickie being a pest and concentrated on getting out of the maze of narrow, one-way streets downtown and onto the road that climbed up to the house. The local radio station predicted snow by tomorrow, and the chill in the late-afternoon air felt like it.

The approach of winter, specifically December 31, gets my juices flowing. Impressive numbers of Americans hang on to appeals for important causes—soup kitchens, battered women's shelters, and community food banks—for November and December donations, and good for them. They make the world go round, and I salute them for it.

In my corner of the fund-raising business, the end of daylight saving time is the signal to get serious about avoiding capital gains, giving away appreciated stock, setting up trusts, and otherwise dancing with the tax man. Long days talking to accountants and lawyers aren't the best part of my job, but being present when Fed Ex brings a donor's signed agreement to give you—well, your museum—a rare Dogon mask, or enough stock to purchase a set of authorized Andy Warhol prints is like opening up the biggest box under the Christmas tree. So the hint of winter in the air made me smile as I drove back to Vera's and pulled into the driveway.

As I opened the front door, Mrs. Ortega called from the kitchen. "Someone is on the phone for you."

Aha, I thought. *Like minds and all that.* It was probably Teeni with a question about revocable trusts.

Mrs. Ortega continued. "He's called a couple of times. He needs to talk to you right away."

Not Teeni, then, and not Dickie. Mrs. Ortega would have known if it was Dickie. Could it be Charlie Sugerman? I hoped it wasn't more criminal activity at my apartment. Neither Fever nor Yvette would do well with a second bout of lawlessness. Mrs. Ortega held out the phone. Worry lines creased her forehead, and her free hand clutched her apron.

"Hello?"

"Thank God I found you," said a raspy voice. "It's Rowland. I'm calling you from the hospital. Our car was in a hit-and-run. Suzy's in surgery." He was talking fast and panting, as though he'd been running up a hill.

"My God, Rowland. How serious is it? And how are you? You don't sound too good."

"I'm okay. Shook up. Suzy has some kind of internal bleeding, and the docs don't know how bad it is yet. She was conscious but in shock, I think, when the paramedics got there."

"Are you in Santa Fe? I'm coming right down."

Reynold didn't argue. I explained to Mrs. Ortega what had happened, grabbed some warm gloves, and filled a travel mug with hot coffee to keep me going.

Santa Fe Memorial Hospital was just a few blocks north of downtown. Its parking lot was half full, and, in the harsh white floodlights mounted at its corners, it looked dreary. Reynold was sitting on a worn couch in the waiting room with his head between his hands, looking at the floor. As he rose to meet me, I noticed he was moving stiffly and his right hand was bandaged. I plopped down next to him. He looked haggard and at least ten years older than he had at brunch.

"How is she?" I asked.

"No news since I called you. I'm just waiting." His face was gray.

"Rowland, that looks and smells like ancient coffee. Let me get you some juice or some tea instead. You probably need a sugar fix right now. And what about food?"

"I couldn't eat."

A heavyset nurse's aide looked over at us from a table in the hallway. She got up and brought over a pitcher of bright red liquid and a plastic glass. Her name tag said she was Hazel. "See here, Mr. Reynold," she scolded. "Your friend is right. I told him he needs some fruit juice, miss," she said, turning to me, "but he wouldn't drink it. The doctor won't like it if he comes back and finds you've fainted, you know. I'll get into trouble."

Reynold looked blankly at her for a moment, then took the glass she had poured, downed it all at once, and handed it back like an obedient child.

"Thanks, Hazel," I said. "Would you leave a refill? I'll make sure he drinks that too."

Hazel nodded again, set the filled glass on the coffee table in front of us, and took herself back to her post, listing a little from side to side as she walked, like a sailor on the deck of a ship.

I turned back to Reynold. "How did it happen? Where were you?"

"After leaving you, we found a jewelry store she liked, then dropped in at Milton's. Then we drove out to the Folk Art Museum. I detoured on the way back to show her a building site I'm interested in up on a ridge near the opera house. This SUV came out of nowhere on one of the roads leading down from the summit, slammed into the car on her side, and almost ran us off the road into a canyon. The guy never even stopped."

"Did the paramedics tell you anything?"

"Not much, just that she was conscious and had no obvious broken bones. The surgeon said her spleen may be injured. It happened so fast. I called 911 from the scene. Turned out someone working a construction site not far away saw the crash and called it in too."

Reynold explained that he'd hurt his hand trying to pull the passenger door open by himself. The door was bashed in, and even with the airbag deployed, Suzy apparently took the force of the crash, jammed in between the door and the gearshift console. The man who saw the accident came down in his pickup and helped pry the door open just as the paramedics and the police got there. Reynold convinced the crew to let him ride in the ambulance with Suzy, promising the police he'd stay at the hospital until they could interview him.

Reynold was clearly running out of steam. Adrenaline's great when you need to fight or flee, but when the rush is gone, you feel like you've swum the English Channel towing an elephant.

I heard a clanking sound coming down the hall toward us. I looked up and saw two uniformed policemen—well, actually one policeman and one policewoman—stumping toward us. About the same height, with turned-out feet in thick black leather shoes, they looked like penguins on their way to the South Pole. They were weighed down by black leather belts from which swung sticks, handcuffs, and who knew what else.

"Mr. Reynold, how are you doing? Feeling any better?" asked Ms. Penguin, resting a hand on her belt. "How's your friend?"

"Hey, Haze," said Mr. Penguin, lifting a hand to Hazel, who smiled broadly and waved back.

"Want some juice, Junior?" she asked brightly.

"Nah, thanks. Just had coffee."

Reynold had unfolded himself from the couch and stood, slightly bent from fatigue. I stood too, making a foursome with the police, who now turned their attention to me.

"You a relative?" the policewoman asked.

"No, a friend. From San Francisco," I added for no reason, except that I didn't want to sound as brusque as she did. "Suzy doesn't have family in Santa Fe, or in New Mexico. I'm a good friend," I burbled on, eager to establish my rights in this waiting room.

"Uh-huh," the policewoman said, not much impressed. Turning to Reynold, she continued, "Mind if we ask you a few more questions, sir? Have you seen the docs yet?"

"Oh, I'm not hurt," Reynold said. "A bruise and a scrape. I just wish I knew something about Ms. Byrnstein's condition."

His voice trailed off. It flashed on me that Suzy might be really hurt—I mean, near death's door. In my rushing around, I had held that scary thought at bay, but now, in the quiet of this room, with two cops standing around trying to be polite, it hit me. I felt as if I might cry or faint.

The policewoman introduced herself to me as Patrol Officer Culpepper before turning her attention back to Reynold. Reaching behind her and producing a small notebook and pen from somewhere on her tool belt, she pulled up a chair opposite the couch and sank into it with a grunt.

"If it's okay with you, sir, I'll finish up my interview while we're waiting. They'll come out as soon as there's something definite to report."

While Junior hung around fingering his cell phone, she walked Reynold through the accident. The winding road that he knew well. The rearview mirror picking up a fast-moving car catching up with them as they slowed for the curves. The shoulder beyond the narrow paved surface falling abruptly away to a steep, wooded arroyo on the driver's side. Suzy chatting, not noticing the car until it attempted to pass them on the right as they approached a turn in the road. Then, suddenly, the SUV slamming into their door as Reynold tried to control his car. The door on Suzy's side getting bashed, glass breaking, Suzy screaming, the SUV lunging around them as they skidded onto the red dirt of the shoulder and toward the ravine.

The policewoman wanted more details. Reynold didn't seem to have them. I could understand why. I mean, who would have the presence of mind to be looking for license plate numbers, face recognition, clothing, or even the make of the car that was whacking into you at forty miles an hour?

At that moment, the double, swinging doors behind Hazel opened, and a man in rumpled, pale blue cotton scrubs and booties came out, looking around the room. A matching blue face mask dangled from his neck. When he saw our group, he came over.

"You're with the woman in the car accident?" he asked. Reynold and I both said yes.

"I'm Dr. Wilson. I performed the surgery on her for internal bleeding. Your friend is lucky," the doctor said, smiling encouragingly at us. "She lost her spleen, but her other organs were spared, except for some bruising. I don't think she's going to have more internal bleeding at this point, but we need to keep her here for a few days."

"What will happen to her if she has no spleen?" Just thinking about it freaked me out.

"How much anatomy do you know?" he said, making this sound like a teachable moment.

I was miffed. I mean, why did I have to know anatomy? All I needed to know was if Suzy was going to be okay. I must have communicated something of my annoyance, because he decided to treat his own question as rhetorical and get on with it.

"Her liver will take over cleaning the blood," he said. "She'll be fine, although she'll have to be supercareful about infections. When we're sure nothing else is going to develop, you can take her home."

"How are you feeling?" Dr. Wilson asked Reynold. "Should we get you down to emergency to check for shock or blood pressure irregularities?"

"Been down already. I'm fine." Reynold waved away the offer, but I could see he was exhausted.

The cops weren't finished with him, but first they asked the doctor when they might talk to Suzy. Not until tomorrow, he replied. She would be in the intensive care unit for the rest of the night. He suggested we all go home and call in the morning, by which time he'd have an update and she would probably be ready to move to a regular post-operative ward.

Wilson's pager went off, and, excusing himself, he headed back through the double doors.

My phone rang softly from inside my bag, but I ignored it.

"If you're sure you don't need some of this excellent care,

I'm going to take you home," I said to Reynold. Poor guy. Twice in one week careless drivers had put him into danger. "You can see he's beat," I argued to the cops. "And he doesn't remember anything more, at least not right now."

Officer Culpepper looked as if she was going to argue, but her partner spoke first. "Not a bad idea, Crissy. We can't do much more tonight except file reports. It's getting too dark to check the scene, the other witness has given his statement, and everyone on patrol's been alerted to look for the hit-and-run car."

Crissy closed her mouth and nodded. Reynold agreed to come to the police station the next morning, before coming to the hospital.

The cold air, with a whiff of snow coming on, cleared my head on the drive to Reynold's house, a huge place that meandered across what must have been four or five city lots in a neighborhood of estate-type properties several miles from Canyon Road. He didn't say much during the trip except to thank me and to mutter about the punishment drunk drivers deserved. I saw him to his front door, got back to Vera's strictly on reserves, and blessed Mrs. Ortega for the low light and thermos of hot Mexican chocolate left for me in the kitchen. In fifteen minutes, I was in bed under a down comforter. In sixteen minutes, I was asleep.

Chapter Seventeen

I dreamed I died and went to heaven. The whole deal: music, smells, bright lights. On second thought, I don't believe coffee will be on the menu beyond the pearly gates. Bach, yes. I mean, how can you have heaven without Bach? And, lucky me, as I squinted from under the puffy comforter, the sky beyond the open blinds was a celestial combo of blue background and fluffy white clouds. So much for weather forecasters. My dream state lasted only a few seconds before I remembered Suzy, Reynold, and our hospital interview with the local cops. Bach continued to pour out his passion from the alarm clock CD player, but heaven retreated from my grasp like the last wisps of fog from the Golden Gate Bridge on a sunny day.

Shrugging on my robe and slippers, I meandered down the hall toward the smell of coffee, where I found Mrs. Ortega bustling around, flour on her hands and on a marble slab on the kitchen counter. She nodded toward the counter. "Fresh tortillas and eggs with spicy sausage?"

"Only if you and Mr. Ortega will join me," I said, filling a mug. "And thanks for the hot chocolate last night. What a comfort. I was exhausted."

"Oh," she said with a laugh, "we ate hours ago. Manuel's already clearing brush."

"Yikes, what time is it?" I asked, feeling sheepish and looking around for a clock. "Nine—not too bad, given everything. I'd better call the hospital right away and see how my friend's doing."

"She's good this morning," Mrs. Ortega said. "Mr. Reynold called awhile ago. He said to tell you she can have visitors after eleven. He hopes to see you there. But that's after you eat some of this."

I took the plate she handed me and sat at the counter. "That's good about Suzy. Did he tell you what happened?" When she shook her head, I filled her in quickly.

Her face took on a fierce look. "Whoever hit them should go to jail. If any of my kids were hit by a driver who ran away, Manuel and I would go after them ourselves. It's no better than murder, to drive drunk."

"What makes you think the other driver was drunk?" I asked.

Mrs. Ortega shrugged. "Why else would he be swerving all over the road, trying to race, and then leaving the scene? Unless they were crazy kids. Can you figure why parents let kids have such large cars before they know how to drive right?" she asked, not really expecting an answer.

I changed the topic, and we talked while I ate, me catching up on Vera's comings and goings.

Ninety minutes later, I was sitting on a plastic molded chair doubtless designed, manufactured, and sold with the argument that it would be comfortable for many body shapes, plus being washable with a hose. As I fidgeted outside Suzy's hospital room, I silently congratulated the designer for putting one over on the world. Not only was it unlike any sentient being's body shape (and here I include our primate cousins), but it was grimy enough to make its original color a mystery.

I had plenty of time to review the chair. A different doctor, who was with Suzy now, had slowed down long enough in his headlong rush to her bedside to assure me she was not in great danger as long as she stayed put for a while. I asked him what he meant by "stayed put." The bed, the hospital, the town? "Ha-ha," he laughed merrily, nodding to acknowledge my wit. Then he plunged into her room, a nurse close behind, closing the door behind him.

For the third time, I jumped up from my four-legged instrument of torture to pace to the window and look down at the parking lot. Reynold had not arrived yet, and I hadn't seen Suzy in the flesh. I was eager to talk with her this morning or, if she was still too sick, to get some fresh air while I waited to see her. It was almost eleven—the start of visiting hours—and bells were ringing at the cathedral a couple of blocks away.

"Well, then, who are you?" said an animated voice. It was the doctor, emerging from Suzy's room, clipboard in hand, stethoscope loosely draped around his neck. A pad of paper seemed to be falling out of his plaid shirt pocket. He was about my age and height, with a buzz cut, high cheekbones, and a dimple in his chin. His white hospital coat was too small for him, so that his forearms looked stuffed into the sleeves. He smiled and stuck out a beefy hand. "I'm Dr. Concha."

I introduced myself, explained why I was hanging around, and asked what he could tell me about Suzy's condition.

"She told me about you, so it's okay to share the information. I'm the resident internist. She lost her spleen, which is not that big a deal, believe it or not. But her other internal organs took quite a bruising, and there's no way I'm going to let her out of my sight until I know she's not going to start bleeding again. No shopping sprees, I'm afraid, but you can visit all you like. She has pain, but we'll make sure she gets meds for that. She mentioned Mr. Reynold too. Is he with you?"

I explained that he had been in the same accident and might be moving a bit slowly this morning but that I'd make sure he got the update.

"Okay, then. I'll be here all day, and the nurse knows to call me if something develops. But I honestly don't think it will, so feel free to go in whenever you like. Please keep a lookout for her to get tired, though, and when she does, give her some quiet time."

So saying, off he went, his coat billowing out around his legs just like a doctor's on TV, the same nurse trailing in his wake.

I eased over to Suzy's door, which was partially open, and pushed it gently. Peeking around it cautiously, I saw her, eyes closed, tubes attached here and there, and a shiner on her right eye. I hesitated in the doorway, wondering if I ought to leave her in peace for a while longer. At that moment, her good eye opened, and she spoke.

"Come in, Dani, and stop looking at me as if I'm on the way to the morgue, will you? It's bad enough being stuck here without makeup or decent clothes without you making faces at me." She attempted a smile.

"Oh, boy, Suzy," I said, a lump forming in my throat. "You may look like hell, but you sound awfully good to me." I gave her a tentative peck on the cheek, gently squeezed the hand she held up to me, and pulled a chair up to the bed. I was fibbing slightly. Her voice was weak, and her smile was wobbly.

"Well, I feel crummy, but I hear from the doc that I'm good enough to be dragged out of bed this afternoon for a short walk down the hall. Sounds like a terrible idea to me, but Dr. Cheerful seems to think it will do me good. How's RR?"

I filled her in on what I knew and told her he was due any minute.

"Keep an eye out for him, will you, Dani? He lives alone, and he's a bit old to be dealing with trauma, no matter what he says." She paused for a minute, obviously fatigued herself, then said, "It was weird, the accident. I don't remember much except the other car coming closer to ours, then side by side. Scary."

"Did you see the driver? Do you have any idea why he bumped the car? My aunt's housekeeper is pretty sure it was a drunk driver or stupid kids showing off."

"I didn't see him until right before he bumped us. But if he wanted to pass us, I can't figure out why he would pull to the right, drunk or not." She paused. "I looked over when he first pulled up, but the windows were that tinted glass, so I couldn't see in. Come to think of it, I'm just assuming it was a guy. After that, I focused on the road. I was scared we were going to veer over the edge. RR did a great job of keeping us on the pavement."

"Not great enough, I'm afraid," said a voice in the doorway. We both looked up.

"RR, I'm so glad to see you," said Suzy, struggling to sound energetic.

I could see she was already flagging from talking with me. I got up and pointed Reynold to the chair. "Sit down, and see how well Suzy's doing," I said. "But don't plan on staying long. The doctor in charge warned me that short visits are all she's allowed right now."

Reynold moved stiffly to the chair, his brow furrowed, his eyes on Suzy. "How are you? I've been so worried. It was all my fault."

"Whoa," Suzy said. "No talk about fault—you were side-swiped, and your driving may have saved my life. Right now, I'm worried about you. So, let's compare injuries for a couple of minutes and then move on to more interesting stuff." She tried to laugh, but it ended in a low groan. "Okay, no belly laughs for a while."

Seeing no other chair in the room, I went looking while Reynold brought her up to date on his interviews with the police, the state of his aches and pains, and the condition of his car. We sat with Suzy for another fifteen minutes, until it was clear she was exhausted. A nurse came in and shooed us out until midafternoon. We promised to return.

"Dani," Suzy said as I was pushing the door open. "Would you drop by the inn and grab me some basics—makeup, a book, maybe a sweater? If they need me to, I'll call the front desk and explain it's okay. No rush but sometime today or tomorrow?"

Reynold admitted he hadn't yet eaten, so we stopped by the hospital's cafeteria for stale coffee and plastic-wrapped croissants.

"Milt called this morning," he said, wiping crumbs off his shirt with a paper napkin. "I filled him in. He was really upset. Wonders if you and I are still coming to the party tonight. I told him I didn't think I was up to it, but I think you should go. It's a spectacular house, and the art in it is worth seeing. The people are from LA originally. They don't open their house for visitors very often. When they do, it's more likely to be for a group of donors and trustees from another museum. Go, you'll love it."

I left it open. I wouldn't know anyone except the Thornes and Dollar. If Suzy and I were going, she could help me get Lisa alone for a few minutes. Without her, I doubted I'd have much success, especially if Win monopolized her as his shield against a pack of strangers.

"You know, if Maslow hadn't died," Reynold mused, "this is the kind of private collection he would be in someday. He had the same California spirit, the fearless application of dynamic color on the surface of the canvas. I had the highest hopes for him. Peter agreed, you know."

I looked at him while he picked at the pastry and sipped his coffee, all the while staring down at the table. I remembered the slight push at my back as the SUV had screeched around the corner near Suzy's. I recalled seeing him at the door to my office right after Clint was pushed out the window, and that he knew it was Clint right away. I pictured those hooded gray eyes and his comment about how Clint was moving away from his influence. And Kendall had described a free-for-all art market in which people were playing for high stakes.

Nice of me or not, I decided to prod him a bit. "Can you tell me anything about Clint's state of mind recently, or about his finances? The police keep asking me questions, so I'm involved, like it or not."

"I can't think of anything you wouldn't already know," Reynold said slowly. He looked older today, the fine lines on his face more visible and his skin pale and papery. I wondered for an instant if Suzy would find him so attractive right now.

"I'd say he was plenty sure of his talent. He was selling more, and his prices were going up fast, which pleased him, naturally. He was happy to be on the Devor's radar, but you know that. He invited me to join him for Peter's dinner in part so Peter could hit me up for a donated piece. You weren't there, were you?"

"If I'd known you were going to be there . . ."

"Nonsense. Peter's a fine host. It's only that I remember noticing that when we arrived and Clint saw that the Thornes were there, he was annoyed. Said they weren't fans of his and vice versa. You know anything about that?"

"Win's hard to get along with. I'm guessing he was jealous."

Reynold fiddled with the thin wooden coffee stirrer and seemed to be gathering himself to get up. I jumped in quickly. "Clint never mentioned any other patrons. Did he have any other major collectors?"

"Not that I knew about. Well, at least not until recently." His lips straightened into a hard line for a minute. Then he shrugged. "His star was rising almost too fast. I heard he'd asked his New York dealer—the dealer I got him—to introduce him to a Texan swimming in money. I don't much like being elbowed out, and that's where it was heading, I have a hunch."

Good reason for murder? I wondered.

Reynold continued. "We didn't talk too often. Most of the time he sent me e-mail updates on what he was doing, with photos attached, and if I liked a piece, I bought it sight unseen. You know I have—or had—first dibs on a lot of his stuff? One of the perks of being the first collector to help him along, especially when the art market's as hot as it's been these last few years."

Sighing audibly, Reynold unfurled his lanky frame from the cafeteria chair before I could question him further. He explained that he had some business to attend to at the office and that he would come back later in the afternoon. I offered him a lift, but he explained that his office was only two blocks away and the fresh air would do him good. The wind was picking up, and I turned up the collar of my lightweight coat as we parted.

It really was a bummer of a trip, I reflected as I unlocked the car door. My own gut hurt just from looking at Suzy. And now, here I was, rattling around with nothing to do except fret. Going to the party tonight might be a good way to distract myself. But first, I would sift through what I knew that related to Clint. After tonight, I decided, I would either have enough information to justify calling Inspector Sugerman, or I'd drop the whole thing. Well, maybe I'd call Sugerman in either case. Those green eyes were hard to forget.

Chapter Eighteen

It took me a minute to recognize the soft ring coming from my pocket and another to fish out the phone and flip it open as I slid behind the wheel.

"Where are you, kiddo?" said the breezy voice. "Pirates let you go yet?"

My ex. I forgot to call Dickie back yesterday.

"Hi, Dickie. Suzy's been in an accident."

"Suzy Byrnstein? Is she okay? You still in Santa Fe?"

"Yeah. It happened on one of those narrow canyon roads north of town. She had surgery, and they took out her spleen. Amazingly, she's going to be fine."

"You weren't by chance in the same car, were you, angel face? Is there more to this than you've told me?"

"Dickie, I wish you wouldn't call me names like that. It's not funny. No, I was not in the car."

"So how did it happen?"

"She was with Rowland in his car. A crazy driver over-took them on a curve, then left the scene after the crash.

Elana thinks whoever hit them was drunk." I slipped the key into the ignition. "So, remind me why you're calling."

"Well, Sherlock, I'm wondering if you figured out who pushed Clinton Maslow out your office window, or who broke into your apartment, or who suggested to your boss that I had enough influence with my mother to make her part with the Henry Moore. It wasn't you, by the way, was it?"

"Definitely not. No one knows your mother's ability to resist the charitable impulse better than I."

"Ouch. I'd resent that if I didn't know the lady myself. What about the murder?"

"I'm not sure of anything. Clint was making money, finally, but he wasn't rich. He was ambitious, but I never heard anything about him sabotaging anyone else's career on the way up. But there are some odd things I've picked up, and I don't know whether to tell the police about them or not."

"Why wouldn't you?"

"They're not clues or anything. And I'd hate to point fingers at people I know."

"Is that what you were going to tell me when we talked yesterday?"

"Yes. For one thing, Suzy told me she thought Lisa Thorne and Clint had an affair awhile ago. Since Lisa was in my office when I got there, I thought she might have a motive and the opportunity."

"I'm sure the police are checking her alibi. Have they asked you about her?"

"Only briefly, and I didn't remember Suzy's comments then. Anyway, she's here, isn't she, so they can't be too suspicious. Inspector Weiler acts as if he thinks any of us could have done it. He's talked with me three times so far."

"No kidding? I feel left out."

"Couldn't have anything to do with the name, could it, Richard? You'd have to be standing there with a knife in your hand before the local cops would dare haul you in for questioning. Listen, I can't drive and talk at the same time, and it's getting chilly sitting here. I don't have more to tell you, I'm not learning much, and I'm not sure what if anything I can do. If it weren't for Peter's . . ." I stopped. I hadn't told anyone about the cache of paintings I'd seen at Peter's house. Telling Mr. Spontaneous Action was not a good idea.

"What? Peter's what? You're not holding out on me, are you?"

"No, it's nothing. I just remembered something I have to do for work. I'll be relieved when they find out who did this."

Dickie was silent for a moment, then said, "I spoke with someone in the DA's office yesterday. One reason I wanted to talk with you is that the police found evidence during the postmortem exam that the poor guy had struggled with someone before he died. Some scratches, skin under his fingernails—stuff like that."

"Oh, my God, that's awful." I shuddered. "What else did he tell you?"

"She. Remember Patsy, my University High School classmate? Not much. The homicide inspectors feel it would have taken a lot of strength to open the window and push a reluctant, fighting man out."

"That must mean that they don't think Lisa is a likely candidate. She's a pencil."

"I said the same thing. Tell you what, though, and this worries me. I think they found something in your office that links you to Clint's death. And I couldn't get anything out of Patsy on that."

"I know what they found. It was a letter supposed to be

from me asking Clint to come to my office. It was in his pocket. I have no clue who wrote it or sent it to Clint."

Dickie's voice shouted out of the phone. "Hell, I should have insisted on the lawyer! I'm calling my guy tomorrow."

"Look, I appreciate your help—honestly, I do—and if this doesn't get solved very soon, I'll get an attorney, I promise. But right now I'm nearly freezing. I'm heading back to Vera's and then, tonight, to a posh event some collectors who live in a gated community are having. Maybe it will take my mind off this."

"Okay, but, speaking as someone who doesn't want to wake up to headlines that say someone I'm closely related to by marriage is in jail, I say, lawyer tomorrow, like it or not. In the meantime, want some company? I've been working on my tae kwan do, you know."

"That won't be necessary. Remember, I'm an innocent bystander here." I turned the key, and the car's heater came on with a rush.

"Think so? What about the fact that someone chose your office to do the deed in? That someone cased your apartment and broke in?"

I thanked Dickie for his concern, promised I'd call tomorrow to let him know how Suzy was doing, said a firm goodbye, and put the car into gear. As I pulled out of the lot, I noticed two police cars with their flashers on parked on the block Reynold had headed for when he left the hospital. Probably nothing, but I was spooked enough by yesterday's events to drive slowly in that direction.

A uniformed cop was standing next to one police car, speaking into a walkie-talkie. I recognized Officer Culpepper from the hospital. The two-story, adobe-clad building behind her bore a polished brass sign next to the oversized front door that read REYNOLD DEVELOPMENT CORPORATION. I swerved into an opening in front of a hydrant across the street and jogged over to the cop.

"Officer, remember me? Dani O'Rourke? I was with Mr. Reynold at the hospital yesterday. The automobile accident Suzy Byrnstein was injured in? He and I visited her in the hospital this morning, in fact. Does this have anything to do with him?"

She squinted at me, held up a finger, and then turned her back and continued to talk into the receiver. I couldn't hear what she was saying, but I took the finger to mean "Stay," so I did, shifting from one foot to the other to try to keep warm.

Within a minute, I heard a siren and looked up the street to see an ambulance pulling out of the hospital parking lot. It arrived as Junior came out of the building. The driver yelled something through the open window, pointing at my car. *Whoops.* I held my keys up and ran back to the car, pulling out as the emergency tech shook his head and glared. Fortunately, there was a twenty-minute space around the corner.

By the time I got back, Culpepper and her partner had their heads together, while another cop held the door open for the EMTs carrying black cases and a stretcher. I sidled up to the officers, stood a few feet away, and waited for them to notice me. People were beginning to congregate on the sidewalk and across the street. Drivers slowed their cars and craned their necks to see what was going on.

"Excuse me," I said, stepping in closer to the cops. They ignored me, and I tried again. "Hello? I'm a friend of Rowland's, and I just left him. I need to know what's happened. Please."

At this last, they stopped murmuring to each other and turned toward me. Junior spoke. "If you'll give us your name and number, we'll contact you if we need your help."

"Look, tell me if it's Mr. Reynold, please. You were on the scene of the hit-and-run yesterday. He was the driver, remember? My friend was injured?"

Officer Culpepper stepped closer. "I remember you. Your friend fell down the stairs. Maybe he got dizzy—some delayed reaction to the crash. He was able to call 911 on his cell phone. They're taking him to emergency. Why don't you wait there?"

The EMT's voice behind us called out, "Coming through." There, strapped onto the stretcher with a collar around his neck, straps around his chest, waist, and legs, was Reynold. A tube was threaded into one arm, and the oxygen mask over his nose and mouth obscured his face. His eyes were closed. It seemed to take them forever to get him into the vehicle. The cops went into the building, and the other pair of patrolmen came out of the building. I took advantage of the changing of the guard to sneak up to the open back doors of the ambulance.

"Excuse me? I'm a friend of his. Is he conscious? Could I come with you to reassure him in case he wakes up?"

"Sorry, ma'am," said one of the EMTs. "No passengers allowed. We're taking him right up the street"—a jerk of the head toward the hospital—"so you can go there and wait if you'd like. Easy now, sir," he said, turning around to the stretcher. Apparently Reynold was conscious, at least enough to say something.

"Tell him Dani O'Rourke is here, will you?" I pleaded. "I'm a friend, and I want to make sure he knows I'm here if he needs anything."

The EMT shrugged, leaned down to Reynold, and then looked back at the closest cop. "'Scuse me, officer? The patient says he wants this lady to bring him something from his office—a calendar, he says. Wants her to pick it up for him."

The cop ambled over to the ambulance door, leaned in and said something, then looked around to me. "Tell Crissy it's okay," he said before hitching up his pants and walking slowly back to his partner's side.

Before I could ask again to talk with Reynold myself, the ambulance doors closed, and, with a quick bleep of its siren, it took off for the hospital.

His calendar. Okay, I could do that. I entered the building. There was a glass door that opened to the right, but it was closed. The lights in the office beyond it were off, and no one was visible. The softly lit staircase in front of me seemed more promising. At the top, beyond another glass door, I found Junior and Crissy in a handsomely furnished reception area.

"We're just locking up. No one else is here, so you can't stay," she said firmly.

"I understand," I said. "But Rowland asked me to get his calendar, and the cop downstairs said I could."

"Mr. Reynold wasn't saying much when we saw him," Junior said, frowning.

"I know, but he spoke to the policeman from the ambulance. Honest, you can ask the other officer. I'm guessing it's on his desk."

He and Crissy exchanged glances, and she shrugged. "Fine with me." Turning to me, she said, "Okay, but make it quick. We'll make a note in the incident report that you have it."

She pointed toward one of the doors. "This seems to be his office."

I nodded briskly, opened the door, and strode to the desk, looking as confident of my right to take things off an almost-stranger's desk as I could manage. The desktop was bare. That's one way to separate the captains of industry from us drones, I've observed. I opened the desk drawers, but no calendar.

There was a short stack of art books on a table near the window. For lack of a better idea, I looked at their spines. The one on top was covered in black cloth and had no title. I flipped it open. It was not exactly a calendar but more of a diary with dated, handwritten entries.

There didn't seem to be anything else that fit the description of a calendar, so I grabbed it and rejoined the officers in the reception area. Crissy closed the office door, and we filed back down the stairs. She turned the locking mechanism from the inside and pulled it shut as we stepped out. I offered her Vera's and my phone numbers, and she said they would call me if necessary.

The small crowd was breaking up. People were going back to their own business, turning up collars to keep out a cold wind. One short man wrapped in a thick down jacket with the collar turned up and a wool cap pulled down over his ears looked familiar from behind. As I pulled into traffic, I glanced toward him, but he had turned away down the side street and was hurrying away. I couldn't see his face.

The ubiquitous plastic chairs were waiting for me. After letting the emergency room receptionist know whom I was there to see, I peeked into Reynold's calendar. It was that or the crumpled August issue of *Parenting,* featuring an article on how to survive your toddler's tantrums and another on safe summer picnic food (hint: no bones, no mayo).

The diary entries seemed to be mostly about his research into artists and the works he was buying. Written in an angular, masculine script and using some personal form of shorthand, the text was made up largely of dated notes about auctions he had attended, artists and their prices, negotiations with dealers, and so on. Flipping to the last couple of pages, I sat up straighter. *Went w Maslow to Devor dinner. Talked with P re $5 M loan—finally met T. Quite a gal!*

The *T* might refer to Teeni, it occurred to me, especially given the comment that followed. But I knew she hadn't been invited to the dinner.

The reference to a whopping five million dollars bothered me even more if it meant a loan to Peter. That's a lot of money, no matter how you cut it. I remembered Jane's obscure reference to Peter's finances. Why would he need that much money?

"Hi, Ms. . . . ?" said a voice close by. It was the same young doctor who was taking care of Suzy. "Are you by any chance here with Mr. Reynold?" Frown lines creased his forehead, and he slapped a clipboard against his thigh rapidly. There were, if possible, more pieces of paper sticking out of his shirt pocket than there had been this morning. He looked harried.

"Yes, yes, I am. I'm Ms. Byrnstein's friend. I'm spending rather a lot of time here, aren't I? First the car accident and now his fall. Is he okay?"

"I'm a little worried. First, are you okay? You don't look so hot."

"Yes, I'm fine, but I'm weirded out by having everyone I know in this town wind up in the hospital. You know what they say about bad things happening in threes? If Suzy and Reynold are one and two, where does that leave me?"

He squatted in front of me. To my surprise, he took my

Susan C. Shea

hand. Offering comfort? I could sure use a shoulder to cry on. Instead, he turned over my palm, placed two fingers on my pulse point, and looked at his watch.

"Your pulse is fine," he said, tipping my chin up and peering into my eyes. "Are you dizzy? Have you had anything to eat today?"

Somewhat put off, I assured him I was fine, thanked him for his concern, and told him I was simply unused to being in hospitals so much.

"Understood," he nodded, smiling slightly. "Well, if you're sure, let me ask you about Mr. Reynold. Did he complain of dizziness or nausea after the accident?"

"Not to me. I dropped him off at his house last night, and I saw him here this morning. Other than having a bandaged hand and looking supertired, he seemed all right and never said anything. He is going to be okay, isn't he?"

He sighed. "I'm concerned. He's not a young man. His heartbeat's irregular, and he may even have had a small stroke. We won't be sure until he's had some tests."

"Could a stroke have caused the fall?"

"Can't say until we can talk to him. He's drifting in and out of consciousness, and we have him under light sedation, in part because he's cracked some ribs and breathing's painful. But he's mentioned you by name a couple of times. I think he wants to see you, and that may help him rest easier. But it has to be very brief. He's not in any condition to talk, and I don't want to add any stress to his system."

"Got it," I said. He probably he wanted his calendar, which I now thought I didn't have. The black book was less a schedule for the future than a recording of past business.

Dr. Concha and I walked into Reynold's room together. It was dim, lined with machinery that blipped every few seconds and displayed green LED data. The doctor pulled a chair up to one side of the bed, and I plopped down.

"Mr. Reynold?" murmured the doctor. "I've brought your friend in to see you for a few minutes."

Reynold's eyes opened slowly.

"She can only stay a short time, Mr. Reynold. You really need to rest, okay?"

Reynold's eyes focused on the doctor's face for a few seconds, and he blinked and mouthed "Okay" in response. Then his eyes turned to me.

Dr. Concha said, "The nurse is available if you need anything. Remember to keep this short." So saying, he disappeared.

I turned back to Reynold and tried to smile. In truth, he looked awful. I wasn't sure what to say. "Rowland," I managed, "you've had a bad weekend. I'm so sorry about this. I wish I could think of a way to be helpful."

"Book?" he mumbled, his voice slurred but raspy in its urgency.

I held it up and asked, "Is this what you meant? The paramedic said you asked for your calendar, but I didn't see one."

Roland's eyes left mine and focused on the black book from the instant I held it up. He nodded slightly and then winced. One hand lifted slightly from the bed. "My book. They know. Peter . . ."

"You want Peter to know something?" I said, perplexed.

His eyes closed briefly, then opened again. "Suzy's in danger . . . she'll know . . . in the book . . ." His voice drifted off.

"I'm sorry, Rowland. Suzy's in danger because of something in this book?"

"Make sure Suzy knows."

Whatever he was trying to tell me was agitating him, and

I felt like an idiot asking him to repeat it. "Suzy needs to know something in the book?"

He tried again. "She does. See if Peter knows too . . ."

He was losing me, and I didn't much like *Suzy* and *danger* in the same breath. "Are you saying Suzy's in danger?"

He moved his head in what could have been a nod or could have been an effort to get more comfortable. "Tell her . . ." His voice trailed off, and his eyelids began to close. He tried to say something else, but it came out as a mumble. His head relaxed on the pillow.

The beeping machines didn't change their rhythm, and none of the green lights started flashing wildly, so I didn't think anything was more wrong than it had been ten minutes ago except that I was now really worried, still clueless, and holding a book that the owner did or did not want some unidentified "them" to see, a "them" that might include Peter.

I waited fifteen minutes more in the darkened room to see if Reynold might surface, but he seemed to be in a drug-induced dreamland, so I scooped up my coat and the book and tiptoed out.

Chapter Nineteen

My watch said lunchtime had come and gone. I was tired, hungry, and spooked by the dramas of the past several days. The nurse at the station said Suzy was off getting some kind of CT scan or X-ray and would likely not be back for an hour. I left word that I'd come back.

I considered calling the police station but decided I'd rather talk to Inspector Sugerman first. I headed back to Vera's, where I could scour Reynold's book in private. When she heard the car, Mrs. Ortega came out to the kitchen, determined to heat up some food she had prepared "just in case." I practically wept with gratitude as the aroma of chicken, cilantro, and garlic began to waft from the warming oven. While I ate and she sipped coffee, I filled her in on Reynold's accident, leaving out my suspicions. Even without them, the fall alarmed her. Reynold was a major player in Santa Fe's business and civic community, and this would be all over town in no time.

My cell phone rang as I scooped the last of the creamy black beans onto a soft tortilla.

"Dani, it's Suzy."

"Suzy, what's the news?" I asked, hoping she hadn't heard about Reynold from someone else.

"I surprise myself, to tell you the truth. When they said I had to sit up yesterday, I was ready to sue for malpractice. But I'm better. The doc says as long as I don't pick up an infection, I should be out of here in a few days. No traveling, though, so I need to extend my hotel reservation. In fact, that's why I'm calling. Could you do that for me, and bring me those few things from my room? My insides may look great, but I don't want anyone other than you to see me with this charming yellow skin, ratty hair, and cracked lips. Ugh."

She sounded so upbeat that I decided to wait until I got to the hospital to fill her in on Reynold's fall. Instead, I got instructions on where to find her makeup bag and the cardigan sweater she wanted to put over the hospital gown. "But I have a better idea about where to stay. I know Vera would insist on your staying here, and Mrs. Ortega and I can take much better care of you."

Mrs. Ortega was pumping her head in agreement. Suzy didn't take much persuading, so we agreed I'd handle the hotel business and drop off her makeup and sweater before heading off to the party tonight.

"One more thing," I said. "Do you recall Rowland's keeping notes in a kind of diary? Does that ring a bell?"

"No. Why do you ask?"

"Well," I said, tiptoeing around his fall down the stairs, "he mentioned something about it to me. If he kept notes about artists and their work in it, maybe it would have something useful about Clint in it."

"Sorry. You'll have to ask RR. He never mentioned it to me."

We rang off, and back downtown I went. The clerk at the Red Desert Inn was sympathetic, but it wasn't until the manager called the hospital and talked directly to Suzy that I was given a key and went up to her room.

"By the way," he said as I turned away from the reception desk, "someone else apparently came by to get things for her the day she was admitted to the hospital. I'm sorry we couldn't let that person in. I'm sure you understand that we can't allow that without our guest's permission."

"Of course. Who was it?" I asked, puzzled and a little alarmed.

"I'm afraid I don't know. Another manager was on duty, and the only reason I know is that she told the desk clerk to let me know the request had been made. Sorry."

As I opened the door to her suite, my first thought was that Suzy on the road was a lot less organized than Suzy at home, which was saying something. I packed up clothes, books, papers, shopping bags with Santa Fe store names. The same bag Suzy had left in my trunk had spilled its contents again, this time all over the bed. I scooped everything up and stuffed it back in, not bothering to sort it out. That would be a good exercise for Suzy during her stay at Vera's.

Dusk was settling over the town as I sped up the hill. I decided I would dress first and detour to the hospital on the way to the party. I knew I was postponing giving Suzy bad news about Reynold for fear it would affect her own recovery. When my cell phone rang, I was tempted to ignore it but decided I'd better not, given that so many people I knew were in bad health.

"Hey, Dani, it's Teeni," the voice on the line said. "I heard Suzy Byrnstein's in the hospital, and things don't sound so good."

"Automobile accident. She needed surgery. She's well enough today to be demanding lipstick, but she had a close call. How did you hear?"

"How else, since you're not keeping me in the loop? Prince Charming, of course."

"Prince . . . Ah, you mean my ex? *Charming* is hardly the term I'd use. How did he happen to tell you?"

"He called me. Said there's something funny going on in Santa Fe and wanted to pick my brains about it. Rowland Reynold, the big collector, is involved, he said. What's that all about?"

"He was driving the car in the accident. You know him, right?"

Silence. To be fair, she might be thinking. "I may have met him," Teeni said in a neutral voice.

"Through Clint?"

"I don't know. Is it important? Have you talked to Peter today?"

"Nope, why do you ask? Should I?"

"Not if he hasn't checked in with you."

"Well, he hasn't, and I'm not expecting him to. It's Sunday, remember? But I'm really glad you called. You know that silent call you picked up in my office that night?"

"Yeah?"

"Well, I got one at home, and, a day later, someone broke into my apartment."

"Yeah, Dickie told me someone had vandalized the place. I was going to ask if you needed anything done."

"It's taken care of, but I think whoever it was wanted to make sure the place was empty. Someone called my office too. Unfortunately, I deleted the voice message, but now I wonder if it was the same person."

Teeni said, "The police are making a big thing about finding my prints on your phone, by the way."

"They don't suspect you, do they?"

"Hard to tell. I told them about the call from upstairs. I had to. But, honestly, I think they're looking at you."

I'm sure my squawks registered over the line.

"I know you didn't do it, for heaven's sake," Teeni said. "But I get the sense they're frustrated and under pressure to close this case. And, let's face it, you're an obvious target. Your office, your former boyfriend, your letter . . ."

I was too angry to say much more than, "I hope they do check Peter out, then, to see if he made the call. I'm not going to sit around waiting to be arrested when I am totally, totally innocent."

"I hear you," Teeni said soothingly, "and I hope you're talking to an attorney."

"I promised I'd contact a friend of Dickie's if I needed protection. It seems so ridiculous, though."

"I'll tell you something, Dani. Whoever the caller was, it wasn't Peter. I asked him yesterday. He was surprised that someone got to his phone, and he asked me not to tell the police, since it would confuse the issue. There were a few VIPs invited into his suite during the gala. That could be sticky, and, let's face it, it's hardly likely Geoff Johnson or his wife ran downstairs and pushed poor Clint out the window."

"Peter's altogether too interested in keeping things quiet," I said, my loyalty to the boss oozing away as a vision of handcuffs and the look on my sister's face pressed in on me.

"Well, I've screwed it up for him, then," Teeni said. "I told the cops he was on the floor all night and it certainly wasn't him. Someone must have gotten in. Maybe Dorie was in the office for part of the time. She could have left her desk for a minute."

"So, are you covering up for him, Teeni?" I said. Her loyalty was touching, but the intensity was new.

Teeni didn't say anything for a while. Then she abruptly changed the subject. "Are you okay? I know this is a tough time, but you did say you were going to try to have some fun down there."

This trip had turned out to be as much fun as programming the auto-record function on the television set without the instruction manual. "Well," I said, trying to shake off my uneasiness, "I'm going to a party tonight at a house that made it into *Architectural Design* recently. That should be interesting. But I'm also using the time to follow up on some odd things I've heard, which seems like a better and better idea if the cops are so short on other leads that they suspect me."

"Odd things? Like what?"

For some reason, I hesitated telling Teeni more about Peter or Reynold. "Never mind. Take my mind off this. Tell me what's up at the office."

"Haven't you been checking your voice mails, girl?" Teeni said in her normal tone of voice. "That cute detective's been asking when you're getting back. You can't tell me he isn't interested in you personally. I can hear it in his voice. Will you call the man Monday, please, so he doesn't keep leaving messages for you here?"

"I gave him my cell phone number. Do me a favor, please? Call and tell him I'm still here, and give him Vera's number and my e-mail address?" I wondered if he was following up on the apartment break-in. Or planning to read me my rights. Of course, he might just want my help in getting a date with Yvette.

"Okay. New topic. Peter said you needed to be thinking about Muriel Prendergast."

I love Mrs. P, who must be ninety. She's a real firecracker, excited about the idea of her late son's name adorning a room in the museum. The half-million-dollar ask needed to be scripted right down to time of day and menu choices, and I owed Peter a plan of action by the time I returned.

By the time I got off the phone, I was running late. Changing quickly, I searched out Suzy's cosmetics case, the sweater she wanted, her address book, and a couple of novels.

The hospital parking lot was still only half full, and I was in Suzy's room in a New York minute. She did look better, much more alert but definitely ready for a makeover. I kissed her cheek and put the bag next to her on the bed.

"They won't let me wash my hair yet, but they can't object to mascara, can they?"

"Nope, mascara and blusher are federally protected rights in my book. I have to run, but I want to ask you something. When I was picking up your clothes from the hotel, the manager said someone came by the day of the accident. Any idea who that might have been?"

"No, unless it was this friendly woman in my yoga class who's staying there too. We were planning to get facials the next morning. Uh-oh, bad on me. I never called her after the accident. I'll do that tonight for sure."

On the drive over, I'd decided I had to tell her about Reynold. I didn't want her to hear about it from him, should he recover enough to come by, or from the police.

"Suzy, I don't want you to worry. After Rowland left the hospital this morning, he walked over to his office. Apparently he fell down the stairs from the second floor and called 911. He's here in the hospital."

"What?" Suzy said, her voice rising. "Is he badly hurt?"

"Well, he spoke to me when I went in to see him earlier. That's a good sign. The doctor said his age is a factor, but he wasn't going to tell me anything more, since I'm not family."

Suzy said, "I'll get the nurse to take me to see him. Poor RR. Two weeks in my company, and he's had two accidents. I feel like I should apologize or something."

"Remember, he was with me when we almost got run over in an intersection near your house. That makes three."

Coincidence? Hard to believe. I had a strong feeling the near miss in San Francisco was deliberate. But if Reynold had been the target then, were the car crash and his fall not accidents? I'd thought *I* was the target in San Francisco. I even thought Reynold might have pushed me. My head was spinning, and Reynold's muttered "danger" rattled around in my brain. Teeni's call had interrupted my plan to read the black book right away. But I had to pass along at least something of his warning, just in case he was right and Suzy could be vulnerable.

"You don't know of something to do with an art purchase or some kind of secret deal, do you?" I asked.

Suzy looked at me. "Want to tell me what you mean? It sounds nasty, the way you say it."

"Rowland seemed to be saying there was something you and he knew. Maybe Peter too? He was kind of drugged, though. He did seem to think it might be . . . well, he used the word 'danger.' " There, I'd said it.

"Danger? Who in the world would want to hurt RR?"

"And why?" I added, as much to myself as to her. I didn't know anything about Reynold's work as a developer in a mostly anti-development town where locals tangled regularly about land and water rights. Reynold could have lots of

enemies. If that was the case, Suzy might have been an innocent victim of someone getting back at Reynold. *But,* said the
little voice in my head, *why was the black book so significant?*

"I'll ask him when I see him," she said. "Promise. Now,
you'd better get going. I want to hear about this palace of lux-
ury first thing tomorrow, okay?" It didn't seem like a good
time to press her with talk about possible danger from some
unnamed "they," so I bit my tongue and left, telling her to get
lots of sleep.

Dollar's directions got me to the party easily. Cars parked
up and down the road clued me in that I had arrived. The host
and hostess were obvious near the wide-open front door, she
in a classic Dior tux and he in a beautifully cut dinner jacket
ruined by one of those strange bolo ties. They professed to be
delighted that their dear friend Milton had invited me. The
hostess waved her hand, weighted down by a gold charm
bracelet I'd kill for, in the direction of the luminaria-lit patio
where she said the gallery owner was "holding court with
that wonderful new artist of his." If the artist was Win, it was
clear that the hostess hadn't spent much time with him. *Wonderful* was not an adjective people normally used in connection with Win Thorne.

I made my way to the bar, intercepted several times by
waiters bearing morsels of fashion food: tuna carpaccio br-
uschetta, and individual endive leaf cups laden with crème
fraiche and caviar.

After a quick tour of the open rooms, which featured stunning combinations of softly painted pink walls and blue tiled
floors that definitely were worthy of a magazine spread or
two, I repaired to the patio. A larger than life, magnificent Vi-
ola Frey sculpture of a chunky woman cast a benevolent eye
over the guests.

Win, true to form, was glowering at a white-haired lady in a skirt accessorized with a silver medallion belt. "Marjorie was telling us about her trip to Venice," Dollar told me. "She met several of Venice's greatest contemporary painters."

"And Mr. Thorne," rasped the woman in a deep, whiskey-and-cigarettes voice, "was informing me that there *are* no great artists in Venice. I sure wouldn't want to be the one passing along that assessment. They seemed pretty sure of themselves."

With that, she rattled the ice cubes in her empty glass and stomped off to freshen her drink. Silence fell as everyone didn't look at Win. He seemed oblivious to any awkwardness, upending his own drink and handing the glass to Lisa with a gesture that said "Get more."

Lisa obediently slipped away, and I followed her. She had been in my office right after Clint went out the window. Granted, she was not likely to have pushed him out, but I wasn't so sure her explanation of looking for a bathroom made sense. Especially since the door to the whole wing was open. What I couldn't begin to guess was why she might have been involved if Peter and Rowland, or Peter on his own, were stealing Clint's artwork. Had she been romantically involved with Clint? Her being married wouldn't have bothered him, alas, and she might have decided to switch allegiances from the has-been to the new star. In any case, I'd be damned if I was going to let myself be the only suspect. If Inspector Weiler wasn't interested in her, so be it.

"So, how are things?" she asked as we eased toward the bar. "You having fun going shopping with Suzy and that cowboy friend of hers—what's his name?"

"Rowland Reynold. But you've met him, haven't you?" I asked. "I thought he said that the other day."

"Oh, I guess we did, briefly. But I didn't remember his name."

"Lisa, I'm glad to have a chance to compare notes with you," I said, as girl-to-girl as I could manage. "I'm still so bummed about Clint and feel, you know, kind of responsible, since it happened in my office. Can we grab a glass of something and sit somewhere quiet for a couple of minutes? Since you were there, I figure you might be able to help me get a fuller picture than the police have given me."

Lisa stiffened slightly and kept walking, looking over at me as if to check that I was still with her. "I don't have much to add. It was all a blur."

She handed the glass to the bartender manning a table, behind which was a large, delectable painting of cakes with frosting painted on so thickly in pastel colors that you could almost smell the sugar. Wayne Thiebaud, I mentally cataloged. First-rate. Mid to late career. Worth having in any major museum.

"I understand that, Lisa. That's what I feel too. But I do wonder, well, why you were in my office, actually. Not that I mind," I hastened to add, not wanting to sound confrontational. "But I don't quite understand . . ." I let my voice drift off, hoping the question in the air and the silence would pressure her to speak.

She turned from the bar, Win's refill in hand, and started back, not meeting my eyes. I trotted around to get in front of her and turned back, stopping in my tracks. She was stuck. She pulled her shoulders back and stared at me.

"The door to the offices was open, the alarm was on, and then I heard a scream and thought maybe I could help. I looked into the room with the open door—I didn't even know it was your office—and your assistant was there. She looked really upset, and it must have been her who screamed, so I went in and asked if there was a problem. She wasn't making much sense, but I understood it was something about the window, and I understood somebody fell. I felt faint, so I sat down. And then everyone else came in."

"Do you remember seeing anyone else in the hall? Anyone you knew?"

"No. Look, I'd better bring this back to Win before the ice melts." She attempted to get by me. By now the crush of guests was large enough that I had her effectively pinned for at least another minute or two.

"Before we go back, can you tell me more about the door from the gallery?"

"There's nothing to tell. It was open. I walked through. Didn't seem like a big deal."

"Yes, but the thing is, it's built not to stay open. It closes behind whoever walks in."

"Maybe your assistant propped it open when she heard the alarm? Maybe it wasn't closed all the way? I don't remember, okay?"

Lisa moved deliberately around me and toward the patio. I could only follow at this point, so I did, catching up to her at the doorway. "One more thing, Lisa, and then I promise I won't bother you again. It's not about that night at the Devor," I added hastily as she turned a gimlet eye and a thrust-out chin in my direction. Clearly, I had passed the bounds of what she considered polite questions.

"Did you go to Suzy's hotel the other day?"

Her mouth dropped open, and she stared at me. When nothing emerged from her mouth after a few beats, I felt compelled to continue. "Suzy's in the hospital, and I had to go get some of her things. The manager said someone looking a lot like you came by, looking for something. If there is something, maybe I could find it for you." It was a guess, but my goal was to shake her up.

"Let me see if I have this straight," Lisa hissed, swinging around to face me. "First, you imply that I was more than an accidental observer in your office after Clint died, then you accuse me of trying to steal something from your friend's hotel room? Have you lost your mind?"

She stepped closer and looked up, all pretense of friendship gone. "Now, listen to me. It was pure bad luck that I wandered into your office at the wrong time. I'm bloody sorry I did, for sure. I think maybe you had something to do with Clint's death, and this is your way of trying to shift the spotlight. Everyone knows you two had an affair that ended in a nasty fight."

She paused for breath but not long enough for me to stop sputtering. I noticed that a couple of guests were glancing our way, picking up on the vehement tone of Lisa's voice. "Furthermore, I didn't go snooping around your pal's hotel room. You find the person who says I was there, and prove it. In the meantime, leave me alone. Win has an important exhibition coming up, and I haven't got time for this crap."

She spun around and hurried over to Win, who was rooted in the same spot, making a halfhearted show of listening to someone. She handed him his glass, reached up to peck his cheek, and smiled at the woman speaking. I stood where I was for a moment, feeling my face get red, wondering if Lisa's outburst meant I had touched a vulnerable spot, or if I was the biggest fool in Santa Fe.

I might have stood in the same spot, feeling like an idiot, for the rest of the evening if I hadn't heard my cell phone ringing from deep inside my bag. The call was coming from

Vera's. I answered it as I slipped out the front door into the frosty night air.

"Dani, I'm glad to catch you." It was Mrs. Ortega, her voice tight with tension. "Your friend called from the hospital. Poor Mr. Reynold. He passed away."

Chapter Twenty

My brain refused to process the news right away. I had been talking to Reynold a couple of hours ago. Mrs. Ortega had to ask me if I was there. "Sorry, Mrs. Ortega," I said, finding my voice while my thoughts continued to roll around in my head in a disorderly fashion. "Suzy called with the news?"

"Yes, she asked if I would call you. She was really upset. She tried your cell phone but couldn't get through, so I said I'd try again."

"I must not have heard it. Okay, I'll go to the hospital right now."

Privately, the news shocked me for another, less charitable reason. I had just about convinced myself that Reynold was Clint's killer, alone or with someone else. He was furious with Clint because he stood to lose his buying advantage if Clint turned to another patron, as he suspected might be happening. If Clint died before that happened, Reynold's existing collection would be gold. I remembered those wolfish

191

eyes and the fact that he knew Clint was the dead man before everyone else did.

But then I conjured up the Rowland Reynold I'd seen lately—the gray face, the old man's bent posture, his anxiety about a mysterious threat, and his genuine concern for Suzy—and I admitted to myself that I might have been chasing the wrong hunch.

Reflecting sadly that I was spending far too much time there, I hurried into the hospital's reception area, noting it was only dimly lit and empty. I made my way down the darkened and silent corridor toward the post-op unit and Suzy's room without being seen or stopped until I reached the nurses' desk.

The nurse on duty was not interested in my reason for being on her ward at that time of night and was not about to let me into Suzy's room. It looked like an impasse until a call light in front of her buzzed. To my relief, the nurse told me it was Suzy's. She instructed me to wait while she checked with the patient. When she returned a minute later, she said I could go in for five minutes but to keep the noise down and try to avoid upsetting the patient further.

Suzy, looking pale in the low overhead light, was lying almost flat in her bed, still connected to drip lines. Her eyes were red-rimmed, and she was clutching a wad of tissues.

"Oh, Dani, thank heavens you came," she cried.

I sat down so she could see me without lifting her head. "Tell me what happened. Rowland was a little out of it when I saw him earlier but still conscious. Did you get in to see him?"

"Only for a couple of minutes. He was so weak."

Suzy didn't look very good either. No wonder the nurse had said not to upset her. "I'm really sorry. But accidents happen, and Rowland was, well, not young, you know." I had no intention of worrying Suzy even if my inner voice was telling me that Reynold's death might have had nothing to do with his age and a lot to do with whoever "they" were that he had been trying to warn me about earlier that day.

Suzy turned her head on the pillow. "Dani," she said, and her voice dropped to a whisper. "I think he was trying to tell me it wasn't an accident. He tried to say something about how I had to watch out. Kind of what he said to you. What do you think he could have meant?" She groaned softly. "I'm sick from all of this stress. My gut hurts, I feel awful, and I can't do a thing about anything. Poor Rowland." She burst into tears.

I held her hand and didn't say anything. This trip had turned into a nightmare. Reynold dead. Suzy seriously injured. Even if I wanted to, I couldn't even retreat to my own home as if it were a cocoon, since it had been broken into. On top of everything, I was still a suspect in a murder case, and now the person I thought might have killed Clint was dead, and I was nowhere in my search for answers.

Suzy stopped crying and wiped her eyes. "I really appreciate your coming in," she said in a soft voice. "Go home and get some sleep. I'll feel stronger in the morning. There's nothing I can do for Rowland."

I squeezed her hand. "Good idea. The quicker you get better, the quicker we can get you back to Vera's."

"The doctor usually comes in around nine or ten in the morning to see me. After that, I should have a better idea of when I can get out."

I agreed there was nothing either of us could do right then and got up to leave. "I wouldn't worry too much about what Rowland said. But in case there's something important we don't understand about all this, is there anything you have here that might be best to let me keep for you?"

She shook her head. "Honestly, I can't think of a thing. Somehow I think RR meant something I knew, not something I had. But you decide, Dani. Just leave me my wallet so I can buy my way out of this place when the time comes."

She sighed and then added, "By the way, someone stopped by to see me when I was down with RR. Didn't leave a message but said she was a friend."

"Who do you think it was?"

"Probably the yoga instructor from the hotel. We got along great, and I was going to go walking with her. Right now I'm not in the mood for company. Can you arrange it so I don't get visitors other than you?"

I agreed and gave her a kiss as I left. The night nurse was at the desk. She looked up from her swivel chair and raised her eyebrows in a question.

"She's okay, but she'd appreciate a sleeping pill," I said, keeping my voice low. The nurse nodded and got up, pulling a metal clipboard from a rack. As she made an entry and searched her key ring, I added, "She's asked that she not have visitors other than me for now." I smiled encouragingly but got nothing back but a casual nod as she turned to the medicine closet.

I retraced my steps back through the darkened corridors to the empty reception area and the parking lot. My breath came out in a small cloud; it was getting colder. I was worried about Suzy facing some unnamed danger. I considered going to the police station, but what could they do? They weren't going to send a cop over to watch the room merely on my report that Reynold thought an unnamed "they" knew or didn't know something. The cops had no reason to believe Reynold didn't tumble down the stairs, or that Suzy hadn't had some bad luck in a collision with some wild kids.

I glanced at my watch. One in the morning. No wonder Suzy and I were so tired. I promised to call Sugerman with my suspicions first thing in the morning and to go see Crissy Culpepper in her office before the day was over.

The streets were virtually empty, with only an occasional car's lights now and then visible in the distance. I crossed the rim road and climbed toward the winding street Vera's house was on. At an empty four-way intersection, the lights of another car came slowly up behind me. It took the same route out of downtown, turning onto Vera's street well behind me. Ordinarily I wouldn't even notice, but after everything that had happened, I was getting a little paranoid.

The car wasn't gaining on me. On impulse, I signaled a left turn, even though the house was straight ahead a mile or so. I slowed down as if I were turning. So did the other car. At the last minute, I hit the accelerator and kept going straight. The other car didn't turn but didn't speed up either. In a minute, it had disappeared from my rearview mirror. It had been a co-incidence. I was upset and needed sleep, period.

Chapter Twenty-one

I woke up early Monday morning with a list of things to do, first of which was to call Sugerman. Enough of this fooling around. I was in over my head, and it was past time to turn it over to the pros. As I sipped coffee and scooped up the last of the melted cheese from my huevos rancheros, Mrs. Ortega handed me the local morning paper, folded open to a small story headlined *Prominent Developer Injured in Fall*. They had gone to press before Reynold died. The story mentioned a recent lawsuit his firm had won and listed his roles on the boards of a number of local organizations.

It was still early in San Francisco, but I decided to leave a message with Sugerman's office anyway. I was taken aback when Inspector Green Eyes answered. First I stammered something; then I took a deep and apparently audible breath, because he said, "Ms. O'Rourke, are you all right?"

"Not too great," I said, shaking my head to untangle any cells that had been thrown into confusion by the sound of his voice. "I understand you've been trying to reach me. I'm sorry I didn't call before. I'm in Santa Fe. Oh, I guess you knew that, since we talked after my apartment got broken into. Anyway, I have some news to tell you, and I'm getting kind of worried." Getting all of that out in one breath deprived me of oxygen, so I sucked in air again.

"Are you out jogging or something?" he said. "I hear it's a higher elevation there. Maybe you should take it easy until you adjust to the place. You could call me back later."

I struggled for a minute. I liked the idea of his seeing me as a determined athlete braving cold wind and steep hillsides in pursuit of a great body. But since the last of the buttery tacos was still in my free hand, I didn't think I could pull off the deception. Plus, I definitely wanted to talk to him now, not later.

"'Fraid not. It's pretty cold, could snow today. I'm at a friend's house." No need to explain that I was staying with my ex's relative. It would be another nail in the coffin of our relationship. If we had one, which was pushing the facts. "But there's bad news. Rowland Reynold, the collector who owns a lot of Clint's work, died yesterday, and I think he may have been killed."

Silence for a count of ten. Then, sternly, "If you think this person may have been the victim of a homicide, have you told the local police?"

"Well, not yet. It's way too coincidental that Rowland knew Clint so well. But Rowland told me before he died that he thought someone might be a threat to him and to Suzy Byrnstein, even though Suzy can't figure out who or why. She said Rowland said something to her also. She's in the hospital too." I was talking fast, I knew, but I had this feeling he thought I was imagining things, and I didn't want him to dismiss me as some kind of nut.

He was silent for a minute again, although this time I heard voices and a phone ringing in the background. "Ms. O'Rourke, you're going to have to go over this again. If I have it right, you think something's going on in Santa Fe that relates to our investigation here. You understand that you still have to talk to the police there, since this Reynold guy died there?"

"Um, can you call me Dani? Yeah, I know I have to talk to the local cops, but they're not going to know anything about Clint, are they? So it's going to sound crazy."

"Tell you what," he said, ignoring my pathetic attempt at breaking the ice. "I don't have a lot of time right now, but why don't you give me the information you have, tell me how you think it connects with the Maslow homicide, and I'll call the Santa Fe police and request that they interview you today."

As I licked the butter off my fingers, I told him about the near-miss incident in San Francisco, the car crash, Reynold's fall, and his vague warnings about the black book. I included what I knew about the mysterious visitor to Suzy's hotel room and about Peter's lost keys, hoping Peter wouldn't fire me for it.

Sugerman was noncommittal about the importance of the information to his investigation but promised to call Officer Culpepper and see what he could learn. In the meantime, he urged me to keep my suspicions to myself. "If there is a bad guy out there, we don't want him to know you're interested, and, if not, well, you don't want to go making everyone nervous, do you?" I couldn't tell from that if he thought I was a sharp-eyed amateur sleuth or an idiot who had to be humored.

He switched gears. "Before I forget, can you give me some idea when you're coming back?"

"Today's Monday, and I have to be back in the office Thursday. Why?" Was this a feeler for a date?

"Weiler wants to interview you." *Let me down easy, why don't you?* This flirtation with Charlie Sugerman was going nowhere. *Best to forget it and have a Snickers,* said my inner voice. "Have you seen today's San Francisco paper?"

There had been a new murder, a particularly lurid one, and he and his partner had drawn the case. That's why he had to get off the phone, he explained, and why the Maslow case might have to wait a few days. "When someone's killed, we try to break the case within the first forty-eight hours, while the evidence is fresh. The older the case gets, the harder it is for witnesses to recall what actually happened, for physical evidence to remain in place, and so on. So, it's all-out today and tomorrow on this, then we'll pick up the pieces in the murder at the Devor."

The murder at the Devor. Great title. Was that bad for business, or what? I wanted this solved almost as much as the police did, partly so that we who admired Clint Maslow could feel that justice was done and partly so the headlines would fade. Unless, of course, the killer turned out to be the director of the museum.

I wasn't too happy about being put on hold just when I'd figured out there was someone out there chasing after people I knew. I told Sugerman how I felt, trying not to pout or whine. This was getting creepy, I said. What if Rowland really was murdered? What then?

He tried to reassure me. He even called me Dani once, before he forgot I was a suspect. I could tell he was eager to get off the phone, but the more he tried to extricate himself, the more I clung. Ultimately, it did me no good. He promised to call the Santa Fe police soon, reminded me to be available in San Francisco on Thursday, and dismissed me. I sat there, chewing absently on a sausage and wondering what to do next.

In spite of the threatening weather, I decided to take a walk. When it comes to divining where we're going to find the money for a touring exhibition of Venetian glass or what argument will get me another development staff person, I find that walking provides good thinking time. Whether or not it would also be good for solving murders I didn't know. It would clear my head, however, and maybe make a dent in the calories I was piling up as a result of Mrs. Ortega's four-star cooking.

The sky was gray, and the round sagebrushes rolling purposefully across the road, all in the same direction, looked like intergalactic insects on a mission. No one else was on the streets. There are no sidewalks in Vera's neighborhood. I guess people drive everywhere. The occasional pickup or car passed me, as did an empty yellow school bus. I concentrated on a calorie-burning pace.

It dawned on me only after I'd turned around at the top of the hill and started back that a pickup I'd seen in front of a house near Vera's was now parked on the block ahead. A maid service, perhaps, or some kind of delivery? As I got closer, the driver looked at his watch, then snapped open a newspaper. I couldn't see his face. I shrugged mentally but kept an eye open. Sure enough, as I turned into the driveway, the same truck zoomed past me headed down toward town. The driver didn't even glance my way. I stood next to the gate until the pickup vanished from sight. Nothing suspicious. But I promised myself to keep an eye open from now on.

Forty-five minutes later, showered and dressed, I was

emerging from the guest room when my cell phone rang. It was Cecilia, the Devor's PR person.

"Dani, I'm glad I caught you. I wanted to give you a heads-up before this goes public. Are you sitting down? Peter's resigned."

"What?" I yelped. "When? Why?"

"He called me at home yesterday but asked me not to say anything until this morning. He's leaving immediately, he says. Geoff Johnson's coming in this morning, along with a few members of the executive committee. We'll do some kind of public announcement by the end of the day."

"I can't believe this. He never said anything. Did something happen between him and the board? It's so sudden."

"Johnson hasn't told me anything, so I have no idea if he asked for Peter's resignation or if it has anything to do with the incident at the Devor. Expect some coverage starting tomorrow. Sounds like you're as surprised as I was."

Was I surprised? More like freaked out. When I got my breath back, I asked her to check with Geoff to find out if I should fly back today and if she could patch me into any conference calls so I'd be up to speed. We agreed to talk again in an hour or two.

"If you have a minute with Peter when he gets in, would you ask him to call me? Tell him it's about Clint's death and the police investigation, okay?" That would get his attention, if his sudden resignation had something to do with this mess.

"Lord, this had almost made me forget about that crisis. Have you heard something from the police? I need to be in that loop."

"No, I wanted to run an idea by him. No information. You'd be top of the list if there were any."

"Okay, good. You're more likely to see Peter than I am,

though. He's in Santa Fe, or at least he was when he called me."

"What?" I squawked again, this time jumping to my feet. "Here in Santa Fe? Are you sure?"

"That's what he said when he called me. Said he thought he could get back to the Bay Area tomorrow."

"But why was he here? I haven't seen him, that's for sure."

"He didn't say other than that it was personal business. I kind of thought it had something to do with his decision. Do you have any idea why Peter might choose to leave the Devor? I mean, he's doing so well, everyone loves him, and the big bucks are rolling in."

"I'm clueless, Cecilia. Did he tell you where he was staying?"

"Nope, although he said he spent most of Saturday hiking. That's all I know."

Peter in Santa Fe when Reynold tumbled down the stairs. When Suzy was hurt in the hit-and-run. Peter possibly needing a large loan from Reynold. Could Peter be the "they" Reynold had tried to warn me about? Peter and someone else? What did they know about? Did it have anything to do with the paintings in Peter's closet?

I had already put a thorough examination of Reynold's book onto my list of things to do today, and, as Cecilia and I wrapped up our call with mutual promises to share information during the day, I made reading the book my highest priority.

But first, I needed to reassure myself that Suzy was okay. She answered her hospital phone, sounding tired. "I picked up some kind of infection, but they tell me not to worry. They added something to the IV, and that should cure it. All

I know is that it gave me hallucinations during the night. I thought there was someone in my room."

Peter? I thought. *Because of the black book?* I shivered.

"I woke up trying to scream. You know that sensation when you open your mouth and nothing comes out? I hit the call button, and a nurse came right in. I made her turn on the light, but there was no one there. That's another reason I'm so worn out, I guess. Not much sleep, Bummer. I won't be getting out of the hospital today."

I urged her to leave the no-visitors instruction in place, and she agreed. "You and the docs are the only exceptions. Man, what a crummy idea it turned out to be—visiting Santa Fe, I mean."

"Suzy, think for a minute," I said. "Rowland obviously felt he had information that was dangerous. Have you had time to think about what that could be? Even if it seems wild and improbable? For all we know, he could have been delirious from the fall, and it could have been only in his mind. But if it wasn't, what might make someone want to hurt you or him?"

"Try thinking about that at three in the morning, when you're captive in a hospital in a strange town. Yeah, I've been thinking about it. I start with art because that's what connected us. Then, buying art, which was his passion. Then the Devor, where his protégé died and where you work."

I said, "Wait a minute. I'm not part of this."

"Think about it. You dated Clint. You're deep into the museum world and the art community. Your boss was getting tight with RR, and that probably would have involved you at the donation level. And—I'm sorry, but it has to be faced— Clint went out your window after getting that bogus letter from you."

I fumed silently. It kept coming back to me, even from people who knew I wasn't the killer.

"After that, I'm baffled," she continued. "Oh, I know. I said Lisa had an affair with him, but that was ages ago. It hardly seems worth murdering about in this day and age. And, even if she did sleep with him, how would that involve RR?"

I agreed that none of it pointed to anything useful. "What did you mean about Peter and Rowland being close?"

"All I know is they were set to meet privately while RR was in San Francisco. It was important to him."

"Well, hold on to your hat. I just found out that Peter is here in Santa Fe. And he's quit the museum."

"No way," she said, sounding shocked.

I told her the little I knew, but I was reluctant to share my wild theory that Peter and Reynold might be engaged in some kind of fraud involving Clint's work. I've read about the market being flooded by fakes from time to time, but that's work by dead artists. *Clint is dead, isn't he?* said my alter ego.

Since Reynold was the best-known collector of Clint's paintings, he was in an excellent position to create a false provenance—a history of the work that supposedly proves it is authentic—for well-executed fakes. I'd been sure at first that the paintings I saw in Peter's closet were real, but that could be the talent of a great forger.

"Suzy, did Rowland ever talk about how much he stood to make if he sold Clint's paintings?"

"Not really. I think he was pleased he'd discovered Clint's work first. He felt it upped his status as a collector of con-temporary American art. But I never heard him talk about selling it. Why?"

"I'm trying to make sense of a lot of separate things, and right now, I'm grasping at straws. Did Rowland ever lose any paintings in a burglary?"

"No. Something's nagging at my memory, though— something about missing paintings."

The cache of paintings I'd stumbled onto had to be part of this mystery. Suppose they were stolen, not faked? Peter couldn't sell them to Reynold to raise funds, because Reynold would be suspicious. But what if Reynold was in on the scheme to sell them to a third party? Clint would have to be out of the picture before they could move.

Maybe the police were getting closer to figuring it out, and Peter panicked. Peter was high-strung. I could see him losing control long enough to shove the older man in a quarrel. But Clint's murder was premeditated, and that didn't sound like Peter to me. Reynold was at the Devor that night. He could have maneuvered Clint into my office. He could have found the keys during the dinner in Peter's office, or Peter could have given him the keys.

This was giving me a massive headache. Suzy sounded tired but clearheaded on the phone. I felt better about putting off my visit for a while. Settling into a chintz-covered love seat in the living room, I rooted around in my bag until I found the black book. I turned to the first entry and began my search for a clue to this tragic mess.

The first half dozen or so pages had to do with a trip to New York three years ago. Reynold had attended a Sotheby's painting auction, the Whitney biennial, and met a dealer for dinner at the Carlyle.

The next pages summarized a series of meetings he had had with a university president who was hoping to attract

funding for a fellowship program. Reynold had added paren-
thetically, *Ask GJ. Hope to interest C. GJ* might be our board
chairman. Could the *C* have been Clint Maslow?

The next entry was more than handwriting. It included
some simple sketches that suggested blocks of space within
a frame. Reynold seemed unhappy about something. His
written notes referred to something being *dm good* but mentioned that whomever he was talking about was *uptight.* I
made a mental note to return to this entry later and kept
reading.

Subsequent entries covered trips to Los Angeles, Chicago,
Minneapolis, and Oakland, plus what seemed to be a reference to his last trip to San Francisco. The last couple of pages
contained two recent entries. *SB* was mentioned. That had to
be Suzy. Reynold liked her work, apparently thought it was
appreciating in value, and intended to purchase two of her
large canvases and introduce her to a gallery owner in Soho.
He also liked her: *Dinner w SB—haven't had so much fun in
yrs. Knows where all the bones are buried!* The *bones* must
have been gossip, knowing Suzy.

The last entry was more sober. *Not sure who to talk to re:
what I saw—who'll believe me?! Need to prove it. Told S today.* At the bottom of the page, removed from the note and
surrounded by doodling, was a question. *PL? No deal now?*
Unlike most of the book, these notes weren't dated, and I
couldn't tell if they had been written before RR left San
Francisco last week.

Mrs. Ortega appeared in the doorway to tell me the phone,
which I'd dimly heard ringing, was for me. I picked up the
receiver next to the chair. It was Officer Culpepper. Would I
come in? They'd gotten a call from the San Francisco police
department and thought I might have some information to

share regarding Mr. Reynold's fall and subsequent death. I said I'd be there in forty-five minutes, and she thanked me.

She sounded curious and irritated in equal amounts. I guessed it was like doctors who weren't awfully fond of their patients' desire for second opinions. Santa Fe could handle its own investigations without some big-city cop poking his nose in. I shrugged mentally. *Get over it.* The possibility of some-one aiming cars at my friends or tossing other people out windows trumped turf wars any day.

I tucked Reynold's black book into my tote bag, told Mrs. Ortega I'd be in town until midafternoon, and headed out. Hospital first to ask Suzy about Reynold's last entry, then straight to Crissy Culpepper's office. *Finally,* I said to myself as I slammed the car door behind me, *some traction.* Maybe in an hour I would have some dramatic evidence to share with the cops and, not incidentally, clear my name.

Chapter Twenty-two

The weekend visitors were gone, and Santa Fe was a small, high desert town again. The sky was getting progressively grayer, the wind was kicking up, and the air smelled like snow. Santa Fe is lovely with a coating of fresh snow, but I wasn't in the mood. I didn't know if Reynold's death had ended the threat or if Suzy was still in danger. The last thing I wanted to do now was go to another art opening, this one for an artist I didn't much like and his hostile wife. I was tempted to skip it and head back to San Francisco. But I couldn't leave Suzy until I knew she was safe.

I braked at a stop sign, then accelerated through it. The SUV behind me didn't do a full stop, and, when we got onto the next block, the driver passed me too fast. I reminded myself that this wasn't the pickup I'd seen before and that I was in no danger. Whatever Reynold and Suzy knew, no one would have a reason to connect me to the secret unless they knew I had the black book, and Suzy was the only person other than the Santa Fe police who knew that now.

The hospital lot was almost full, and the lobby and hallway were humming as nurses and aides traveled the corridor, carrying or pushing everything from wheelchairs to mops. Civilians strolled the hallways, talking to patients in bathrobes or peering at room numbers. Suzy herself seemed less miserable.

"I'm feeling better, and I really want to get out of this place," she said when she saw me. "Whatever meds they added to the stew are working."

I passed along Mrs. Ortega's instructions to call when she was ready for Manuel to pick her up, then closed the door and pulled up a chair. The bed next to Suzy was still unoccupied, and I wanted privacy for our talk about Reynold's black book entry.

"I need to talk with you," I said. "I don't want to upset you, but I'm not convinced Rowland's fall was an accident. Part of that is his own warnings to both of us," I said, as she frowned, "but I want to read you something from his diary. It concerns you."

At that moment, the door opened, and a cheery voice interrupted us. The nurse on duty swept in with a wheelchair and a clipboard. Suzy, it seemed, had an appointment for an MRI. Nope, it couldn't wait. Doctor had to have the results by the time of his rounds.

Suzy made a face. "Sorry, Dani, but whatever it is, it's going to have to wait. They don't take no for an answer around here. It can wait an hour, can't it?"

The nurse had already started folding back covers, handing Suzy her bathrobe, and moving her portable pole with its plastic bags of nourishment and drugs. I didn't have time to wait and still be at the police station when I promised.

"Your friend might be out of here tonight or tomorrow

morning if the results of the scan and this morning's blood work are good," the nurse informed me as she settled Suzy into the chair.

"Okay," I said, stymied. We would be able to talk privately at Vera's. And I had no doubt that Manuel and Elana Ortega would keep Suzy safe from unwanted visitors. Suzy promised to call me as soon as she knew when she would be released.

I drove the short distance to the police station under gloomy skies. The next half hour was frustrating. The cubicle Crissy Culpepper worked in was small and hot. She was no Inspector Weiler. I was quite sure she didn't suspect me of murder. But I got the impression she thought I had less talent as an amateur detective than did the score of Beanie Babies clustered on her windowsill. She walked me backward through my suspicions, from Reynold's accident to the Devor Museum and Clint's death. I showed her Reynold's black book, and she promptly claimed it as evidence, although she wasn't ready to say what it was evidence of.

We went 'round and 'round, with me trying to convince her that people could get killed for art, and she trying equally hard to explain to me that there wasn't any evidence to support my claim that Reynold had been pushed down the stairs.

"Have you checked with Mr. Reynold's assistant to see if anything's missing?"

Culpepper shook her head. The police weren't investigating a crime. She shifted in her chair and played with her ballpoint pen.

"Let's see if I have this straight," she said. "You think Mr. Reynold might have been pushed down the stairs of his office because he knew something about an artist who was killed in San Francisco last week, is that right? But you don't know who might have killed either man, or what Mr. Reynold might have known. And you think the hit-and-run accident Mr. Reynold and your friend were in on Saturday might have been a deliberate attempt to scare or kill them?"

I nodded.

"I was at the scene, Ms. O'Rourke, and I have to say that, as long as they were wearing seat belts, that accident was unlikely to be fatal. The arroyo wasn't deep. In New Mexico, people run off the road all the time. It was a freak outcome that your friend was as badly injured as she was. If I were trying to kill someone, I wouldn't pick that way to do it, frankly."

Well, then. Case dismissed. Maybe she was right, and I was trying too hard to connect the dots. I had to admit that if I didn't know about the Clinton Maslow case, the rest would not seem so ominous. I decided to try once more before admitting defeat. "Did Inspector Sugerman explain that the San Francisco police have concluded that Mr. Maslow's death was murder? And that these people knew one another?"

"Yup," she answered. "But that doesn't mean much in itself. If a truck driver gets himself killed, we don't automatically suspect every other truck driver he knew in six states. I'm listening—honestly, I am. But I can't find the connection, and you haven't provided any evidence to connect these incidents.

"Now," she added, holding up her pen to keep me from interrupting, "I'm not saying we aren't open to reviewing this if something comes up—a witness, say, or some kind of hard evidence. We'll look at this book, too, and see if it suggests something we can follow up on. And, knowing that there are police working on the other death, I'll bring it to my shift sergeant's attention. If he thinks it's a good idea, we'll bring in a detective from Violent Crimes to review the report."

I had to be satisfied with that. I asked her if she'd give me a copy of the last page of Reynold's diary, and she agreed to make the copy herself while I waited in her cubicle. I asked her if they'd share the book with Sugerman, and she was non-committal, saying it was now part of the Santa Fe Police Department's evidence. If the "San Fran" police wanted to come and see it, she'd make sure it was available. I promised myself to make sure Sugerman knew about the diary.

Discouraged, I left the station wondering what I should do next. Reynold's office was close by, and I decided to see if any of his employees were there today. The street-level door opened when I pulled the handle, and I saw lights when I got to the head of the stairs. There was no one in sight in the reception area, but I heard voices and saw that the door to Reynold's office was open.

"Hello? Anyone here?" I called. The voices quit, and a woman's head appeared around the door.

"Yes," she said, coming out into the reception area, "but we're closed today. Do you have a project with us, Ms. . . . ?" She was about ten years older than I, I judged, solidly built, dressed in black slacks and a fuzzy black turtleneck sweater. Her short white hair was tucked behind her ears, revealing small gold beads in her earlobes. Her eyes were slightly red.

"No, no," I replied, "it's not business. I knew Mr. Reynold socially, and he asked me to get something from his office when I last saw him."

"When would that have been?" she asked politely but neutrally.

"Yesterday," I said.

"Yesterday?" She looked startled. "Do you know he's, um, passed on?"

"Yes, and I am so sorry. I'm Dani O'Rourke. I'm concerned

about how it might have happened, and I think he was too."
This was risky, I knew, but my gut told me that Reynold had
died for a reason related to Clint's death. It would be too much
coincidence for another lethal enemy to surface and hit one of
Clint's closest associates at the same time.

She looked over her shoulder as she stepped toward me.
Sticking out her hand, she said "I'm Doris Dell, Mr. Reynold's
assistant. Our VP for operations is here too. I don't know how
you know—knew, sorry—Mr. Reynold or what your concerns
are, but if you want to tell us about them, we'd like to hear. I
worked for Mr. Reynold for thirty years, and he was a good
man—tough in business, but fair."

Two minutes later, the three of us were perched in
Reynold's office. I told them briefly about Clint's death but
mostly concentrated on RR's black book and how adamant
he had been about it. I didn't mention his warning about the
mysterious "them." They knew he collected art, and Doris
had seen the black book going into and coming out of brief-
cases and travel bags many times. But Reynold's art collection was a private pursuit with his own funds, so there wasn't
anything in the development company's business files.

The VP stood up and began pacing the room slowly. "Listen," he said, as much to me as to the assistant, "I don't like
this. Doris and I"—he gestured to her—"are worried. RR
was a vigorous man in great health for his age. We've been
in these offices for at least fifteen years, and he negotiated
those stairs day and night, tired after a long trip, with slush
and mud on his boots, even when the power was off during
storms and we had only flashlights and candles to see by. It's
hard to imagine how he'd fall."

"Was anything missing other than the book he asked me
to take?" I asked.

Doris shook her head. "I can't swear not," she said, looking first at him and then at me. "I didn't even know the diary had been taken. It could have been at his house or in his car."

She looked around the room. "I don't know what I'm looking for, which makes it . . . wait." She strode over to a wall that had three framed paintings on it and held up her hand. I didn't see any sign of anything missing, no blank spaces or picture hooks, but Doris started nodding her head. "He had a small, framed painting set on top of these cabinets, leaning against the wall. I think I would have noticed if he took it home when I was in the office."

"Was it valuable?" I asked. "Do you know who painted it or anything about it?"

"No, sorry," Doris said, shaking her head. "What about you, Al?"

The VP shook his head. I asked Doris if she could describe it, and she closed her eyes, trying to oblige me. But all she could come up with was that it was colorful and abstract. She did recall one other thing.

"I noticed it at some point after he brought it in and asked him if it was a new addition to his collection. He said something about if you can't show a painting, does it really exist, like a tree falling in the forest. He laughed about it. I had no idea what he meant, of course, and he didn't say anything more."

None of this was particularly illuminating, and I couldn't think of any questions that would help me dig deeper. I thanked them, gave Doris my card, and invited either one of them to call me if anything else occurred to them. As I was leaving, I remembered something the police had not wanted to share with me. "Was there any sign of someone forcing their way into the office? Broken locks, scratched wood on the door, whatever?"

The vice president of operations answered this time. "Nothing we could see. But this is a lightly secured office, since nothing of value's in here except for a few computers whose contents are backed up to an off-site server at the end of every day. This is a really low-crime area. Could even be that Rowland left the door open when he came in."

Doris glanced at my card and looked up at me. "Oh, you're the second person from the Devor Museum to come by. I didn't realize you worked there. I guess Mr. Reynold had a lot of friends in San Francisco."

"What do you mean?" I asked, almost afraid to hear.

"See?" she said, going to her desk in the reception area and picking up a business card lying on it. "A Mr. Lindsey was here too." She held out Peter's card for my inspection.

Damn and double damn. When things get complicated, they really get complicated.

"Did he know Rowland was dead?"

"I didn't see him. His card was outside in the mailbox when I checked it first thing this morning," Doris explained. "Saturday's mail was still there, which didn't surprise me. RR wouldn't normally pick up the mail."

"Mr. Lindsey hasn't called or anything?" I asked, careful to sound casual.

"No, not that I know of, and I've been answering the phone since early this morning. If he does, should I tell him you stopped by?"

"Sure," I said, my brain spinning. *Okay,* I said to myself. *Peter could have dropped by anytime during the weekend. If*

he had argued with Reynold and had a role in his fall down
the stairs, he would hardly have left his card, would he?

There wasn't much more to say, and, thanking them for their
willingness to talk with me, I headed out. The mailbox with the
Reynold company name on it was one of those contraptions
you could slip mail into but not open without a key. Which
meant that my boss, now my former boss, could have left the
card any time after Friday's incoming mail was brought up
from the box. Did he have an argument with Reynold Sunday
morning? It would be hard to prove anything, since no one
could say specifically when the card was deposited. However,
the presence of the card made me sick to my stomach.

A missing painting with mysterious provenance seemed
as if it ought to count for something in this investigation, but
without a clue as to whose it was or how Reynold came to
have it, I was stumped there too. If I were betting, I'd say it
was Clint's, although it occurred to me that Reynold must
have had other artists in his collection. Reynold's comment
to Doris suggested he was hiding the painting, at least from
people who weren't likely to visit his office. But if he'd taken
it surreptitiously, why? Clint would surely give or sell him
anything he wanted.

Wishing I still had Reynold's black book so I could reread
entries to see if there was a mention of the small abstract, I
sat in my car wondering what to do next and looking at an
appealing little bookstore and coffee shop across the street. I
wouldn't have noticed him if he hadn't snapped the newspaper open the same way, but there he was, sitting at a table
next to the window. My stomach flipped. It was the same guy
who'd parked near Vera's. This time I didn't see his car, but
there was an SUV parked a couple of doors down that looked
like the one that had passed me. I was sure it was the same

man. Maybe whoever tried to run Reynold off the road had decided that I knew the same thing that made Reynold dangerous. Hastily I turned the key in the ignition.

My cell phone rang. "They tell me I'm good to go, at least with a kit full of antibiotics and as far as your Aunt Vera's," Suzy announced with more energy in her voice than I'd heard in a long time. "I passed the walking and peeing tests, and I think they're as eager to get me out of here as I am to leave."

I told her I'd alert the Ortegas and come over to help her check out. As I wheeled out of my parking space, I looked in the rearview mirror. No one jumped into the SUV and ripped out of the parking space like in a Bruce Willis flick, thank heavens. I did an extra turn around the block anyway before heading up the street, reflecting that if anyone had been trying to sideline my friend, that, at least, had failed. Now we had the Ortegas on our side, and not much got past them.

Chapter Twenty-three

T here was no one following me as I drove Suzy home. No one passed us, and I didn't notice anyone reading newspapers in parked cars.

To say the Ortegas rolled out the welcome mat would be an understatement. Within an hour, Suzy was enveloped in a cloud of comforters and pillows in another guest bedroom, furnished with a little sterling silver bell and the firm directive to ring it day or night if she needed anything at all.

Mrs. Ortega quizzed Suzy about menu requirements. Soft, bland food appeared to be *de rigueur.* Mrs. Ortega didn't miss a beat. "Flan," she said firmly, and she marched off to the kitchen.

I flopped down into an easy chair when we were alone and read Reynold's last entry to Suzy: *Not sure who to talk to re: what I saw—who'll believe me?! Need to prove it. Told S today.*

"Oh," she said, surprise in her voice. "I remember it, but

it's no big deal. I didn't realize RR was so upset. He and I both thought Win's new paintings borrowed a lot from Clint's when we peeked at them the day Win and Dollar were hanging the show. You know, brush techniques, thematic ideas. It happens sometimes. It's not classy, but it's not criminal."

"Did you say anything to Win?"

"Of course not. It was sad, though. The teacher copying the student who got more successful than he was, you know? It annoyed RR because he has a lot invested in Clint. But that's all it was."

"Darn. I was sure I'd stumbled onto something. He seemed so worried."

"I'm guessing he had a bad concussion and wasn't thinking clearly. Deliberately killing someone over anything less than a roomful of Rembrandts seems pretty over the top," Suzy said, squirming a little in the bed and grimacing.

"Well, what about this?" I continued, quoting again. "PL? No deal now?"

"Jeez, that means nothing to me. Do you think he's talking about Peter?"

"I do, but I was hoping you might know if they had some business dealings."

"I knew they were going to meet, but I assumed RR was going to make a gift to the Devor. He never said a word to me, though.

"You did the right thing, going to the police. It's so muddled. I'm glad it's their job, not ours." She reached a hand toward me, and when I grabbed it, she said with a sad smile, "This business with me in the hospital and RR dying has stressed you out. I feel responsible for dragging you into what my German grandmother used to call *Sturm und Drang*. Why don't you kick back, have a martini, and tell me a bedtime story, even though it's early? I'll enjoy the booze vicariously at least. Believe me, when I'm back in shape, I intend to start every day with a vodka martini."

Since her eyelids were drooping and the mug of home-made chicken broth on the bedside table was still half full, I figured this was total bravado. I stayed with her until she had taken the last dose of meds for the night. The kitchen light was on, and both Ortegas were still there. Mrs. Ortega hastily brought a heaping plate of something that smelled wonderful from the warming oven for me.

"We'll take turns tonight watching Ms. Byrnstein," Mrs. Ortega explained as we all sat at the counter. I made Mrs. Ortega promise to wake me up if Suzy needed anything and crept off to my own room. The cell phone rang while I was brushing my hair, and I glanced at the time. Only nine o'clock. My body said it was a lot later.

It was Sugerman, and he sounded as tired as I felt, but he had good news. There had been a break on the other high-profile murder case he and Weiler were working on, and a slimeball with nasty habits was in custody. "His girlfriend ratted on him," Sugerman said with grim satisfaction.

That meant they could turn their attention back to Clint's murder.

"Since we seem to be hitting a wall with what we have here, I've arranged to come down to Santa Fe tomorrow morning. I talked to your cop there, so she won't think we're horning in. I'm still focused on Maslow, but I'll look at the accident reports and see if I can find something. And they'll let me see the diary you told me about."

I was so relieved, I almost cried. I wanted nothing so much as to dump everything into his lap. We agreed that since Suzy was at the house and he might want to talk with her, we would meet here.

"By the way," he said as the conversation wound down, "you'll be glad to know that your apartment hasn't been broken into again. I dropped in on my way to check on something else, and your cat sitter says everything's been quiet. Your ex-husband called the chief over the weekend, though. Raised quite a stink. Said you needed police protection. You know anything about this?" He sounded a little peeved.

I winced. "Definitely not. I haven't spoken to him in a couple of days." I changed the subject. "The opening for Win Thorne's art show is at six tomorrow. If you want to stick around that long, you could come. Both the Thornes will be there." *Not a date,* I told myself, *strictly detective work.*

"My plane leaves Albuquerque around nine, I think. But thanks."

Can't blame a girl for trying. I had been removed from the concept of romance so long, I'd forgotten how to signal interest. Unless I had done fine and he was signaling no interest. I made a face in the mirror. *Stupid, stupid.* We said good-bye, and I went back to brushing my hair.

I wished I knew more about the status of the investigation. By now, they might know whose DNA was on Clint's hands, if Dickie's information about the autopsy results was true. If there were clues in my office, the cops had those to work with too, thanks to their CSI team. When Sugerman came, I intended to ask him straight out.

As I tossed and turned, I debated with myself if I should tell Sugerman about my speculations about a conspiracy to pump up the market for Clint's work. Had Reynold been killed because he knew too much, or was getting cold feet, in a plot to make money off Clint's appreciating stock of paintings? It frightened me to pursue that line of reasoning to its conclusion, since it led to my boss.

When I woke up, it was to the smell of coffee. It seemed unnaturally quiet until I opened the drapes. Snow. You forget when you live in a temperate climate just how transforming snow is. The sky and land were almost the same color; near and far were mere concepts; shapes blurred into suggestions of cacti and low walls and driveways. The air was still, and the large flakes fell straight down. Above all, it was quiet, like a French Impressionist painting, daubs of whites and pale grays almost magically conveying heavy ice on rooftops, frozen branches, and rutted tracks.

To my surprise, Suzy was in the kitchen, chatting with Mrs. Ortega in Spanish. Her hair was sticking up in jagged waves, she had no makeup on, and she was pale, but she was upright.

"This is the best coffee I've had since I left San Francisco, maybe the best ever. And that smell is actually making me hungry. Elana swears she can turn my share into a flan," Suzy said.

The aroma of sautéing sausage, tomato, and peppers jump-started my own salivary glands, which are the sworn enemies of my wardrobe. The radio was on, and at one point we all stopped what we were doing and listened to the local forecast. Snow most of the day, tapering off this evening. Snow-plows and salt trucks out, schools closed.

I wondered out loud about Inspector Sugerman's trip. Albuquerque's airport would be open, Mrs. Ortega said, and the highway between there and Santa Fe was a high-priority road, so it might be slower but not a real problem. I was relieved. Now that I was prepared to hand everything off, I couldn't wait. Retreating with my mug, I showered and dressed for the weather, borrowing a heavy sweater from the stock our hostess kept in the hall closet for visitors. My cell phone rang as I pulled the garment over my head, and I grabbed for it, shrugging into the warmth of the soft turtleneck.

"Hey there, how're you this beautiful morning?" said an all-too-familiar voice.

"Dickie, isn't it a bit early to be calling? Is everything okay—Fever and my apartment, I mean?"

"Perfecto. I checked right before I left. That Yvette is one responsible person, I'm telling you. Loves your cat. And has a nicely turned ankle, I might add."

Oh, give me a break. There are two men in my life—well, as much in my life as any men are—and both feel the need to hover around my cat sitter. Not that I'm jealous. But if I ever meet someone who might become a real boyfriend, I might do well to imitate her French accent and girlish air of helplessness.

"I'm so glad you noticed. Is that why you're calling, to tell me Yvette has a cute figure? Déjà vu all over again."

"Not funny," he said in an aggrieved tone of voice. "You know I made a whopper of a mistake, and I've apologized at least a hundred times. When are you going to believe me?"

"When cows fly. Dickie, I appreciate what you did when my apartment was broken into. I think it's under control. Inspector Sugerman seems to have found time to drop by and chat with the same lady of the well-turned ankle, and all is well. He did say something about you bugging the police chief to give me a bodyguard, though. I had a hunch from his tone of voice that the suggestion didn't sit well with the SFPD."

"I only asked if they had thought of that, since you're at

the heart of this thing. Cops don't always see the big picture, you know."

"I'm nowhere near the heart. I'm a capillary on the little finger of this case. It's as if you're trying to make sure they suspect me, for God's sake."

"Calm down, princess. But you've got to admit, you are key. Body goes out your window. You knew the guy well, and you mixed it up in public. You're getting hang-up calls, and your house is burgled. Your best friend is creamed in a hit-and-run. You understand the art crowd better than the cops, for sure. I think you may even know why that guy got killed, without realizing it. You're key."

I was silent. Suzy had said the same thing.

"That's why," my unnaturally cheerful ex continued, "we need to solve this thing fast. How about we meet for breakfast?"

What is it about Dickie that leaves me speechless or stupidly repeating what he says so often? Maybe he moves too fast for my plodding brain to follow. Maybe he darts in too many directions at once for me to comprehend exactly what's going on when he's around. Whatever it is, he had me again. "Solve it? Breakfast? Where are you, Dickie, and what are you talking about?"

"Hey, you didn't think I was going to let you get into trouble on your own, did you? We may not be *à deux* anymore, but I'm not crazy about having a dead ex-wife. I'm at the inn downtown, the one with the great restaurant, and I saw cactus pancakes on the menu. How about meeting in a half hour?"

"'Dead'? Are you trying to scare me to death?" I sputtered, protested, and generally resisted for a few minutes. But Dickie on a mission is a force of nature, and I gave in ultimately. I also realized he didn't know about Rowland

Reynold's death. I had to tell him, but I wasn't looking forward to it. He'd get fired up again and insist I was the next target or something equally guaranteed to frighten me.

The doorbell rang as I snapped my cell phone shut. When I went out to see who it was, Mrs. Ortega was struggling back to the kitchen with an over-the-top arrangement of deep orange chrysanthemums, evergreens, and purple leaves. It was for Suzy, who said, "Hah" as she read the card. "Are you absolutely sure you don't want Dickie back? Playboy he may be, but he has style." She tossed the card in my direction. He has his moments.

Bundling up in a thick sheepskin jacket I borrowed from Vera's closet for the trip into town, I promised to be back long before Inspector Sugerman arrived. I left Suzy stretched out on the living room sofa, covered with a down comforter, the remote control at her side along with a pile of art magazines.

The citizens of this town know how to drive in snow, although they apparently don't pay enough taxes for a fleet of snow-removal vehicles. However, this snow wasn't ice in disguise, and traffic was moving well. At Dickie's hotel, the one Suzy had stayed in, the same doorman in a designer version of a long cowboy coat came rushing out with an umbrella, and my car was whisked off to the garage. I found Dickie in the almost empty restaurant, talking to a couple of appreciative waiters. At the conclusion of what must have been a joke, they guffawed loudly. Only then did one turn to see me headed their way. Quickly his face assumed a neutral expression, and he refolded his white napkin over his forearm as he seated me across from Dickie.

"Isn't this a great place? Turns out these guys were bartending at Lake Placid last year when I was there for the slalom races. Ski bums, like me. Can't get enough. So, want to try those pancakes? The guys say they aren't bad."

Full from Mrs. Ortega's bounteous breakfast, I said I'd settle for a cappuccino. Orders given and waiters out of hearing range, I leaned forward. "I really appreciate your concern, but Inspector Sugerman will be here soon, and I'm going to hand off to him. I've given up trying to figure the whole thing out. It's too confusing."

"Sugerman's SFPD, right? What's he doing here?"

"He's flying in this morning. He said he wants to interview me again about Clint's murder and doesn't want to wait 'til I get back to work Thursday. Something else happened that I haven't had time to tell you about. Rowland Reynold fell down his office stairs in town and died."

Dickie's response was predictable. I waited until he had finished choking on his coffee and reading me the riot act.

"Sugerman will check out Reynold's death with the Santa Fe cops. If he thinks it's suspicious, he'll be on top of it. Anyway, he'll be at Vera's at two." I looked at my watch.

"Wait a minute, ducks. He's coming all the way from San Francisco to interview you about the Devor murder and Reynold's fall? I'm not sure I like that. What if he shows up with handcuffs?"

"Dickie, quit joking. Of course I'm not a suspect in either one. . . ." My voice trailed off. Why not? There was that weird letter that no one had admitted writing. I suppose, in theory, I could have slipped away from the party long enough to argue with Clint. I was in Santa Fe when Reynold fell or was pushed down the stairs. The coincidences made me shiver.

While his waiter buddy slid a huge plate of pancakes in front of him, Dickie sat there, head cocked, watching me to see if I was figuring it out. When the guy left, I said, "Dickie, you're forgetting one thing. There's no motive. I didn't want Clint dead. I liked Clint, for God's sake."

"Okay, but who else has a motive? I don't know much, but I did poke around a bit and found out there aren't any obvious skeletons in Clint's life. No threatening ex-wives or boyfriends, no big debts he was hiding, no family feuds."

"You did what?"

"Hired a private detective—no big deal. They do these background checks all the time. Anyway, the cops are scratching their heads, as far as I can tell. That's why I think you're so important to this thing. The cops don't know squat about the backbiting in the arts community, but you do. Who hated Clint? Suzy probably knows. She knows everything, bless her pointy little head."

"I'm sure Clint didn't have real enemies, not the kind who kill people," I protested. "This is the art world, Dickie, not the Mafia."

Dickie might have one point, I conceded. Maybe I needed to spend some more time with Suzy before Sugerman came, if only to decide if it was wise to mention my crazy theories about my boss and stolen paintings to the police, who would doubtless run right to Peter with my suspicions.

A long time ago, Dickie had warned me not to play poker for money. Now, he said with a smile, "Yup, that's what I think too. These cactus cakes are oversold, and I'm pining for Mrs. Ortega's eggs and salsa. What do you say? If Suzy's too tired, I won't bug her—promise." Without waiting for a reply, he jumped up, signaled the waiter to put it on his room bill, and practically pulled my chair out from under me.

Snow was still falling as Dickie propelled me into the lobby, the flakes so large they looked fake seen through the big glass doors. They drifted down, sticking on the bare heads and knitted caps of the pedestrians hurrying past, the roofs and windshields of slow-moving cars and pickup trucks, and the tops of downtown Santa Fe's ornate lampposts. Before I could open my mouth, Dickie told the valet we'd take his car. I started to protest, and Dickie nodded as if in agreement, although he actually was not agreeing at all. "The weather's crummy. I'll drive you back this afternoon so you can pick up your car."

I didn't argue. It would be enough to drive home after the opening if the snow hadn't melted. Turning up the collar on my borrowed sheepskin coat, I scooted into the passenger seat of his rented SUV without argument. On the way, I filled him in on the black book, Reynold's rambling warning, and the fact that Peter was in town and had resigned from the Devor. I didn't mention the closet full of paintings. Dickie was too well connected in San Francisco, and a few words from him could torpedo Peter's future, even if he was ultimately proved innocent of anything illegal.

Mrs. Ortega almost swooned when Dickie emerged from the car into the hallway. Manuel appeared at the sound of his voice, wreathed in smiles. Suzy drifted slowly but gracefully from her room, having applied mascara, blusher, and a dab of her signature perfume.

"Oh," Dickie groaned a half hour later. "I can't eat anything else. Stop, *por favor,* Mrs. O. No, not one more tortilla. I'll burst."

Beaming with pride, the chef slid a last cinnamon-and-butter-drenched pastry onto his plate. I peeked at my watch. We only had an hour, assuming Sugerman was on schedule.

I told Mrs. Ortega that we would do the kitchen cleanup so she and Manuel could rest after their night duty. When the plates were loaded into the dishwasher, we moved to the living room. Suzy settled on the sofa while Dickie lit a fire in the kiva, the traditional, stove-type fireplace common to houses in the region. We filled him in on what I'd found in the diary and what Suzy thought it meant.

Dickie agreed with Suzy that imitation didn't seem like a killing offense. "I do think there's a clue buried somewhere," he insisted, "if we could only see it. What are the chances Reynold found out that an artist he admires is a forger working for some syndicate, and the syndicate is trying to keep the truth from coming out?"

"The world of fakes and big-money art fraud is notorious, and there are dozens of cases where the money involved is in the millions," I said doubtfully. "But I've never heard of anyone getting killed. If you're caught, it can mean prison and megamoney in damages, not to say total humiliation as an artist. I can't see Clint stooping to that."

Suzy shook her head. "I don't think Win Thorne fits that model either. True, the new paintings looked familiar, but not famous-familiar, if you know what I mean. I wish I'd seen the picture that's gone missing from RR's office. It might jar my memory."

"His staff didn't have any idea who'd painted it or where Rowland got it," I said in frustration.

Dickie had been drumming his knuckles on the arms of his chair and now leaned forward. "Could Reynold get into a situation where he'd be going through a Dumpster? That doesn't sound right to me. Maybe if we could figure that out, we'd know whose work it was."

Suzy paused to sip her coffee, pursing her lips and looking out the window. My gaze shifted too. It was still snowing, although more lightly, and the landscape was all but obscured in the quiet blanket of white. I had a strong hunch that the ultimate answer included Clint Maslow. There had to be a connection.

Suzy was looking for the connection too. "Win would hardly copy Clint's work," she said. "Clint's too new to the major market, and, anyway, he would hear about it if fake work was showing up in the market."

"Unless . . ." Dickie said, his voice rising in excitement. "Unless whoever was trying to make money from Clint's work knew that Clint was going to die soon and was stock-piling fakes."

That was the what-if I had been trying to avoid for days, since it led directly to my boss' closet.

"So someone else pushed RR down the stairs to keep him quiet?" Suzy asked. "Someone who thought he knew about the fakes?"

"Rowland was Clint's biggest collector," I said. "He had a lot to lose if forgeries undercut the value of his collection. Think about the Jackson Pollack paintings someone found in an attic." Some recently discovered splatter paintings attributed to Pollack would fetch mucho millions for the finders if the paintings were authenticated and sold sparingly over time. If they were ultimately judged copies or deliberate fakes, they wouldn't be worth a dime.

But Clint? A gallery full of work "discovered" after he was murdered might fetch a couple of million dollars at most. And whoever stepped forward with the paintings would surely become murder suspect number one.

Dickie shook his head. "It's like musical chairs. If Reynold killed Maslow, who killed Reynold?"

Peter, I thought, but didn't say out loud. *Damn and double damn,* said my inner voice.

Suddenly, Suzy yelped, startling me out of my internal

debate. "That's it," she blurted. "Clint told me a couple of years ago that he was depressed. He felt he had hit a wall and that what he was doing was junk—derivative, pretty, meaningless. I'm sure it was then that he told me he tossed a series of partially finished canvases into the trash. Lost his temper, he admitted. When he realized he could paint over them to save money, he went out to the Dumpster behind the Institute, and either the bin had been emptied or someone else with the same recycling plan had grabbed them all."

"Okay," Dickie said slowly. "But that means Reynold was the guy who cleaned out the trash?"

"I don't think so," I said, suddenly excited, "because Rowland asked me if I knew where they might be the night in San Francisco when we almost got hit by the car."

Dickie turned to Suzy. "Why . . ."

The doorbell chimed. It had to be Inspector Sugerman. Before I could decide how much of this to share with him, in he walked, his nose and ears bright pink from the cold. He looked pinker when he noticed Richard Argetter III sprawled comfortably on the sofa, grinning up at him in an alpha male smile. Suzy, quick to pick up on these things, turned toward me and rolled her eyes before settling back into her cocoon of eiderdown, looking from one man to the other.

Chapter Twenty-four

Inspector Sugerman didn't take his eyes off my ex as he unwound his camel-colored scarf and said to me, "I didn't realize you had company."

"Oh, you mean Dickie and Suzy?" I said, waving my hands airily in their direction. "Well, Suzy's staying here recovering from the car accident, and Dickie, well, he happened to drop in."

"Drop in? From San Francisco?"

"I didn't know he was in Santa Fe when we talked on the phone. This is his aunt's house."

I stopped. Why did I babble whenever I talked to this cop? Better I should shut up and remember that I was, if Dickie was even half right, at least a minor suspect in a murder investigation Green Eyes was conducting right here in Vera's living room.

Dickie, having established his squatting rights to the living room, now stood up gracefully and held out his hand, still smiling but less fiercely. "Inspector Sugerman. We met at the

Devor the night Clinton Maslow died. We're glad you're here. This business has gotten out of hand, and I know it's harder dealing with it since the two murders happened in different jurisdictions."

Sugerman shook hands but didn't relax an iota as far as I could see. "I remember. I'm not sure why you think we're looking at two murders, Mr. Argetter. Far as I know, Mr. Reynold's death was an accident. I expect I'll know more after I talk to Ms. O'Rourke. Which I need to do. Alone."

"I'd prefer to be present, Inspector," Dickie said with a chuckle. "But," he added, sweeping his arms wide, "I'm not her attorney, so I know I can't insist."

"Ms. O'Rourke has offered to assist us with our investigation," Sugerman said, frowning. "If you have some information to offer, I'd be glad to talk with you later. Same," he said to Suzy with a nod, "for Ms. Byrnstein. I understand you knew Mr. Reynold well and that you and Ms. O'Rourke think the car crash you were in might have been attempted murder."

Suzy jumped in. "I think someone was trying to intimidate RR, at least. We've been comparing notes, trying to figure out who could be behind this and why," she said, gesturing at Dickie and me. "In fact . . ."

"I know your time is tight. Why don't we get on with our meeting, Inspector?" I blurted, not yet sure how much speculation I was prepared to share formally with a policeman. I wanted a definite sign that Sugerman didn't think I killed Clint, that he did not, in fact, have a Miranda card in his coat pocket.

It was more than that, though. Neither Suzy nor Dickie knew my suspicions about Peter, or that I still thought Teeni was holding something back about him. Thinking about telling anyone made my stomach do flips. If it got out, I could pretty much kiss my career good-bye. How many people would hire someone who was known to have accused her last boss of fraud and murder?

Sugerman started by running me through what I had told him on the phone. I added what Reynold's assistant had told me about the missing picture, what Suzy had told me about the Dumpster diving, and about my argument with Lisa.

"Okay, let's go back to the night of Mr. Maslow's murder. Can you tell me where you were fifteen minutes before the alarm went off?"

"I was on the third floor. I'm not sure when the alarm went off, because I didn't hear it. I was in the ladies' room when Len Hightower called me. Why?"

"The Devor's system only has audible alarms for the public spaces," Sugerman said. "The basement workrooms, staff offices, and security points like upper-floor windows are all connected to the security office and monitored by computers. Alarms register as flashing signs onscreen."

"I didn't know that."

"So," Sugerman continued, rolling his eyes, "when your window was opened, it registered visually on a computer monitor in the security room. Which was, unfortunately, unoccupied at the time. Seems the mayor and his entourage were arriving, and your security chief decided a flourish was needed at the front entrance. Maybe a little bit of one-upmanship with the uniformed division?"

"You're kidding," I said. When the board found out, Hightower would be in deep doo-doo.

"The guy on duty in the monitoring room knew one of the mayor's bodyguards, and they stood around chatting for a while. By the time he got back, he had a plate of food, and I'm afraid that distracted him further. When he finally noticed the alarm message, he hit the bell alarm for that floor. So we'd like you to try to recall exactly what you saw as soon as you heard someone had fallen. Was there anyone suspicious, anyone running down the stairs, for example?"

"No, I'm sure I would have remembered. But . . ." I stopped and closed my eyes.

"What is it?" Sugerman asked.

"I'm not sure. I . . . wait. There was a guard getting off the elevator downstairs at about the time you think all this happened. I saw him from a landing and assumed he was headed to the security office on his break. The way the security office is laid out, he would have seen the monitors right inside the door when he went in. Did you interview him?"

"I'm not sure who you mean. You didn't mention him previously."

"I didn't remember it, and there wasn't any reason to. But there was something about him that made me think he was a temp hired for the night." I was struggling the way you do when you're trying to recall a dream and it's slipping away faster than you can hold it in your memory.

"A hat. He was wearing some kind of hat. That's probably why I can't tell you who he was. I didn't see his face, and I wasn't paying a lot of attention, but it wasn't the normal outfit. In fact, I'll bet he was the same guy who propped open the door to our offices. One of the regulars wouldn't do that. It's totally against the rules."

Sugerman looked thoughtful, tapping his pen against his notepad. "I wish we'd known this earlier. I don't know if it's significant, but we like to have everyone identified and accounted for, and this guy isn't ringing a bell for me. I'll check it out first thing tomorrow."

I was silent for a moment as he went back to his notepad.

"Inspector, could I ask you about something else that's bothering me?"

He looked up noncommittally.

"Have you considered that it might be someone who wasn't in the office when the cops arrived? Someone none of the rest of us saw?"

"Is there someone you have in mind?" he asked.

"Yes, although I'm not sure it's relevant anymore. Rowland Reynold showed up outside my office door after Hightower told the security guard to keep everyone out. I wondered how he got there."

"Apparently a lot of people just appeared. Your guard wasn't too effective. Anyone in the vicinity of the suite's door could have slipped in or talked his way in." He shook his head. "The security staff could use some additional training."

"I'll be sure to tell Len. He'll appreciate the suggestion," I said.

"Anything else I should know?" Sugerman asked.

"Yes. I have to tell you something that might be related to Clint's and Rowland's deaths, and I am begging you not to say where you heard this. I'm serious. There are other ways you can verify it. Can you consider me a confidential source?"

"I can't make any promises. You could be an accessory to a crime if you hold something back that would lead to a conviction in a murder case, you know."

Way to go, my inner voice said. *You just led yourself into a trap.* Hell with it. I was tired of going around in circles trying to figure this out on my own, so I did a data dump of sorts, telling Sugerman about the cache of Maslow paintings, my elderly donor's comment about Peter's finances, my general suspicion about ways to profit from an artist's death, and the shock of Peter's resignation and presence in Santa Fe. He listened carefully, asked some questions about the nature of putting stolen or copied art onto the market, and agreed it was worth checking into.

"Could be blackmail involved. Maybe the collector was blackmailing your boss, or the artist was blackmailing the collector. Thought about that?"

I had to admit, I hadn't thought about blackmail for money, and I didn't see a wealthy man like Reynold extorting money. Clint had a difficult side, but I couldn't get my head around him as a blackmailer either. Peter, on the other hand, supposedly had money problems. And why else would Reynold be entertaining the idea of a huge personal loan to Peter, as the note in his black book indicated?

"We'll check out your theory about putting fakes onto the market, but that will take time and may involve another agency, especially if there's fraud operating across state or international boundaries. When I get back to San Francisco, I'll get in touch with Maslow's brother to see if he found records that account for all of Maslow's paintings. We'll get his financial documents from the bank, in light of the blackmail angle. And I'll ask for Santa Fe's help getting Reynold's bank transactions to look for large withdrawals. But, keep in mind, Reynold's death may turn out to be an unlucky coincidence after all of this."

"May I ask you something? You said there were fingerprints on my office window. Won't that help you find out who did it?"

Sugerman looked down and wiggled the pages of his open notebook for a few seconds before straightening his back in the chair. "I can't say much, but, no, they haven't helped, unfortunately. It happens sometimes."

I had been hoping that, somewhere along the way, a blazingly clear piece of evidence would turn up that would exonerate me once and for all and nail the creep who'd killed Clint. I was also hoping any evidence would clear Peter and Teeni, because wondering about my boss and my assistant was depressing.

Knuckles rapped on the door, and Dickie poked his head in. "Sorry to interrupt," he said, "but if we're going to the opening, we'd better get organized. It's still snowing, and that means a slow ride."

Charlie Sugerman gave me a look that suggested I might have exaggerated how free I was of my former spouse. I felt my cheeks get red. He said we were finished and that he'd like to talk with Suzy if she felt up to it. She was back in bed but willing if he wouldn't mind asking his questions there. I fluffed her pillows and handed her a hairbrush before retreating to my bedroom to change. Given the weather, I might have opted for comfort over fashion, but I loved my new stiletto heels, and I'd be in a car when I wasn't in the gallery. I compromised with the borrowed sheepskin jacket.

It was almost dark, and the snow had begun to outpace the plows. It hadn't, as the local weatherman predicted, stopped, and I thought it was a long shot that a big crowd would brave it for the Dollar Gallery's opening party. When we arrived at the hotel, Dickie said he could be ready in ten minutes if I didn't mind waiting.

I had news for my ex. "We" were not going to the opening. Dickie had been in charge of my day so far, but I was not about to let him take over any more of it. He had an unfortunate way of smothering people until something or someone else captured his interest. I had no intention of letting him do that to me again.

He argued. I insisted. He sulked. I got out of the car and marched over to the valet station with him trailing. "Fine, if you don't want company, I won't go. I'm not interested in the show, and I can't stand Thorne's greedy little wife. I swear she has dollar signs in her eyes."

"Well, I expect a lot of people have dollar signs in their eyes when they see you, Dickie, including a lot of your girl-friends."

He opened and closed his mouth a couple of times. "Okay, he said, his voice rising slightly. "Got it. I won't bother you anymore. Have a great evening. Maybe I'll see you in San Francisco." He spun around and headed for the elevators.

My rented car glided up to the hotel entrance, snowless from its stay under cover. As I slid into the driver's seat, I told myself I didn't need company. I figured I could stay for less than an hour and call it a night. I would look at the work with Suzy's accusations in mind, but I wouldn't say anything to Win. That was Sugerman's job now. I was off the hook and out of the detective business.

Chapter Twenty-five

In the summer, parking along the narrow, picturesque streets in the main shopping area of Santa Fe is almost impossible. Tonight, plowed snow was the only obstacle. I found a spot around the corner from the gallery, next to an alley. Yellow light, puffs of steam, and joking voices speaking Spanish wafted from the open alley door of a neighboring café. The unmarked door next to it must be the delivery door for the gallery.

I locked the car and trudged around the corner, pulling the coat collar up as far as it would go, already sorry I had not worn sensible shoes. The Milton Dollar Gallery was lit brightly. There were about twenty people there so far, glass cups of what smelled like mulled red wine in their hands.

Win's voice, a little slurred, rose over the mellow sounds of jazz coming from speakers somewhere. Milton Dollar headed in my direction eagerly. With the practice of an experienced host, he introduced me to a few clients, made sure his assistant had delivered me some of the fragrant brew, and waved his arms around. "Now that they're properly hung, I hope you'll take a good look. Quite wonderful." He beamed.

I let the assistant take my coat and mostly listened to Dollar's regular clients talk about recent car purchases, the trouble with public schools, and the other topics that seem to govern cocktail parties everywhere.

As an owlish-looking older man began to tell me about the dispute he was having with his tile installer, my cell phone chirped from deep inside my handbag. I reached inside, but too late. It stopped as I got my hand around it. Dickie, most likely, with ten good reasons I should do or not do something. *Divorce* didn't seem to mean the same thing to him as it did to me. He didn't want to be pinned down, I was quite sure, so what was he doing trailing me around? I toggled the ringer off so I wouldn't have to field another call.

When I could untangle myself from the conversational group where Dollar had inserted me, I wandered over to the nearest group of paintings, looking for evidence of what had upset Reynold. Abstract, like all of Win's work, they were looser, more assured, with broad, fat brushstrokes and an almost musical sense of rhythm and color. But spooky, because they did look something like Clint's. Not his unique hand and ferocious brushwork, but well composed and confident. Question was, who'd painted them?

"What do you think?" said a voice at my side.

I hadn't seen her come up to me. "Hi, Lisa. Wonderful." Given that she'd reamed me out the last time we met, I was cautious in my greeting. But she seemed not to bear a grudge against me.

"Win worked so hard on these and had doubts as late as

the other day that they would hold their own. But I think he's pulled off a real coup. I'm hoping the New York dealer we've been trying to interest will take Win on."

I looked over at Win. His glowering face was a dull red, and he had retreated from the group of well-wishers to stand by himself next to the table on which the punch bowl and a platter of fruit and cheese sat. The young assistant presiding over the refreshments peeked nervously at him. I hoped he wouldn't blow off the small crowd who had come to the opening.

"Do you think we could show these to your boss?" Lisa was still beside me.

"It's actually one of the department curators who looks at portfolios. But that only happens once a year and mostly by invitation. It's really hard to get their attention. I know it's a flawed system, but that's what it is, alas."

"But you could mention Win, couldn't you? That would make a big difference."

I shifted from one foot to the other, wondering how to extricate myself. As if on cue, the lights flickered, and conversation slowed. Guests peered out the window at the snow, which was blowing now. A jolly couple complimented Dollar loudly for having the foresight to put lighted candles around the room "just in case." I heard grumbles about the local utilities as I slipped away and headed toward the drinks table for a refill. Win had moved off. The assistant smiled when I asked her if she thought the weather was getting worse. "Depends," she said with a shrug. "I don't think it's likely to warm up for a couple of days. If you don't like skiing, that's not good news, I guess."

One couple left, pulling their coat collars up as they pushed open the door. Someone else slipped out behind them. I had the sense that this party, not lively to begin with, was melting away. I strolled along a wall of paintings, noticing the thick buildup of paint, slabbed on with a trowel in some places. It gave the work a fierceness and energy and also added dimension.

The work reminded me more of Thiebaud's cityscapes. Thiebaud's work had skyrocketed in value in recent years as museums and major collections snapped it up. No wonder Dollar was rolling out the red carpet. If critics and collectors had the same reaction, Win's fortunes might be looking up.

In one corner, hung close together and specially lit to draw out the sweep of color and line that connected them thematically, was a series of three paintings, like nothing of Win's I'd ever seen.

The lights flickered again, this time a bit longer. A sprinkling of laughter came from a small group standing across the room. The men broke away and came over to the assistant's table. "That's it," one said with a laugh. "Time to mush home, get out the candles, and fire up the kiva." He took a couple of coats from the assistant, only to have his place taken by another man. It signaled the end of the evening, and, without losing a beat, Dollar thanked each for coming and invited them to come back during the show. With all the skill of a great salesman, he implied that Win's work was going to sell quickly and was a great investment.

I used the cover of the general exodus to get my own coat. In spite of my promise to myself to let Sugerman do all the heavy lifting, I wanted to talk with Suzy about what I'd seen and what it might mean. As I turned away from the table in front of the screen where the assistant was stationed, Win reached out and grabbed my jacket sleeve. I jumped.

"Listen," he said, looking at me owlishly and moving his lips with the exaggerated care of someone who was conscious

he was not speaking clearly. "Can I talk with you, confidentially?" He attempted to lower his voice, but it was still a stage
whisper.

"Um, what about?"

"I want to discuss my work with you." He smiled briefly,
evincing a jack-o'-lantern grimace. I guessed Lisa had given
him instructions to butter me up about promoting him to the
Devor, and I was embarrassed.

"You want to talk now?"

"No," he said, looking out over the room. "Too many
people." He hiccupped abruptly. "Later."

I was annoyed. Was I supposed to stand around on a freezing night so he could bully me? I didn't think so.

"Can't we do it by phone?"

"No, no," he said, shaking his head slowly. "Not a phone
matter—need your help." By now his voice really was a whisper, urgent and low, mouthed almost into my ear. He had a
strong hold on my forearm, and he was squeezing. I pulled my
arm away as diplomatically as I could, but Win didn't back
off.

"I already told Lisa I don't have any influence with the
Devor acquisitions committee, Win."

He glared at me. "Not about that. About that bastard
Maslow. Something you need to know."

"You know something?" I stopped breathing. "Did you
tell the police?"

"No way. But I want you to know. I definitely want you to
know."

The look on his face made the hair on the back of my neck
prickle, and I was torn. I wanted to hear whatever it was that
Win felt I needed to know. But he was acting strangely, and I

wasn't crazy about the idea of meeting him alone while he was in this mood. Lisa's laughter sounded behind us. She was saying good-bye to the last of the guests as the young assistant lugged the punch bowl back behind the room divider to the storage and work area. The gallery owner flitted around, gathering up used napkins and cups.

"I'll wait at the Sagura Bar and Grill next door for a half hour, but that's it," I said reluctantly, my voice as low as his. "Is Lisa coming too?"

"Just me. Order me a whiskey. This punch is making me sick. I'll be right over."

As if the whiskey won't make you sicker. I shrugged on my coat and said my good-byes to Lisa and Dollar.

"You'll try, Dani?" Lisa said with a smile that seemed to carry an indefinable whiff of menace. I smiled noncommittally.

The wind had picked up, but the snow was only flurries. My high-heeled shoes weren't getting a lot of traction, so I was relieved that the Sagura was next door and my car around the corner. I ordered an Irish coffee and sat at the nearly deserted bar. Good time to call Vera's. When I pulled out my cell phone, the blinking light signaling a call was on, but since the phone was set at vibrate and buried in my bag under gloves and assorted junk, I hadn't heard it.

Mrs. Ortega answered the phone. "Suzy's been trying to get you on your cell phone, but it doesn't seem to be working. I'll get her for you."

Suzy came on, sounding stressed. "Thank God you called. I've been trying ever since your detective left. I remembered what was bugging me. I wanted to catch you before you went to the opening."

"The opening's over. The weather put a dent in the party. But Win is acting strangely. He asked me to meet him— says he has information about Clint I need to know."

Suzy's voice sounded far away. "I've been thinking about what Rowland wrote in the diary. I told you we both thought Win's newest work was derivative—not original enough in style, subject, and execution. Okay. Well, later that evening I told RR something more was bugging me about them.

"See, I realized at least one looked exactly like one of Clint's pieces, and I mean exactly. I remembered it because Clint had been so self-critical when I saw it in his studio. It was part of a triptych, and I sketched it because I was intrigued, even if he wasn't happy with it. I wanted to convince him to stick with what he was working out. I dumped it into my tote bag and just found it after you left."

"The folded paper?" I asked in amazement. "That was Clint's?" Something was banging in my brain, something that fit with what Suzy was telling me. But what?

"My sketch of the center of Clint's triptych, yes. But this is what I really wanted to tell you. When I showed it to RR, he said, 'My Dumpster diving treasure.' "

"Omigod."

And then it came to me. The specially lit pieces in Dollar's gallery, the three paintings. The triptych.

"I saw it, Suzy. I saw the triptych. Just now. It's in the gallery. What should I do?"

"Get the hell out of there." Suzy's voice was sharp. "I'm ready to bet Win's new paintings are really Clint's, changed a little by Win. And I think Win has figured out that I know. I was showing Rowland the sketch when we were at the café, and Win walked past the window. The picture in RR's office?

Rowland must have grabbed it from the studio or the Dumpster when Clint told him he planned to throw them away."

"That's crazy," I muttered, "over-the-top crazy."

"Win's got such a temper, I think he may have killed Clint and Rowland to keep it a secret. You need to get out of there right now, Dani."

"I'm not in the gallery. But Win couldn't have killed Clint. He has an alibi for the time. Did you tell Sugerman about this?"

"No, it didn't come together for me until after he left. You should call him."

"I don't know how we can prove it, but I'll stop by the police station. If I can't see Crissy Culpepper, I'll leave a message for her to call me. Then I'm coming back to Vera's."

I looked around to make sure no one could overhear my end of the conversation. The bartender was telling the only other customers at the bar a joke that had them guffawing even before the punch line. Even so, I lowered my voice.

"Why would Win do something so dumb and self-destructive? Sooner or later, people would find out. His career would never survive it."

"Obviously, he thinks no one else has seen the work Clint threw away."

I checked my watch. "I'm going to leave now. Are the Ortegas there?"

"Yes. Is Dickie with you? Can he drive you up?"

"No, but I'm fine to drive myself." As I spoke, the Sagura's lights dimmed briefly. The bartender looked up, shook his head in annoyance, and broke off his conversation with the man and woman holding up the other end of the bar. I told Suzy I'd see her in a half hour.

"I'd better get the candles out," the bartender said. "I'm willing to bet we lose power soon. Want another Irish, miss?"

I shook my head, asked him how much I owed, and headed out the door. I peeked into the gallery next door. There was a dim light coming from the area behind the screen, and the candle displays were still lit, although I didn't see anyone. The wind hit my face as I picked my way carefully across the snow-crunchy pavement. The gallery door was open, and a little pile of snow had edged onto the wood floor. At the very least, I could close it.

"Hello?" I called, poking my head in. "Anyone here?" I figured Win and Dollar might be talking about prospective buyers before they called it quits for the night. That would explain why Win hadn't made it over to the Sagura Bar and Grill. As long as I wasn't alone with him, I ought to be okay.

No one answered. Standing on the threshold, I thought I heard low voices in the back. I walked only far enough to call out to Dollar that his door was open.

Just as I got to the spot where the drinks table had been earlier, a strong gust of wind banged the front door closed. At the same time, the lights flickered and went out, leaving only scattered, dancing pinpoints of candlelight. The streetlights went out too. I glanced toward the front picture window, only faintly visible as a lighter block against black walls. The Sagura's lights were gone, too. The whole street was dark. *Time to leave,* my inner voice shouted.

I turned toward what I thought was the front room. My leg bumped a table edge, and I almost tripped over a bag set next to it. Confused in the dark, I had turned into the alcove where Win had been setting out paintings when I'd stopped by before the opening. I moved my foot away from the bag and put my hands out in front of me to help guide me forward.

And then I screamed. Or tried to. I sounded more like a mouse being pinched. I was touching someone. A voice close to me, too close, said, "Shh . . . shut up." It was Win. His voice was rough, pitched low. His hand grabbed my arm and pulled me closer to him. I gargled and managed to get a few words out.

"Let me go, Win."

He was pulling me farther into the alcove. My heart was banging so hard, I could hardly speak over it, and my feet kept bumping into the bag. I was using my other arm to try to detach his fingers from my sleeve.

His voice was close to my ear when he spoke again. "Don't say a word. Keep quiet. Get down on the floor."

Somehow that didn't seem like a good idea. If I were on the floor, I couldn't run. And run was what my brain was telling me to do in no uncertain terms, as in, *run for your life, idiot.* Why I should be running for my life was unclear, this being, for God's sake, a fashionable art gallery in the middle of a friendly town.

Win pushed me hard, and I tripped and sprawled, hitting my head on the table and then landing on top of the bag, which began to groan. I screamed in a mouse voice again, pushing myself up and away from what I suddenly realized was a person crumpled on the floor. *Oh, yuck. How much worse could it get?*

Win must have done something to Milton Dollar, something like knocking him unconscious, and now here I was, scrabbling around the floor about a foot from Win.

I was having trouble getting up. I kept pushing with my outstretched hands but slipping on the floor, which was wet for some reason. I sat on my rear end and scooted as far away from the groaning mass and Win as I could until my back

touched a wall behind me. I scrambled upright, pushing myself off the wall with hands that were unaccountably sticky.
Win's dark shape lurched toward me, and I waved my arms
madly. "Get away from me. Get away!" I shouted, as one of
his hands reached for my hair. From nowhere, something
crashed into my temple, and I slid down onto the floor.

From a great distance, I heard quarreling, a man and a
woman. I couldn't seem to pay attention for long, and then,
when I focused better, I realized they weren't far away and
that my head hurt. Really hurt, not like a headache or a bump
on a cabinet door but as if a vise was squeezing the opposite
sides of my skull together. Tears sprang to my eyes when I
opened them.

I must have fainted for a minute. I was half sitting and half
lying on a cold floor in a dark room, and the argument I was
hearing was close by. Win's voice, and now I recognized
Lisa's. Oh, yeah, that was it. Win had been coming for me. He
must have hit me, and now Lisa was in danger. I had to help,
but it was hard to think, and the gallery was still pitch dark.
My bag was on the floor somewhere, and I knew it contained
a cell phone. I could call 911 if I could find it. Of course, the
bag was black, the perfect camouflage in this nightmare landscape.

Rocking onto my hands and knees slowly, as befits someone with a vise on her head, I looked around, trying to see into
the darkness. Dollar's body was between me and the margin-
ally lighter rectangle that was the main room. The voices were
coming from the alcove where the table was.

I'm sure I wasn't breathing, which probably explained why
I was so dizzy. But something else seemed odd. Win's voice
was not threatening anymore. In fact, he sounded scared,
which didn't make sense.

"Take it easy. Everything will be all right."

"It's never going to be all right now. First you had to leave fingerprints all over her office, so I had to risk getting caught when I went back to clean up. Then you were supposed to keep her from coming. And now that Reynold's dead, you've lost your nerve."

My God, so it was *Win.* He'd killed Clint and Reynold and tried to run me down . . . unless they were talking about trying to kill Suzy. My legs almost gave out, and the whiskey and coffee rose in my throat, burning. I told myself not to even think about throwing up.

But why was Lisa arguing with a man who had a gun? Wasn't that dangerous? Very slowly, I peeked around the corner. I was low enough that he might not see me if he was focused on her. Unfortunately, all I saw in the candlelight flickers were the shapes of legs and feet, one pair in black brogues, the other in rhinestoned cowboy boots. Fortunately, none of the feet were aimed at me.

"How was I supposed to know the old man knew Milt, or that Milt had seen the thing?" Win said with a groan. "I should have known trying to convince Maslow to let it go wouldn't work."

"Shut up!" Lisa shrieked, sending my pulse into orbit. "If you'd done what I told you to, no one would have known about this. I've worked to make you successful for twenty freaking years, always on my own because you never had the guts or the drive."

"That's not true. But I followed you the other day. I know everything!" he bellowed. "You're crazy, do you know that? Crazy."

The brogues headed toward the cowboy boots. They didn't get far. With an explosive popping noise that tightened the vise on my head, the brogues stopped moving. The only sound I heard for a second or two was the echo bouncing around in my brain. Then the brogues took another step, the table was pushed aside with a scraping sound, and Win dropped slowly into view. He looked right at me, and I froze, waiting for him to reach out and grab me. But he didn't seem to recognize me. His mouth was open, and, as his arm touched my hand, his face smashed into the floor.

I screamed out loud this time. And watched the cowboy boots turn in my direction. Two steps and they were next to Win's face. Someone pulled my hair, forcing my face up.

"Well, well, here she is, Miss Goody-Goody herself. I thought you were down for the count. My fault for not hitting you harder. Pity. Win was right. You're too nosy to quit." The voice was Lisa's, but Lisa on steroids. "Get up. Now."

I tried to stop shaking. My teeth were chattering, and I wanted nothing so much as to go to sleep and find out this was all a nightmare of epic proportions. Win's immobile face stared at me sideways from where he lay, its expression conveying I'd better do what Lisa wanted. I pulled myself up. Even though my eyes had adjusted to the darkness, it was still impossible to make out details by the tiny, fluttering lights in the main gallery.

A car drove by on the quiet street, throwing a sudden white light up and across the main gallery space but not into the alcove. As it washed past, I got a brief glimpse of my bag, farther out in the main room than I wanted it to be. I'd have to do something to distract Lisa if I wanted to get to it. And then what? Hold up my hand to shut her up while I rummaged through the purse for my cell phone? It's hard to think while your head is pounding, two dead or wounded men are at your feet, and a harpy with a gun is a foot away from your face.

A draft made me shudder even more, and I pulled my coat more tightly around me.

"Don't ever get married," Lisa said in a completely different, strangely conversational tone. "Or, married again, in your case. Men are so weak, so gutless. But you knew that, married to your millionaire, didn't you? I used to envy you—did you know that?"

As I leaned on the alcove wall, looking toward the outline of my bag and the front door and forcing myself to breathe, Lisa paced back and forth a couple of feet in front of me, waving a small gun in my direction. No one could see us from the street, and no one could come in without Lisa's hearing them.

Pace, pace. A brittle laugh. "We never had any money, Win and me. We used to dream about the day when he'd have a huge show at Pace, you know, or some other major gallery in New York. He had all the right credentials. Yale, an MFA, the apprenticeship with an A-list painter. But he fiddled it all away."

I wasn't following any of this. Lisa was pissed because Win wasn't rich or famous? And? Since when do you shoot your husband because he didn't make it into the Whitney Biennial? A small, functioning part of my brain noted that a lot of great artists aren't in that show, and a lot of people, including art critics, don't think it matters.

Reynold had been concerned that something he knew put Suzy and himself into danger. Then he died. Suzy thought it was the painting in Reynold's office. Suzy also said she and Reynold believed Win had been copying Clint's style. What if it went further than that? What if these were actually Clint's paintings? What if that's what Reynold had figured out?

Lisa was still pointing the gun at various parts of my

anatomy as she walked back and forth. Win was still under-
foot, a reminder that she was quite capable of pulling the trigger if provoked. I took a deep breath. The oxygen reminded
my brain all over again that it was hurting.

"Lisa?" I cleared my throat, faking a calmness I didn't
feel, "help me understand. Was Win bullying you into something? Did he force you to cover up something illegal?"

"Hah," she said on a rising giggle. "That's one way of
looking at it, Miss Know-It-All. Don't move."

The last because I had edged one small step away from the
wall toward the main gallery. She was acting crazy, but crazy
like a fox, it turned out. I sagged against the wall. Nothing to
do but stall for time, in the hope that she'd lose some of the
adrenaline that was pumping her up and get tired before deciding to shoot me too.

"Does this have something to do with the paintings in this
show, Lisa? What's going on? Can I help?" *Like maybe call
911 and get you locked up tight, for example?* I strained my
eyes into the darkness, not sure if having the lights go on
again would help or hurt my chances.

Lisa cackled as she paced. "Help? I asked you to help, but
it's too late now. We needed to get these paintings authenticated as Win's and into a museum right away, you see? There
are more, plus Win was working on some based on these—
his own, this time. We were counting on this. It had to work.
We'd done so much for it already, and Win was getting cold
feet." Her voice rose to a keening wail. A truck was grinding
its gears somewhere outside, and another cold blast of air
rose from the floor.

"What is it about these paintings that's so important?"

"You don't know? We weren't sure. I didn't see any of
Clint's artwork in your apartment. I flew all the way there and

back for nothing. Then Win saw Reynold and your pal Suzy sitting in the café looking at the drawing. I couldn't believe it, and I couldn't get into Suzy's hotel room to destroy it. I thought she might have given it to you. But Win was sure you didn't know.

"Of course, when I saw Clint's little painting in Reynold's office, I knew he'd figure it out. I mean, what would he say to Dollar when he saw the rest of them? And then it turned out the old bastard had already told Dollar what he suspected, and we found out tonight after the opening, so what could I do?"

"You mean you shot Milton Dollar?"

"Had to, didn't I?" Lisa was talking fast, sucking in air noisily. Every once in a while, her head snapped in my direction, and her eyes, denser black holes in the darkness, locked on my face.

"But what was it they knew, Lisa?"

"Clint's canvases, of course. The ones Win took from the Dumpster. The best work Clint ever did. No, the best work Win ever did." Lisa snorted. "The student passed the teacher long ago, and they both knew it. Worse, when Clint signed with the gallery in New York and got into the MOMA show, he had to rub it in Win's face."

She blew air out of her mouth in a noisy gust. "He was so full of himself, said he'd hit the jackpot. Decided the series of paintings he was working on weren't up to MOMA standards and threw them all away. Poor Win. He could see that Clint's throwaways were better than anything Win had done in years. So my fool husband stole them—can you believe it? Locked them in his studio at home—said he was saving them until Clint wanted them back. But that was a lie. Truth is, he couldn't leave them alone."

"But surely Win didn't think he could pass them off as his own?" I asked, caught up in her story in spite of myself. "Even if no one else realized it, Clint would know."

"Taking the paintings wasn't my idea," she snarled at me. "But he made them his own. They turned into something much better. If no one who knew Clint saw the first batch, it could have worked."

Lisa seemed determined to make me understand the crazy logic of all this. As the headlights of another slow-moving car arced through the gallery, she turned in that direction, and I edged toward the alcove. I remembered the door next to the neighboring café's kitchen. If it was an emergency exit or de-livery entrance, maybe it wasn't locked on the inside. My hands were numb with cold, and I shoved them into the pock-ets of the borrowed coat.

She giggled again. "We should thank you, Dani. It was your letter to Clint that solved the problem, at the end."

"I don't know what you mean."

"Your letter asking him to meet you in your office. Don't you remember? Oh, maybe not, since you didn't actually write it. But your stationery and the keys Win found in the men's room the night of Peter's dinner party did the trick. Clint made the mistake of calling to say he knew Win had taken the paintings. An artist who saw Win do it had told Clint a few weeks before. Clint said he was calling the police. Win only wanted to scare Clint that night, but Clint laughed at him."

"The police said Win had an alibi," I said, confused.

Lisa nodded. "Win borrowed a guard's jacket and cap he found in the caterer's kitchen, used the elevator, and was back downstairs before the alarm rang. He mentioned what time it was to Goldie while they were talking—the wrong time, of course—and she never checked her watch. Then everyone was focused on Clint's body, so when Win told me he panicked and forgot to wipe his fingerprints off the door-knob, I thought I had time to run upstairs. But I hadn't fin-ished when I heard people coming, so I ducked into the ladies' room."

"But then, why were you in my office when I got there?" I asked, as much to keep her talking as anything. My voice wobbled.

"I decided to say I was looking for the bathroom and fol-lowed the noise. Smart, huh?"

I coughed. Suddenly the barrel of the gun pressed into my side. "Why am I telling you all of this? It's not like you can fix it."

"Did you shoot Win deliberately?" I asked, a lump in my throat making it hard to talk. There were dead people in this room, and I might be one of them soon.

"He was going to call the cops. He didn't like that I killed Reynold. But these paintings are mine. I worked for them, and they're my future now. Just Suzy now, and after we're done here, I'll manage that. After all, she's not in good health. Any-thing might happen, and it would be sad but not unexpected."

I didn't like the way this conversation was headed. Lisa had a plan, and she was sticking to it, while I had no plan, only cold feet—literally as well as figuratively—and a vague sense that my best and worst options might be the same—to make a run for the dark corridor behind the alcove. Even if it led to the door and the door opened into the alley where I had parked, I'd be out in the snow in my fake Manolos, and more visible. The other option was to send Lisa toward the back door and make a run for the front. Every once in a while, a car drove past. Maybe I'd get lucky, and one would stop, or at least serve as a barrier between me and Lady Macbeth long enough for me to reach the Sagura Bar and Grill.

Eeny-meeny-miny-moe. Which of my lousy ideas should I try? My fingers, slightly defrosted, curled around something in the pocket of Vera's sheepskin coat. A small stone, by the feel of it. Large enough to make a noise, even if the noise sounded like a small stone bouncing around a floor. *What do you have to lose?* my inner voice pointed out. First, keep her talking.

"Wouldn't the dealers figure this out anyway? If they had seen Clint's work, they'd know right away."

"Yeah, but if we convinced them that Clint stole the work from Win in the first place . . ."

I was about to tell Lisa what a dumb idea that was when several things happened at once. First, my instinct for self-preservation kicked in, and I shut my mouth, threw the stone toward the dark corridor, and started running toward the front of the gallery. The cell phone in my bag began to chirp as the annoying draft that had been swirling around the alcove became a major wind. A lot of people were yelling at once. Beams of light jumped all over the ceiling, Lisa yelled, a gunshot cracked, and someone pushed me to the floor. I curled into a ball, waiting for the bullet to hit me.

"Are you okay?" someone shouted. I could hardly make sense of the question because so much else was going on. To top it off, bright lights suddenly shone, making me blind. The power was back on, just what I didn't need—bright lights to help Lisa with her aim. Lisa, however, was still hollering from the alcove, and I was next to the front door, trying to make my legs move.

"Dani, answer me. Are you okay?" Gingerly I picked my head up an inch and looked behind me. A few feet away, Dickie, on all fours, was scrabbling toward me, eyes flashing.

"Dickie?" Beyond him, a flock of uniformed cops flooded the alcove. Three of them were hanging on to a thrashing Lisa Thorne. Behind them, smoothing his hair with one hand, a gun in the other, was Inspector Sugerman. Crissy Culpepper was barking into her walkie-talkie.

"What's going on? How did you get here?" I asked as I sat up slowly, rubbing the elbow that had hit the floor hard.

Dickie reached me and pulled me toward him. "You're not shot, are you?" he said into my hair.

"I don't think so," I answered, "but maybe I was, and I'm in shock. I've never been shot before."

Dickie pulled his face away and frowned at me. "Well, that's good," he said, articulating his words carefully, "but I think I may be. Shot, that is." And he turned and looked down. I did too. Saw blood and—what else?—screamed.

"Help!" I yelled. "Someone help, he's bleeding." Dickie smiled vaguely at me, then collapsed slowly to the floor as Officer Culpepper's partner, Junior, and Charlie Sugerman ran over. They asked questions, he murmured answers, they looked him over, and I sat in a heap, no use to anyone.

Not one but two teams of paramedics compounded the confusion right about then. One young man did a quick examination of my ex and announced he had been hit in the thigh, but no bones or arteries were involved. He'd live.

Win, I heard them say, was dead. Dollar, still hunched under the table in the alcove, was not in good shape, but he was alive. They bundled him onto a stretcher first, and I heard a siren at the back door as they took off for the hospital. Lisa, hands cuffed behind her back and demanding something incoherently at the top of her voice, was next out, flanked by at least four uniformed cops led by Crissy, still talking into her walkie-talkie.

The paramedics finally got to Dickie, who had rallied a bit and was holding my hand as we sat there on the floor. As they moved him onto a gurney, he gritted his teeth but was otherwise calm. "So, you'll meet me at the hospital?" he said with the little-boy smile that was my Achilles' heel.

I scrambled to my feet, felt an arm helping me up, and turned to see Green Eyes, no longer waving a gun and looking at me worriedly.

"Yes, of course," I hastened to say as the gurney wheels clattered away.

Inspector Sugerman still held my arm, which was a good thing, and not for romantic reasons. My legs felt like mush.

"After the paramedics check you out, you should go to the police station to give a statement," he said, almost apologetically. "The Santa Fe police have jurisdiction, and there are two patrolmen waiting with a car out back. They say I can sit in, given that what happened here also affects my case. You're all right, aren't you?"

I nodded, sick of all this. What I wanted was, well, I didn't know. Not a police station, though. We moved slowly to the door, Sugerman pausing to pick up my bag. With the lights on, I could see bloody smears on the floor and the wall, the table angled half into the main gallery, a stack of paintings leaning crazily out of a storage bin. Signaling Sugerman to wait, I went over and looked closely at them. All Win's—or Clint's— I wasn't sure any longer—the closest two slashed and torn. Poor Win. I'd bet anything he was doing that when Lisa found him.

"Crime doesn't pay," I said as I rejoined Sugerman.

He chuckled as he took my arm again and gave it an interesting squeeze. "May I quote you on that?"

Chapter Twenty-six

I now know several things about myself. One: when faced with something really scary, I scream like a mouse being pinched. Not particularly useful, but at least I know.

Two: I have smart friends with good instincts. Around two o'clock the next morning, sitting in the kitchen with hot Mexican chocolate courtesy of a teary Mrs. Ortega, Suzy told me she hadn't thought it was a great idea for me to go talk with Win about the possibility he was a forger. Fortunately for me, Charlie Sugerman had given up on getting back to Albuquerque in the snowstorm, and she was able to reach him on the cell phone number he'd left with her "just in case."

Three: stubbornness in an ex-husband has its upsides. Dickie wasn't happy about the chain of events that included people being pushed out of windows, off roads, and down stairs. Seems he had hired someone to keep an eye on me for my own good—the newspaper-snapping driver I'd noticed around town—and when the private detective called him at the hotel and said the lights had gone off in a building I'd

261

just entered, Dickie had called Culpepper before heading over to the gallery on foot. Lucky for me, she and Junior were on patrol duty.

At police headquarters, Crissy told me I was "brilliant. How you kept her talking all that time is beyond me, but we heard all we needed to know." Sugerman admitted that the San Francisco cops had been looking at Reynold once they realized the significance of his rift with Clint and in spite of finding Win's prints in my office. They couldn't shake the alibi Goldie had given Win.

When Reynold died, they were stymied, since, as Charlie explained sheepishly, they never saw me as a serious suspect. "Too nice," he said with a shrug and a little smile. What I'd told him about Peter had taken him by surprise, and he had been on the phone with Weiler to see if they could find grounds for a search warrant to collect the paintings I'd described.

Crissy Culpepper had bought Sugerman's request for big-time help after Suzy reported that Win wanted to meet with me and I hadn't arrived home. She'd called the gallery first, and when there was no answer, even though a cruiser said the front door was slightly open, corralled almost everyone on duty and surrounded the gallery silently. The street was blocked off, no red-and-blue cop-car lights, no sirens, and unmarked cars deliberately drove past the gallery to see if their lights would give the police any information. The cold drafts I'd felt were from the back door being opened silently, so cops could position themselves along the corridor.

In my book—and in her supervisor's—Officer Culpepper was a hero.

Sugerman, second into the gallery behind Culpepper, had heard everything. Crissy laughed when she explained what had set everyone into motion. "Your rock bounced off Junior's head before it hit the floor. He jerked, and your ex-husband started running at the same time the perp's gun went off."

The other hero, I had to admit, was my ex. Propped up in his hospital bed, Dickie was barely awake when I came over after my interview at the police station. Sugerman was waiting to drive me to Vera's, but I needed to see for myself that my former husband was all right. God forbid his mother got the idea I had abandoned her only son to the care of strangers in his hour of need.

He opened one eye and raised a hand languidly from the covers, motioning me over. I took his hand and looked at him. "Dickie, how's your leg? Does it hurt a lot?"

"A lot?" he answered in a faltering voice. "Well, no, not too much, I guess."

My eyes filled with tears. He had risked his life for me, jumping into a dangerous situation without hesitation. He had actually taken a bullet for me. I leaned down to kiss his cheek. His reflexes are good. Before I could move, his head whipped around, and we were locked in a real, no-holds-barred, lips-to-lips kiss.

"My Amazon detective," he said, closing his eyes. "I'll be out of here in no time. Crutches will add to my appeal, don't you think?"

"I'm sure," I said, withdrawing my hand. "But, please, don't ever do something so dangerous again, do you hear?"

Dickie looked slightly abashed as I started crying. Once I started, I couldn't stop, my weeping getting louder and louder.

"I'm sorry," he said, holding his hands up in a placating gesture. "I didn't do anything, really. But I couldn't let that witch shoot you, could I?

"Tell you what," he said as I subsided into hiccups and

nose blowing, "I'll be out of here tomorrow, and I'll come up to Vera's. We need to talk."

"Talk? What about? I never want to talk about this horrible business again."

"I mean about us, sugar."

Charlie Sugerman poked his head around the door, and the nurse on duty decided at that moment to come in and shoo me out.

Peter found me the next day and solved lots of riddles for me. Reynold had persuaded him to become the founding director of a new museum in Santa Fe dedicated to the cutting-edge work of artists from the western states.

"It was a chance to make my mark with a more *avant garde* collection," he said. "I knew it was a risky venture, but I'm young enough that if it didn't work out, I could find another job."

Sheepishly he admitted he wanted to hire Teeni as his head curator, but she wouldn't go without my blessing. Since last week, in fact, she had been avoiding him. She seemed to think he'd had something to do with Clint's death.

"She said I had called down to your office right after it happened and hung up when she answered. I didn't, of course. Someone must have used my extension, since that's what showed up on your phone console. I was afraid the same person had used my keys to get into your office. It didn't take a genius to realize that that person must have killed Maslow, so I was petrified. I admit, I panicked. I called Teeni when you left my house to tell her we had to keep the new museum venture quiet until the fuss died down."

Clint was to be in the permanent collection of Reynold's museum and the subject of the first solo show. He had lent